HOW TO BECOME
A MONSTER

HOW TO BECOME A MONSTER

Jean Barbe

Translated by
Patricia Wright

McArthur & Company
Toronto

First published in Canada in 2006 by
McArthur & Company
322 King St., West, Suite 402
Toronto, Ontario
M5V 1J2
www.mcarthur-co.com

Library and Archives Canada Cataloguing in Publication

Barbe, Jean
[Comment devenir un monstre. English]
    How to become a monster / Jean Barbe ; translated by Patricia Wright.

Translation of: Comment devenir un monstre.
ISBN 1-55278-579-3

    I. Wright, Patricia (Patricia Anne), 1970- II. Title.
III. Title: Comment devenir un monstre. English.

PS8553.A718C6513 2006   C843'.54   C2005-907840-5

Cover Design by Tania Craan
Interior Composition by Michael P.M. Callaghan
Printed in Canada by Webcom

Study after Pope Innocent X by Velasquez
by Francis Bacon (1909-92)
Aberdeen Art Gallery and Museum,
Scotland/Bridgeman Art Library

The publisher would like to acknowledge the financial support of the
Government of Canada through the Book Publishing Industry Development
Program, the Canada Council for the Arts, and the Ontario Arts Council for
our publishing activities. We also acknowledge the Government of Ontario
through the Ontario Media Development Corporation Ontario Book
Initiative.

10 9 8 7 6 5 4 3 2 1

THE STARS ABOVE

Snow lay at the peak of the mountain. We climbed at night, in silence, stopping to listen. The whistling of the bullets can be heard even after it is over, even when it has yet to happen. Once you've been shot at, you're always a target. The opposite is also true. What I mean is you are always staring down one end or the other of a barrel.

It was very dark under the cover of the trees. We couldn't see a thing, but we couldn't hear anything either. Silence and darkness. You don't know what it feels like, that silence and that darkness. Prelude to the clamour and the fire. Silence and darkness are inhabited by a multitude of fire-eaters all set to roar, but when? You can't see the darkness, you can't hear the silence; you are poised for the beginning of the racket and the fire when the monsters emerge from their den.

War is dreadfully noisy. You no longer hear yourself think. In fact, you don't think. You react. After some time, it's as though you're surrounded by wadding – the noise mutes everything, confuses everything, isolates. You become detached from yourself. In those moments I feel invincible, which is not an illusion. I have never been wounded other than scratched. I've shed more blood in the kitchen than I did in the war, even though I know how to handle a knife. But I'm even better at handling a weapon. It's a gift.

A path wound up the hill to the top, but we walked alongside it through the woods. I was on the right with a few men. The commander was on the left with Mistral and the bulk of the unit. I climbed. I had been told to climb. I didn't know what we were going to find at the top, I hadn't been told and I hadn't asked. I climbed in the deafening silence, yaw after yaw, finger on the trigger. Suddenly there was snow. A carpet of snow, really. It looked like a carpet, growing thicker towards the summit.

How far was the summit? I had no idea and that was fine with me. But the snow . . . The snow was a blessing and a danger. It was a moonless night but the scanty glow from the stars reflecting off the snow was enough to light the mountain. It felt as though I was moving through a dream. At the same time, I was aware that I was visible, a black silhouette against a white background. I didn't care. It was beautiful. The bare trees, the firs in black robes, the stars.

The snow went up to my ankles and would soon be halfway up my leg. The trees grew farther apart and then, suddenly, we reached the summit. It was an observatory. It was old, all white and caked in snow. It wasn't modern and this pleased me. There were useless crowns – no pains were taken to save on materials. Poised as it was on the peak of the mountain, it was reminiscent of a bald head pointing towards the unknown.

I couldn't see the telescope lens from where I stood, but there was a big antenna, which seemed out of place, mounted on the dome like a plastic figurine on a wedding cake. I immediately understood our objective: a communications antenna.

Out of habit, I mechanically gave the sign for the men to move out. It was so beautiful, so calm. It was light as day, almost. I like stars even if I don't know them by name. As a child, I looked at them, lying down in the grass, trying to understand infinity.

There was no sign of enemy forces. The commander must know what he is doing. We stayed there, waiting, ready to open fire. I had to force myself to maintain my gaze in the direction of the big door that opened onto the flank of the observatory, right in front of me. After some time, it opened. A man with a gun in a bandolier stepped out, pulled a cigarette from his pocket and struck a match. One of our men opened fire much too early. The man fell, and for several minutes I saw the smoke from his cigarette continue to curl. The cigarette fell inside his collar and continued to burn against his skin.

After that, all hell broke loose. I don't know why they tried to come out. It was stupid. We had no losses and they dropped one after another. Now they were everywhere, scattered in the snow around the station. It was dry up there. The snow was light and powdered the bodies. Only the blood stayed very bright, like red flowers on a field of snow. The blood drank in the snowflakes one by one as they settled under the soft whisper of the wind and the last sighs. The blood could only be seen in the light of the flares that the commander had set off.

Minutes earlier, there had been nothing in the snow, not even footsteps. And now this. All these fallen bodies in absurd positions, slowly being covered by a dusting of snow. Our men cautiously remained under the cover of the trees, waiting. You never know. The flare accomplished its duty and died out with a soft hiss in the snow. The blood became black. I looked at the sky and then the ground. Up there, white stains against a black background. Down here, black stains against a white backdrop. The glow of the stars reached me after millions of years of travel. I saw the gleam of a dead, mineral, cruel world.

Death had a mineral quality, even in the snow.

That's when it happened.

A white flag waved through the door of the station. The man waving it was cautious and took his time to come out. In one hand he held his flag (a white shirt, I think, tied to the end of a broomstick), and the other was brandished high, palm facing us to prove that he was unarmed. He bellowed that he was surrendering, that he was not a soldier. He moved towards us, slowly, continuing to yell that he was surrendering while waving his white flag.

He was cursing out loud. He made noise. He was disturbing the natural order of things with his voice, his gestures, the blood in his veins.

I put a bullet between his eyes. He fell. Silence returned.

It was the first time.

"The first time you killed anyone?"

"The first time I felt that I found my place in the universe."

ADVOCATE FOR LOSERS

My children bothered me with their presence. Leaning against the door frame in my bedroom they were content watching me pack my bags. But while I laid across the bed the new packaged shirts, the freshly pressed suits and the expensive accessories that completed my combat clothes, I could feel their little eyes piercing my nape right through to the bone of my third vertebrae.

True, I was abandoning them; I was leaving without them. It was also true that I was happy to leave them behind. The pain in my neck was undoubtedly the physiological manifestation of a weighty conscience, too heavy to carry.

But this was my first mission abroad. An international case could only further a young lawyer's career. It was an adventure and I was living it as such. I had travelled somewhat during my studies, but I hadn't experienced a true event since I had passed the bar and later witnessed my wife's two deliveries aided by epidurals.

Following these, I had donned my role as father as one would don a military uniform, careful to exercise my duty and conscious of the sacrifices to accomplish it. I loved my children because obviously I had to love them. I got down on all fours to tickle them, but for some time now, my heart was no longer in it. Where was it? I had lost it somewhere along the way and couldn't recover it.

"Don't you want to watch TV or a movie?"

The eldest just shook his head while grasping the door frame.

How in hell could these children – who shouldn't be able to sit still – how could they stand there, motionless, for over ten minutes? What could be so fascinating about watching a forty-year-old man pack his suitcase?

I would have sent them to the kitchen to bother their mother instead of me, but Florence had yet to calm down since I announced my departure. The only looks she had given me since this morning fell under one of the following two categories: cool indifference or scathing intent. I sighed as I kneeled on my suitcase to close it.

"Daddy, why are you leaving?" asked Arthur.

How could I answer that? After a discreet glance at my wristwatch (I still had a few minutes to spare), I opened my arms and my children threw themselves at me like a barbarian horde. Instead of explaining, I tossed my son on the bed to tickle him – another act of cowardice to my credit. My daughter climbed onto my back and I tickled her in turn, and then we all threw ourselves into an epic pillow fight to which, dishevelled and panting, I had to put an end because it was time to go.

I slipped on my overcoat and carried my suitcase and briefcase to the front door. The children were wrapped around my ankles. Their love for me, unshakeable and uncompromising, was a mystery.

They clung to my thighs and tried to walk on my feet while I was moving towards the kitchen where Florence had been furiously scrubbing the same pot for a good twenty minutes. When it came time to say goodbye, I knew I could benefit from the protection of my children – out of consideration for them, Florence would hold her fire.

"It's time," I said.

She swept the back of her hand across her forehead, moving aside the strands of hair that had fallen from her loosely tied bun. Cautiously, I moved closer to kiss her. At the last second, she denied me her lips and I kissed her on the cheek. Anger still burned in her eyes, enhancing her beauty. I felt horribly guilty.

"I'll call you tomorrow," I said.

Florence took a step back, sighed and then looked me in the eyes.

"Fine," she said after a second. "Have a good trip, François."

She gave me a sort of faint smile. It was unexpected. A blessing in a way. I bent down to kiss my children. Arthur's eyes filled with tears. From her nostril, Margot dug out a juicy booger which she promptly popped into her mouth. I kissed her on the forehead.

"Goodbye! Goodbye!" I said as I picked up my luggage. "See you soon! Be good!"

Hostage to an array of contradicting emotions, I settled in to the back of the taxi that was driving me to the airport. I took a rum-filled flask from my pocket and took a long swig. While the alcohol exploded in my stomach and its heat was released, spilling into my bloodstream, relief gave way to fear, then shame gave way to excitement. I pictured Florence, still standing in the kitchen, pressing our crying children to her and looking at the space I occupied and that I had deserted by escaping. Florence's look haunted me, chased me to the fast lane where my taxi joined the herd of vehicles deadlocked by rush hour. My forehead was covered in sweat. What had taken over me? Why this need to escape? What had I done?

But I was very much aware. Lawyer, father, husband: for too long now, my roles felt as though they had been written by an unimaginative hack for a mind-numbing soap opera. I felt as though I had become a soulless machine running on empty. My days unfolded according to an established routine requesting no contribution on my behalf. I wasn't living my life, it was taking care of itself. It was a reasonable existence up until the point at which "I" dissipated.

I had lost the taste for everything. I came home increasingly late from work because the prospect of another family dinner complete with screams, spilled milk and noodles on the carpet was excruciating to me. I made up excuses that I had appointments when I was out drinking and feeling sorry for myself. I was torn: there was the "me" who was suffering and the detestable "me," no one else. This couldn't go on.

That's when I registered for Lawyers Without Borders.

It was a spontaneous act, somewhat suicidal, as much for my professional life as for my family life. I felt better immediately. What possibilities for adventure remained for a man like me? A sporty convertible for Sunday drives? An affair with the legal assistant? Tango lessons?

The mere chance of being sent abroad returned a lost charm to my existence, a sense of precariousness that rendered it precious. For the first time in a long time, I felt alive.

This went on for three weeks and then came the call. I didn't expect it, at least not so soon. I wasn't ready. I preferred the *possibility* of a departure to the departure itself. I hadn't breathed a word to Florence or to my partners at the firm. I estimated this trip would cost me tens of thousands of dollars in financial losses.

For a few days, I toyed with the idea of refusing to leave. But whatever my reasons, this last cowardly act would have been the death of me. So, I gathered my courage and spoke to Florence.

It went rather well, if you prefer dead silence to vicious screaming matches. I spent our last nights together on the couch. I wore Florence's patience to the bone. She was exhausted, I knew it. Worried about the future. Alone too. But who wasn't?

The taxi climbed the access ramp leading to the airport. I paid, unloaded my bags and headed towards the check-in counter. As usual, it was packed. The new security measures created endless line-ups, eliciting grumbles from the passengers. But the alcohol was starting to take its effect. I smiled mysteriously. I pulled my shoulders back and walked with more determination. I presented my passport to a charming airline employee.

"Boarding is at Gate 32, Mr. Chevalier," she said.

Yes, that was me: François Chevalier, Esquire, riding in taxis and an officer of the Court, defender of widows and orphans, advocate for losers. And now I was heading out on a crusade. I was going to take Justice to foreign soil. Had to drink to that.

In the airport bar, I put back several scotches to gather courage. In the end, I'd had so much that I had to be helped to my seat. A flight attendant leaned over me to buckle my seat-belt. This seemed diabolically complicated. I slipped into a drunken slumber, heavy and dreamless.

When I woke, three hours later, my chin was coated with saliva. I must have snored considerably, judging by the angry looks tossed my way by my close neighbours. I still found the strength to order a drink before taking a file from my briefcase and diving right in. I didn't look up until we landed.

Lawyers Without Borders had assigned me to assist the Monster in preparing for his trial. At least that's what the local press called him, based on the newspaper clippings that I had, after successively rejecting the epithets of butcher (too vague), Hell's cook (too literary) and criminal (too commonplace).

The upcoming trial was not as sensational as those in the Capital or The Hague, which mobilized battalions of foreign correspondents. My client was neither a high-ranking official nor one of the country's leaders. In other words, he had never given an order to anyone. He wasn't responsible for the deaths of millions of innocent people, only a few dozen, and most of these killed by his own hand.

In the absence of the death penalty, he risked spending his life, several times over, in prison. I believed I could help him by pleading extenuating circumstances – after all, there had been a war going on – or temporary insanity. Wasn't he also a victim of war?

The case was nothing like those that Lawyers Without Borders normally took on. This explained the haste with which the file had been processed. Generally, the group got involved in taking care of organizations, implementing legal networks in countries where there is a lack. I knew of few direct defence cases. It made it even more exciting.

For the hundredth time, I scanned the few pages that made up the entire file. Viktor Rosh, a.k.a. Chef. A cook in civilian life. Retired parents. One brother. Long periods of unemployment, first in the Capital, then in the forest region of M. Enlisted voluntarily at the start of the war. Militiaman. Commando unit. His superiors had already been tried and convicted or had gone underground. The file referred to war crimes, without much detail, and to crimes without any detail at all. I supposed that additional information was waiting for me with the appointed lawyer with whom I was to collaborate because I couldn't practise over there.

Two photographs were attached to the file with a paper clip. The first, a mug shot, showed the Monster straight on and in profile. Viktor Rosh was a thirty-six-year-old man with dark, unkempt hair. A few wrinkles crossed his forehead. But were these really worry lines? It could have been said that the man had opened his eyes a little too wide, as if flabbergasted to see what he was seeing. But what was he seeing?

Apart from that, a fairly handsome man, slightly rustic. In any case, he didn't look like a monster, contrary to what was depicted in the second photograph.

This one was incredible, as if it was staged or some kind of bad joke. It more than justified his Monster nickname. It showed Rosh, bare-chested and much thinner, in the middle of the woods. His hair was long and tangled and he had a shaggy beard. He held what appeared to be a long-bladed kitchen knife. Curiously, tufts of hair covered his torso as though he was a caveman not yet convinced that he wanted to be a *sapien*. In addition, he was spattered in a viscous liquid whose bright red colour left no doubt that it was blood. It was everywhere – on his hands, his arms, and his chest, right up to his forehead. Drops pearled at the tip of his knife. On the back of the photograph, a date revealed that it had been taken the same day my client had been arrested.

I kept going back to this photo. The savagery it emanated attracted me. It harboured a mystery, a danger that did not belong to cities and white-collar crimes. It showed a vitality that I felt privy to, that I secretly aspired to. It was a horrible photograph that I would never show my children for all the money in the world for fear of infusing their sleep with terrible, crippling nightmares. But it was undeniable that the creature pictured was a man, by that I mean a being brimming with testosterone; a lean, sinewy primitive body and . . . what exactly? The complete opposite of myself.

The plane landed early in the morning. After collecting my luggage, I had to take a shuttle to the county town in the neighbouring province. The trip lasted a little over three hours. Crossing the town of M., I saw buildings rebuilt in haste with no consideration for aesthetics. Strange, these societies who fought over matters of history always managed to obliterate it.

People walked while hugging the walls as if a burst of machine-gun fire was going to incessantly sweep the sidewalks – but judging from the cigarette butts, greasy paper and plastic bags littering the ground, nothing had visibly swept the sidewalks for some time. It was fairly depressing.

A suite at the Black Bear Inn had been reserved for me. This was to serve as my residence for the weeks to come. I checked in and took up my own luggage.

I unpacked, put away my clothes and my toiletries. On a table near the window, I placed my leather-bound binder, my

Waterman pen, my client's file and a few international law manuals. I took a shower, shaved and changed my clothes, and began to spin circles in my room.

I couldn't sit still. So, I did what I normally did in such situations: I went down to the hotel bar in order to stupefy myself with scotch.

When I woke the next morning, I experienced a brief strange feeling. What? No little person to jump on the bed and cover my face in wet kisses? I stretched my legs and wiggled my toes under the sheets. There was something indulgent about waking up this way, alone, in a potentially dangerous foreign country. I ordered a hearty breakfast that I ate in bed without caring about crumbs. I sipped my scalding, overly sweet coffee. I called the front desk to reserve a taxi for nine o'clock. Shower, shave, fresh clothes. I put my things together and ensured that each of my lawyer gadgets was in order. The phone rang. It was the front desk. My taxi was waiting.

My hand was on the doorknob when, shit! Shit, shit, shit! I had forgotten to call home as promised! But I no longer had time. Tonight. No, not tonight because of the time difference. Tomorrow then. Yes, tomorrow without fail. And I left – and the thought of my family left my mind at the same time.

I was going to the M. prison to meet my client. It was a good half-hour outside the city in a sort of natural basin where the morning mist still lingered. I attempted to concentrate during the trip, but concentrate on what?

The prison where he was held while awaiting trial was modest. I had seen few undamaged buildings since my arrival, but this one was intact as if the bullets and shells had willingly spared it. Perhaps the two enemy camps had preserved it knowing that they would have use for it after the war, whatever the outcome.

The taxi came to a stop. We had arrived. I presented my papers to the guard and was shown in.

While I was escorted through the caged hallways and was shown through barred doors, I wondered if there existed a world association of prison paint merchants who only kept in stock millions and millions of litres of distemper in colours such as pee yellow, puke green and dirty beige. If this was the case, had they presented their collection to the decorating committee and if so, had they been imprisoned for their misdeeds?

It was stupid, I know, but it was so. My brain and I aren't always on the same page. I take the direct route and it takes detours. I've gotten used to it. When this occurs, I feign a state of deep thought by pursing my lips and furrowing my brow, an image patiently perfected in front of the bathroom mirror during my morning shaving sessions.

My escort guard showed me to a small windowless room whose entire furnishings consisted of a small table and two chairs made of white wood. The neon lighting emphasized the roughness of the concrete surrounding me. This was not the ideal environment to foster a trusting relationship.

I sat. The guard left the room leaving the door open. I was grateful to him. On the table, I opened my leather bag containing a pad of yellow paper. For form's sake, I verified that my pen was filled with ink. I was nervous. I was waiting for a monster.

I heard footsteps in the corridor. It was him. I sat up straight. I put on my most professional air. He sat down in front of me, handcuffs on his wrists. The guard left, locking the door behind him, and . . .

"And what?" he asked.

"And nothing," I answered.

"What do you mean 'nothing'?"

"Nothing as in nothing."

"He didn't speak to you?"

"Not a word!"

"That's annoying."

"You don't seem surprised."

He smiled, revealing teeth that pointed in all directions. His white moustache with downturned ends had a yellowish trail caused by the smoke from the big cigars permanently pinched between lips so red that they looked made up. He was a large man, done up out-of-season in a light-coloured striped suit, who welcomed me like a long-lost friend. Ten minutes after having first laid eyes on him, I knew his whole story: his wife, Elena, his two sons and his three daughters, the eldest, poor thing, afflicted with a harelip that sealed her fate as an old maid.

Sure, the man was jovial, but in a slightly exaggerated way. He seemed astonishingly eager-to-please for a lawyer: Mr. Cevitjc, my only ally in this affair.

He was more the Monster's lawyer than I was, but like me, he hadn't chosen the job. The State had appointed him.

"No, it doesn't surprise me," answered Cevitjc. "He's been like that since the beginning."

"Like what?"

"Silent."

"You mean to say that he's never uttered a word?"

"Not one."

"Since when?"

"His arrest."

Dumbfounded, I slumped down in my chair. Ordinarily, I maintained emotionless business relationships with my clients. After all, they wished to sidestep prison or lighten their sentence and I was the man for the job. They had somewhat of a tendency to bombard me with useless details in a stream of words that I recommended they repress if they wanted the slightest chance in front of the judge. No one had ever given me the silent treatment. At two hundred dollars an hour, no one could afford to.

Once the door to the room closed, sealing in our confidentiality, I looked Viktor Rosh straight in the eyes and introduced myself. I spoke of my career, my successes (exaggerating them a little), and then shared my intention to do everything in my power to come to his aid. Next, I asked him, for form's sake, if he wished to plead not guilty. I waited for his answer. He looked at me, no doubt taking his time to reflect. I kept waiting.

"So?" I asked.

He didn't answer.

"Do you understand the question?"

Still nothing. He was smiling nonetheless. I looked around, searching for who knows what, a hidden camera. Perhaps I was the brunt of a good prison guard joke, and my Monster was waiting for me in the next room, this one being an impostor. But no, no camera. And decidedly, the Monster resembled him too much. It came to mind that he was testing me, that through his silence he was making an opening for me to dive into his world, to adapt. I had to earn his trust. But what should I say? I gave him my leftist long-winded speech according to which no one is ever really guilty and we are all victims. I spoke of men and women who had committed atrocious acts but who had suffered for so long that it was a wonder they hadn't killed earlier. The fact of the matter was, these men and women wanted to be loved but didn't know how to ask and didn't know how to give, and trapped in their bodies and in their hearts, from wanting to get out, they wound up exploding, etc.

I had been talking to myself for a good ten minutes. He was still looking at me with his small, vaguely alien smile, not as if he couldn't care less about me or what I was saying, but rather as if he had already heard it all countless times. Or he was crazy. But if he was crazy, he would have been locked up in a psychiatric hospital and not a prison. Or perhaps . . .

It was a test of will. He wanted to determine if I too had the same moral strength to be silent. Well, if that's what he wanted, that's what he was going to get. Abruptly, I stopped speaking, settled into my chair and stared at him in silence.

This lasted a good, what, six or seven minutes. An eternity in which I experienced all the states: determination, confusion, fear, anger, pity. I had blown it. I had barely just arrived and it was already time to leave, with my tail between my legs, another failure in my briefcase. Was it on this reef of silence that the damaged boat of my forties was to run aground?

I had collected my things. I didn't dare look at him anymore. I knocked on the door that the guard came to open and I left without saying a word.

"Someone could have warned me," I said.

"That he doesn't speak? No one told you?" asked Cevitjc.

"No."

"It must be a mistake. But I had hoped that your presence would draw him out of his silence."

"Apparently not."

"Yes, it's too bad."

"How should I take it?"

"Oh! However you like! Think of it what you like! I don't know. He is uncooperative, and he doesn't seem to want to defend himself."

Cevitjc leaned in towards me. The smoke from his cigar made him blink.

"I am his appointed lawyer. Understand?"

"Not exactly."

"A guy like him isn't going to pay for a vacation on the Côte d'Azur."

"Do you go often?" I asked foolishly.

"Every war so far," he answered.

He sat back in his seat and took a couple of puffs and watched the curls of smoke rise to the ceiling. Then:

"Do you know that he's guilty?"

"I am not a judge . . ."

"There are too many witnesses, and his silence is incriminating."

"Our duty is to defend him."

"But he doesn't want to be defended!"

"I did not travel halfway across the world for nothing."

"True," said Cevitjc.

"I can help him," I said.

"Okay. We'll represent him and spare him the legal concerns wherever possible. As for the rest, don't kid yourself. He'll be found guilty on all counts. Here, I prepared this for you."

He tossed on his desk a thick file covered in green cardboard.

"Once you've read it, you'll understand the extent of his guilt."

"There are no attenuating circumstances?"

"That's all that exists here, you know, so much so that it no longer counts."

"He will die in prison."

"Or, with a little luck, there will be another war in ten years, and with even more luck his party will be victorious, he will be freed, exonerated, given a position in the civil service and a park will be named after him."

"You're laughing at me."

"Not really."

"I refuse to admit defeat from the beginning."

"Whether or not you accept it, you must understand that here, the dead are counted by the hundreds of thousands and therefore other thousands of people had to have killed them. These people are either in the good camp or the bad camp. And unfortunately, the two camps have been swapping places for centuries, but it can't be helped. Hate breeds hate, violence breeds violence. Because killing is so routine, we kill routinely. In a country like yours, where you are wary of red meat, the idea of the Beast is quite remote. But here, the Beast is a part of our daily lives. We know it well. It knows us well. And Rosh knows it. And, if we have collectively decided that Rosh is the Beast, too bad for him. It all falls on him. Next time, it will be someone else."

"That's a terribly cynical view."

Cevitjc appeared to pity me. His small eyes, disappearing in the folds of fat, suddenly looked at me with kindness.

"This doesn't mean that we are useless, my boy. Simply that we have to recognize the limits of our power."

"What is this power?'

"We can help him to salvage some of his dignity as a man when everyone is calling him a monster. The trial will be followed closely by the national press and perhaps the foreign one as well. Your job will be to intervene, to protect him."

"But if he doesn't want to talk to me?"

"That's a problem. But I don't think he'll remain silent forever. Each of us wants to talk, to explain the quintessential nature of our personal truth. He'll come around, but it's up to you to help him."

"Why did he want a Lawyer without Borders if he doesn't want to defend himself?"

Cevitjc appeared ill at ease with my question. He blew smoke rings with his cigar.

"Who knows? We all want to be understood. You're a foreigner . . . perhaps he wished to face someone who has a new outlook, who could understand without prejudging. He doesn't seem to want a lawyer. Maybe he needs a friend."

"I . . ."

But I couldn't translate my thoughts into words. A friend? I certainly hadn't travelled thousands of kilometres to befriend a monster. If only I could gain his trust . . .

"What do I have to do?"

"He wants us to take an interest in him, not in his case. His silence is a scream. With what the State pays me . . . But you, you are perfect."

"Perfect for what?"

"Find out who he is, seek out those who knew him well. I don't know. Act as though he has captivated you, become the collector of his facts and his actions . . . Perhaps you'll stumble upon some attenuating circumstances, as you say, that could take a few years off his sentence. Who knows? You have to get him to talk, there's no other way, otherwise . . . can you imagine the trial?"

"Well," I said, "okay. But where should I start?"

"I don't know," answered Cevitjc. "At the beginning?"

A TASTE FOR LIVING

I was born in the Capital, I grew up there, I studied there. But I never really felt at home there. In the big cities, there is this culture of money and a passion for social-climbing that I found disconcerting because I was particularly lacking in money and passion. I was timid, and that was fatal.

My parents were modest and in my eyes they were small. They weren't mean, but they displayed such fondness for normality that it could be qualified as obsessive.

For them, to blend in with the masses was a sign of health. But perhaps this was just a defensive strategy. My father also went to war, before I was born. As a remnant of this ordeal by fire was a gleam of despair in his eyes. With the end of his war came the end of his youth, and a certain way of life that was no longer useful. As a result, he was content to survive, without a peep, on the tip of his toes, always watching his tongue. The war had killed all of his dreams, all of his wishes, all of his joy, all of his love. Unless he had always been that way.

He was . . . a father to me. That is to say that he made me, fed me and clothed me until I was able to take care of myself, and that's about it. For a long time all I knew of the world was what he had told me: you had to beware.

He was a carpenter. Maybe he still is. He chose a trade that wouldn't require him to think. His hands did the work on their own, big calloused hands, more familiar with a hammer than a child's cheek. His hand was happy to plane a wood plank but feared a touch as if I was the one covered in splinters. As for my mother . . . she loved her husband and protected her man by quieting her children's cries. Of course, she loved us as well. She loved us like poor, hopeless creatures that had to be protected from everything, most of all from the hope that one day things would be better. To her, everything was a source of danger. I remember that she held my hand to climb the stairs until I was ten years old, and even then she didn't let go until I threatened to kill myself if she didn't leave me alone. The careful attention she paid us consisted in just that: Be careful! Be careful not to fall, be careful not to run, be careful not to choke, not to get cold . . . be careful, be careful, be careful!

Driven by such encouragement, what a surprise that I was an average student! None of my teachers predicted any type of career for me. I had no characteristics whatsoever to the extent that it was difficult to even picture myself: I didn't leave much of an impression on anyone.

There was always my brother, but he was older. I had shared a few secrets with him that were received with grumbles. And during a few brief years, I felt his protective arm around my shoulders. My big brother . . . He was struck with a passion for politics. He didn't come home much anymore and then one day, not at all. The last time I saw him was on television during a protest. I think he had to flee the country. He never wrote to me. Everyone has their fate.

My parents assumed that I would end up with a hammer in my hand; no doubt this would have been the case had I not discovered cooking.

We weren't wealthy. In order to have spending money, as soon as I turned fourteen, I found a dishwashing job in a restaurant in the centre of town. The work was mind-numbing and exhausting, but what did I know? I was very proud to earn some money and sometimes I was served leftovers that delighted my palate. That is where it all began. My life. The rest doesn't really count, if at all.

But in this restaurant, slightly expensive and too brightly lit for my eyes that were accustomed to the reassuring darkness of my father's house, in this huge kitchen made of aluminium and porcelain, in the fragrant spices, the fumets, reductions, vinegars and cream sauces, meat on bones, crustaceans, shellfish (and me who had never seen the ocean), the game, the wild mushrooms, chanterelles, boletuses, ceps, morels, meadow mushrooms – here, it was here that my eyes were opened while my hands splashed around in greasy water floating with the remnants of all the feasts.

I knew nothing. I was clueless to the nature of a *bouillabaisse* or a *gratin*. A *parfait*? A straight-A student. My ignorance was astonishing, appalling. I was a pathetic being who washed the dishes. But I watched, listened, tasted. I absorbed everything.

It was as though the entire world was rushing through the kitchen doors to bring me its fragrances, its traditions and its history. Framed by piles of dishes and mounds of utensils, I travelled. This restaurant's menu was my first real book.

Timidly at first, then with increasing boldness, I asked questions. I watched the chef closely, getting drunk on his barked orders. The flame, the breaking of the plates and the sizzling of the vegetables sautéed in butter, the almost chaotic fury of the knife-wielding uniformed staff foreshadowed my destiny. I can see that now.

But at the time, it was an adventure. I washed the dishes at superhuman speed in hopes of lending a hand in the kitchen once my own task was accomplished. I often managed and people became used to me. Now and then I was entrusted with the arrangement. As soon as school let out I rushed towards the restaurant to slice, peel, carve, shred and chop. I learned to handle a knife and grew accustomed to animal blood which we used to bind the sauces. I especially enjoyed the days when the supplies arrived by airplane: cases and cases of wine, game, lobsters, anything that wasn't produced locally. I was to keep them cool in the large coolers, hang the carcasses, and lay the bottles on their sides, reading the labels as I daydreamed. Alone in these cold rooms with sides of beef hanging from the ceiling and entire rows of *foie gras* in jars, I was in seventh heaven.

The chef was a surly man who had studied his art in France. It would be exaggerating to say that he had taken me under his protective wing, but he wasn't as hard on me as he was on the others. He was the first to mention the Hotel Institute and he later opened the doors for me with a praising letter of recommendation. He was good for me. I regret having left him in a jam much later on. But all's fair in love and war.

I worked alongside him for almost four years. In many ways, a kitchen is organized very much like a military hierarchy. There is no room for discussion, orders are orders and discipline is crucial. The troops are drawn up in battle formation, each section assigned with a specific mission. But there was reasoning behind all of this, an order that revealed itself in the end, in the plates, in the blend of flavours, in the harmony of textures. The chef was a god, omnipotent, sometimes scolding, sometimes loving, and always feared. I admired this big-bellied man, respected him and perhaps even felt a kind of love for him. He saved my life, or at least gave it meaning. I owe part of what I am to him.

Four years later, I was preparing to leave the restaurant to begin my studies at the Hotel Institute. It was my last day. The chef came to see me and proposed, for the first time since I had known him, that we eat together.

"Here?" I asked.

"No. A well-kept secret. Come on!"

Out we went. I was eighteen years old and had reached my full height but I still went red in the face like a kid, and outside of the kitchen I was awkward and clumsy. Beside the chef who seemed to float on the sidewalks, I had forgotten how to walk. I tripped, made little strange hops and caught my soles on the slightest bumps.

We walked in silence. The chef whistled while looking in the shop windows. I was excited. I imagined the secret table reserved for chefs only in the security of an exclusive club that opened its doors solely to members – and here I was at times ruining a béchamel!

But we left behind the posh neighbourhoods to wind through the immigrant alleyways. The low, run-down buildings each sheltered at least one cheap restaurant with exotic aromas and questionable hygiene. We turned down a smaller alleyway, and then down another that led to a dead end. At the very end, an old man lorded over a board that sat on trestles, in front of a sort of shed whose lifted door put on view a refrigerator and a brazier topped by a grill.

"American hot dogs!" called out the chef with an emphasis that seemed slightly out of place to me.

The old man was named Amir. He had lived in the U.S. for a few years where he had sold merguez sausages. When he returned here for unknown family reasons, the merguez market had been saturated for quite some time. So, he wrote to his American friends who, every month, shipped him a load of pink sausages and little soft buns that he grilled over coals and topped with bottled condiments.

The chef ordered several that we ate standing up in big pasty bites and washed down with gulps of cola. I expected that any minute now, the chef would reveal the reason behind our presence in these parts: a council of wise men, a maxim, a warning against gastronomic misuse. But no. After a loud burp he said to me:

"It's soft, it's fatty, it's warm – just like a woman's breast!"

Then he took me by the arm and we returned to the restaurant where I finished my day of work. I was disappointed. But I wasn't done with American sausages.

At the end of the day, I handed in my apron. The chef hugged me. My colleagues wished me good luck and I returned to my parents' home.

They didn't look favourably on my enrolment in the Institute. If I hadn't won a scholarship they would never have agreed to pay my tuition. That a true satisfaction of the senses could be obtained through food seemed practically indecent to them, borderline pornographic. To them, eating consisted basically of nourishing oneself. For fear that a hint of life remained in the meat and vegetables, my mother never hesitated to assassinate them a second time by cooking them to the point of complete annihilation.

My brother had left the house several years earlier. I had lost him to politics. Now there were only the three of us, two killjoys and me, who was just beginning to live. It was unbearable. Three months after the start of my classes, I told my parents of my intention to rent a room in the city. The scholarship money would just cover it. They appeared relieved. The slight bit of longing that I held, the slightest hope that I nurtured in me made me, in their eyes, the equivalent of a drug addict and thief: my unpredictability terrified them.

I gathered my belongings and they followed me to the door waving as I dragged my suitcases to the bus stop. They didn't say "See you soon!" They didn't say "Come back whenever you want."

I got the message. I never stepped foot in that house again, and they never attempted to visit mine. I imagine that they felt it was enough to have supported me until I was eighteen and that it was no longer up to them. I also imagined that no sooner had the door closed behind me than they crawled back under the rock they had been forced to come out from under by becoming parents, to pick up where they left off their existence as woodlice.

I never looked back. During that period, we had been living in peace for long enough to believe that it was a permanent situation. The Hotel Institute buzzed with activity and year after year couldn't produce enough cooks to run all the restaurants that were opening their doors. It was an era of prosperity and forgetfulness. The Capital preened its feathers and stuck out its chest. For three years I heated cauldrons, bound sauces and stuffed fowl. For three years I sketched the plans for my own little restaurant.

Oh, nothing much! A small restaurant, if not a café. A tiny little space of freedom. I hadn't learned to dream, let alone dream big.

But cooking took you places. Borscht, paella, chicken yassa – three dishes, three continents. Cooking was an invitation to travel and when, overcome with exhaustion, I sank into the dusty mattress in my cramped room, I sometimes imagined myself heading out on an adventure, with empty hands and empty pockets, a nomadic cook like the poets of the Middle Ages. I could picture myself around the world, stopping here and there in cities and towns, and everywhere my knowledge would be welcome. I would wake petrified by this courage, of which there was no trace in the light of day.

The reality was, even though I loved to cook, cooking didn't count me among its favourites. After the first two years of courses that covered the fundamentals of the profession, it was obvious that I didn't have the skills required to ever hope of becoming a master chef. Cooking was like any other art form. In aspiring to be the best you had to first learn the basic rules of thumb – and then break them. And so, Picasso, outstanding in drawing and in anatomy, would position the ears in the place of the eyes and the nose in the place of the mouth.

I was not Picasso. I didn't dare break the rules. I didn't have that kind of imagination. I could put together a complicated dish with ease by never straying from the rules of the art. But faced with an array of ingredients and my imagination, I would freeze like ice cubes in a tray.

And so, wanting to escape the absolute mediocrity of my parents, I found myself confronted with my own. I was devastated. But what was there to do? I looked around me. Some were better and some were worse. Certain graduates, unable to make a successful omelette if their lives depended on it, found work in the best restaurants. They didn't appear to suffer from their incompetence, why should I have to suffer due to my own? I had to be realistic. One could be good without being great. Fair was already pretty good.

Without a doubt I was waiting for a revelation, a swift change in the order of the universe. I believed in inspiration, but it had not yet touched me with its wing. I had to wait and that's what I did. I finished my last year of studies within the average and from one day to the next, found myself a qualified cook without a dime. In the midst of a full recession.

We hadn't seen it coming, the economists even less so. Inflation, stock market crash, what did I know about all that? To me, the economy is likened to a mystical science consisting of putting the swirls of a torrent into words. You can talk all you want but the water is running.

In short, when it came my turn to enter the job market, there was no room left. The Capital was losing its feathers and its shoulders slumped lamentably. I went from one restaurant to the next only to see them close their doors or reduce by half their ambitions like their staff. I was twenty-one years old, with a room that I no longer had the means to live in. I began to understand my parents.

I ended up finding a job as a cook in a hospital kitchen. It didn't pay very well and lacked prestige but I was content to have found something. With the enthusiasm of youth, I vowed to myself that I would create a delicious menu that would enthral the patients and accelerate their recovery, but soon I came up against dietetic principals decreed by the College of Medicine according to which anything healthy must be tasteless.

I spent six years at that hospital. Six years boiling chicken breasts in unsalted water. It was long. Six years no longer knowing how to hope, shut in the basement of an old hospital whose antiseptic odour impregnated my clothes as well as my dreams.

I had given up my room for a small apartment within my means. I worked during the day and at night I read cookbooks; these were my only friends.

I wasn't a hermit per se. I greeted people and they greeted me in return. I smiled and others did the same. From time to time I even took part in group activities and drew a few moments of pleasure out of them. But, agitation for agitation, I preferred the one taking place in my mind to that of the bodies dancing in the discos, whose sole goal was to knock about under the sheets later on.

I didn't have a talent for love or friendship. As in the kitchen, I was incapable of spontaneity. I applied recipes that proved disappointing and I rarely managed a third date from a woman who had gotten to know me on the first two. I didn't dare open the doors to my soul to any of them, I admit. However it was there, behind my closed eyelids. The image of a restaurant, my own, small, without stars, without flair, without pretension except for its name: The Art Café.

I could see the walls covered in book-lined shelves. Movie posters. Photographs of wonderful and exotic locales. The menu written out on a chalkboard. The morning light, streaming through the tall windows, diagonally illuminating the students going over their notes from the day before while dunking a butter croissant in a big bowl of *café au lait*. At noon, they gave up their seats to local merchants there to noisily wolf down a pot roast, fattened chicken with diced bacon, or a *niçoise* salad. And in the evening, in the luminous cocoon of the candles, all the tables occupied by travel buffs, eyes closed while they tasted tiny spring rolls, mahi mahi, fish soup with coconut milk and coriander, the seafood platter, and the brochette of game. Oriental rugs covered the ground. In the background played the delicate notes of chamber music.

I could picture myself as well. I was smiling in this picture. I was floating above all of this. I was never alone again. I moved in between the tables, exchanging a few words here and there.

At the beginning, I chased this image away as soon as it entered my mind, screaming at it to leave and taking on a mean look. Then I got used to its presence. It was like a dog that had chosen me as its master. I gave in, playing with it by throwing it details and colours that it brought back to the canvas.

I let myself be convinced. Once again I began to think it was possible. I told myself, "I just have to save everything I can for enough years." And that's what I did. I cut back on everything, even on shoelaces. I stopped going out – which wasn't a huge sacrifice – and I volunteered for any available overtime. I bought nothing. I recycled everything. For several years, I lived on canned tuna and shredded carrots. I watched a nice little nest egg grow at the bank. It was possible. It was really possible. I just had to wait. Wait for the money, and it came, and wait for the economic crisis to resolve itself. I just had to wait for the wind to turn.

It turned. I lost my job. Based on the number of patients, the old hospital couldn't justify the galloping maintenance costs. It had purely and simply closed by relocating the patients. But not the employees. I redid the rounds of the restaurants to find a job, but six years in a hospital kitchen did not inspire the owners, and in any event, the Capital had never been so poor. Soup kitchens were not providing. People slept on sidewalks. At least I had money. It lasted over a year. I was already accustomed to living frugally so I wasn't changing my habits at all. Before it even had a chance to exist, the Art Café was dead, and something in me died along with it.

I became apathetic. I no longer looked for work, I wasn't interested in anything. I washed my clothes in cold tap water and I sat down to watch them dry on the radiator. I no longer spoke to anyone. I had eaten so much tuna that my skin smelled of fish.

At the bank, my savings were diminishing. I could see the day approaching when I would be on the street, so crushed by adversity that it would be impossible to get back on my feet. I knew something had to be done. Worse yet, I thought I knew what to do. After having given up on many things, I was going to have to forsake my dignity.

I returned to the immigrant quarter. Amir's restaurant was closed, the garage door hermetically sealed on the alley, like the lid of an old woman's eye. I knocked. After a long pause, he opened the door dressed in a bathrobe, all bent over and crippled by rheumatism, his enormous grey eyebrows arched suspiciously. I dropped my old boss's name to open the door. Amir smiled. He let me in.

My new business operated fairly efficiently from the start. The upside was the advantage of being outside. I was constantly on the move. I walked kilometres and kilometres every day. I needed it after over a year of inactivity. At first, my legs made me suffer terribly, and then they became hard as rocks. I had to equip myself with good shoes to avoid blisters and calluses. I also had to take care of my appearance so as not to frighten clients. In short, I was becoming a respectable citizen once again. But at what cost!

I spoke with Amir for a good hour. I already knew that he had ceased his activities two or three years ago.

"Health . . ."

I sympathized.

Then, I offered him a small amount of money to purchase, not his business, but his American contacts. He accepted and thought I was crazy. I ran straight for the telephone, and despite the time and cultural differences, I managed to persuade the person on the other end of the line of my determination to become the herald of ballpark sausages in my homeland, a food barely known by my compatriots up until now.

"With money, it can be done. With money, anything can be done," he said, a continent away.

We agreed on the terms and conditions. I went to the bank to transfer funds to the account he had indicated and waited. I was nervous. What if nothing came of this, and what if I had stupidly been cheated of my remaining wealth?

Then came another phone call and I went to the airport to collect a few cases of hot dogs packaged in plastic, and bags of small, soft, insipid buns, as well as several containers of ketchup and some bright yellow stuff that in no way had the right to bear the name of mustard.

My idea wasn't to imitate Amir's business. I didn't have the means to set up shop. And since people had stopped frequenting restaurants, the restaurant had to go to them.

Down to my pennies, I bought a small gas barbecue that I modified by mounting it on baby carriage wheels. I secured a cooler between the wheels and voilà! I went into the streets yelling "hot dogs"!

The idea had developed in me through the echoing words of my old teacher. *Soft, warm and fatty like a woman's breast.* I pondered . . . If the American hot dog was a breast, it was shaped like a dick. It's not a dish, rather a perversion. People could always be counted on to favour their vices even in times when money is scarce. The unfortunate people who sleep under cardboard roofs always find some change with which to buy a bottle, and in times of crisis, prostitutes are even more numerous. I hoped that the others, a little better off, would find the resources to satisfy their cravings with my wretched sandwiches.

Happily, my reasoning was well-founded. The low price of my hot dogs and the addictive nature of their chemical components drew a good number of satisfied clients from the very beginning. In the name of my own survival, I wandered through all the Capital's neighbourhoods to poison my fellow citizens.

Was I unhappy? I was earning a living. It's always a little depressing to have to earn what was given to us so generously at birth. Let's say I wasn't happy. My social life resumed with periodic telephone calls with my American suppliers and those random, sometimes single, contacts with my clients. At the very least, I could keep my apartment and eat things other than tuna. In fact, business was good to the point where I could begin saving again, but saving for what? I definitely did not want to dream anymore. I saved out of habit and for fear of soon finding myself with nothing.

There are people who are lucky, and others who aren't. I was among the latter. I sought consolation by telling myself that I was not responsible for the state of things, but in the universal lottery, my number hadn't been drawn. Because I didn't believe in God, who was I supposed to complain to? Fate wasn't known to listen attentively to human beings. And anyway, I was not a loser. I simply wasn't a winner.

I had optimized my return by establishing a pedestrian route where the hot dog/step ratio was in my favour. I stopped in specific places where devotees would rush at me instead of the other way around. To my great surprise, I had to restock at an increasingly frequent rate, so much that my little sausage-stuffed buns flew out like hot cakes. After sixteen months, I started to wonder if I shouldn't buy more barbecues and hire some young people to man them. Without dreaming, but more in line with a realistic nightmare, I pictured a flotilla of gas barbecues winding through the city to stuff its inhabitants until their arteries exploded while splattering the walls with bloodstains the colour of ketchup- and mustard-covered sanies. I would have done it if I could have effortlessly increased my wealth and so started to dream again despite myself. But the combined influence of two events ended up dragging me elsewhere.

The first was a restaurant opening that I witnessed because my usual route consisted in a stop right out front. Through the greatest of coincidences, it was called Art Café and resembled the one I had stopped dreaming about in every aspect. It still smelled of fresh paint when, on its first day, family and friends gathered for a free meal and to toast the business's success. The owner, a man my age who could very well have been me, beamed and blushed while kissing the women as two waiters juggled plates as they raced the distance between the kitchen and the tables.

The following day and those thereafter, the Art Café remained almost empty. Until it really took off, the owner took advantage of the time to hammer something, rearrange the tables and water potted plants that had suffered in the move.

On the inside, I wished him the best of luck, but each time my route led me by there, each time my eyes searched the restaurant and I examined the daily menu written out in white chalk on a slate, each time I felt a pang of jealousy, I felt "Why not me? Why did I have to push a barbecue on wheels to sell people beef and pork by-products? Why am I here and he is there?"

I lingered too long. I was hurting myself.

I saw the right colour choice for the walls, the right furniture, elegant and comfortable, the right lighting, the lovely smell of fresh bread, of thyme and toasted pine nuts that wafted into the street and came to tickle my nostrils. It was . . . that. It was my dream turned into reality but belonging to another. It was my abandoned dream that another had gathered delicately in his cupped hands to warm it with his breath and nurse it back to health.

So be it. It didn't belong to me anymore. Let someone else cosset and hatch it. I was obviously not worthy and had resigned myself to my fate to the point where soon I was satisfied with silently encouraging the dream of another. I wanted the Art Café to be successful because this would mean that my former dream was good, that it was well dreamed, that I was right to dream about it and that I wasn't just a dreamer.

But as time went on, there were still no clients. The owner had completed his finishing touches. Now, he spent his time leaning on the front door frame, his gaze growing emptier, just like his business. Day after day, I watched the staff leave, never to come back. I saw the menu change, lighten, the choices melting like snow under the sun.

It was terribly unfair. I couldn't understand it. I couldn't accept it. Right in front of the Art Café, I sold more American hot dogs than should be allowed by the Department of Public Health, but was no one going to allow themselves to be tempted by the *paella valencienne* or the *lapin à la moutarde*? If only the dishes had been overpriced, but they weren't.

They preferred my hot dogs. I was praised as if they were the best thing in the world. I was embarrassed to have studied cooking to then end up grilling sausages. But I did it well! Shit has to have a crispy coating! I despised my clients who swallowed them gluttonously, mustard on their collars, instead of sitting out front to eat like human beings worthy of the name.

The owner of the Art Café was slowly sinking. Oh, he occasionally had clients! But three daily specials don't make ends meet. It wasn't much of a stretch to imagine the bottomless pit that this represented and even more, the inexpressible anxiety of losing everything because, in the end, we know nothing about our equals even though we thought we knew them, even though we thought we knew what was good for them. But they don't want to hear it. And if they don't want to hear it, it's because they don't want to have anything to do with you.

I watched the sinking ship and did nothing. Not once did I eat there. I had the impression that any help from me would merely serve to accelerate its demise. I already believed I was responsible for its failure, because the dream was originally mine and it was tainted. I remained in my spot on the sidewalk, with my sausages, and I watched the owner's stare gradually cloud over, his smile fix into a frown, his wrinkles deepen. It was my mirror. After some time, I couldn't stand it any longer. I altered my route and never stepped foot in front of the Art Café again.

I lost clients, I made new ones. One of them changed my life.

I had chosen a working-class neighbourhood that I had avoided up until then. The poor struggled enough without insulting them with selling my product that gratifies without sticking to the body, and fills you up without nourishment. Whatever . . .

The man was very tanned, broad-shouldered, and every day he ate two, sometimes three or even four hot dogs with moans of enjoyment. With a full mouth, he insisted on making light conversation with me. He badgered me with questions that I had to answer to be polite. When he learned that I had studied cooking, his bushy eyebrows formed a triumphant arc.

He was a foreman in a large sawmill in the M. region. The cook had just handed in his resignation. Would I be interested in replacing him? I shrugged my shoulders. But in the end, why not? I could no longer digest my own sausages, or what my life had become.

The man made some phone calls, talked to his boss, and there you have it. On the strength of my hot dogs, I found myself in the woods, cooking for tables of lumberjacks.

When we are indifferent to everything, we let ourselves be carried away.

TEA IN THE GARDEN
OF RUINS

Cevitjc had provided me with a chauffeur and guide.

"And not just any one! A retired military man," he specified.

I was flattered by the attention up until the time Josef picked me up at the hotel at the wheel of a shiny 4x4 rental, black as night (windows included) that could have been mistaken for one of those combat vehicles the Russian Mafiosos drive when vacationing on the shores of the Baltic Sea.

From it stepped down a debonair old grandpa with swollen ankles and a red nose whose broken veins revealed an immoderate taste for red wine. He wore an absurd fly fisherman's hat, an old jogging suit in outdated colours and on his feet – I looked up to inspect the unanimously blue sky – rain boots. But his eyes sparkled and, with his broad grey moustache that covered his upper lip, he looked like the giant and somewhat damaged version of a fairy-tale elf.

I intended to get myself to the Capital to "start at the beginning," and the thought of hours of sharing the confined space of the 4x4 with such a character did not please me one bit. But I had no choice. I got in.

I had counted on making a round trip that day, so I hadn't brought a bag, except for my briefcase containing the thick green-covered file given to me by Cevitjc. I wanted to read it during the ride but in the meantime, I turned to lay the bag on the back seat, enabling me to catch a glimpse of a large calibre revolver, poorly hidden under a blanket. I pretended not to have seen it but I suspended my motion and returned the briefcase to my lap. I shot a sideways glance at Josef. He appeared more dangerous than he had at first sight. For a good fifteen minutes, we travelled in silence. The silence grew progressively heavier. Finally, I couldn't take it any longer; I turned to Josef and asked:

"Why the gun?"

"Hunting."

"With a handgun?"

He shrugged his shoulders and I heard him mumble under his moustache.

"No, seriously?"

"Seriously? Some of your client's accomplices are still free. They aren't kind."

"You think they could come after me?"

"I don't know. I don't think so. But if ever they do, I prefer to be armed."

"So you're here to defend me?"

"Oh no, I'm only your chauffeur. The gun is for my own protection!"

Josef looked at me, his eyes chuckled and his moustache twitched with a light quiver.

Just my luck. A comedian. An armed comedian.

I dedicated the rest of the trip to reading the green-covered file while periodically glancing anxiously out the window, as if there was an ambush waiting somewhere along the road.

Subsequently, I completely disregarded the scenery I was so absorbed in my reading. War is a terrible story. But there was worse. There was Rosalind.

I was dismayed. How could my client have committed such an act? And why? There was nothing military or tactic involved. Rather, it was a pure barbarian act. Despicable . . . The murder of a child. My mind was spinning: the mere horror of the act committed by my client could definitively prove to be the last hope. For no sane person would knowingly agree to kill a child. Therefore, the answer had to lie in alienation. The Monster is crazy, I decided, and consequently cannot be held responsible for his actions.

I had the address on a piece of paper, the street name written in capital letters. I followed the directions. I had left Josef a few hundred metres back because the roads, full of potholes due to bombings, hadn't been cleared of the mountains of rubble cluttering them. I was alone; I preferred to be in these delicate situations. What's more, I felt a certain embarrassment in walking around accompanied by a sixty-five-year-old elf.

If the Capital's centre had been relatively spared, the suburbs had been caught in the crossfire between assailants and protectors. Many stray shells had thus destroyed targets that were entirely non-strategic, except for those who lived there.

But for now, nothing appeared menacing. A beautiful sun, already setting, made shadows play among the ruins, and under the clear light, one would have thought that this part of the city was not destroyed, but rather still in the project phase. Laughing children climbed mountains of debris. They had piled breeze-blocks to form walls, redoubts, bridges, castles that were reduced models of this neighbourhood that once was and had yet to be. The dust suspended in the air, golden in the light, transformed the setting into a scene filled with innocence.

I had arrived. Here was the address shown on my paper. Only, there was no longer a house. Three walls still stood. The sky could be seen through sections of roof. Without windows or doors, the façade pockmarked by gunfire still bore red-painted numbers that made up its civic address. But there must be some mistake. No one could possibly live here.

I moved closer. Through the hole in the door, I could see swept floors. Further, there was an armchair covered with a tarp. From the back, of what remained of the kitchen, wafted at me the smell of coffee. I shouted:

"Is anyone home?"

No answer. I suspected squatters, people who had lost everything and had nothing to lose. I backed out at once. From the back of the house, I heard a sort of shissing. I admit I was scared. My usual fighting ground was the thick carpeting in my office and my weapons were fat handbooks of case law. Is the pen more powerful than the sword? At that moment, I would have chosen the sword. I could just imagine those squatters who lived in the ruins and drank rain water, stealing stray dogs to eat them and making necklaces from their teeth.

I heard footsteps, scuffling. I looked around for a weapon and bent down to pick up a rock. When I stood up, two small elderly people stood before me, a woman and a man, holding each other by the arm. Two worn-out beings, not withered, but on the road to becoming that way. The man stood straight, as if summoning the memory of his own strength. The woman stood slightly behind, brandishing a small used dustpan that seemed menacing nonetheless.

"What do you want?" asked the Monster's father.

"What are you doing here?" asked the Monster's mother.

It was completely inappropriate but I laughed in relief. I laughed for having been scared of these two fragile, harmless beings. Suddenly, the man was wielding a crowbar that he had hidden behind his back.

"I am your son's lawyer," I hurried to declare.

"Which one?"

"Viktor."

"Oh," said the man.

Dropping the arm holding the crowbar, he turned his back to me and disappeared, through the kitchen, into the garden.

"How is . . . ?" began the mother, but she didn't finish her sentence.

The dustpan fell to the floor with a pathetic metallic ping. The woman did not lower her gaze, her shoulders did not hunch. She looked at me and cried. She wasn't ashamed of her tears. On the contrary, she owned them.

A mother's tears. What huge strength she draws! I looked at her, intimidated. I saw my mother, I saw all the mothers in the world. I saw Florence, the mother of my children. The enormity of maternal love, the enormity of love's powerlessness. Mothers want to hold back the ocean with their arms and irrigate the deserts with their tears. In order to come to life, love is condemned for eternity to search for a gesture, a caress, a word, a kiss. The ghost of love who sighs after life was her, this old woman, in these ruins, the family home where the Monster had learned to walk.

"Come," she said at last.

I followed her into the garden.

Walking through the house in ruins, I easily imagined the crayon marks on the door frames marking the children's growth. I imagined the bursts of children's laughter, the toys on the floor and the slow ascent towards adulthood that is also a swift passage in time and space until separation, sometimes until indifference, until loss.

I had the opportunity to think about all of this during the trip, while reading the green file that was as damning as Cevitjc had said it was. After all, I was also a father.

I thought of my own son. He was still a baby but how severely I punished him when he struck his little sister. I, who played continually with the fine line between good and evil, drawing it here instead of there and there instead of here, I knew that it existed. How many times had my son's guilty expression given him away while his transgression was still unknown to me? He suspected the existence of this line as well.

What if he became a monster? What would I do with my love for him? How do you hug a monster? How did Viktor Rosh's mother do it?

If the house was demolished, the bombardments had miraculously spared the small shed at the back of the garden which, I imagine, had housed garden tools, bags of earth for potted plants and a lawnmower. It was a tiny, windowless sheet-metal shelter, two by three metres, and they lived inside. A bed, a foldaway table, two straight chairs, a watering can, a few saucepans, glasses, plates and a gas stove. They lived there, in a functional and sparse setting, but everywhere around the garden shed, arranged on the lawn as if for company, lay the remains of their real home: furniture, armoires, easy chairs, dining-room table with its chairs, kitchen table with its chairs, dressing table, china cabinet, sofas, carpets, pedestal tables and their knick-knacks, clocks, lamps, candlesticks, photographs in their gold frames, mirrors and a massive old-fashioned bed with sculpted ornaments, an accumulation of objects compiled over a lifetime, their feet bathing in the garden dust.

The Monster's parents had emptied the ruined house and put everything back in its place in the garden as if walls, and not air, separated the rooms. On the ground, I saw paths being worn between what could pass as a living room and what served as a library because the shelves had suffered and there were no books. Not everything was in good condition. Broken, patched up, lopsided, filthy and amputated objects seemed to be treated with the same infinite respect of their past. They too seemed to wait for a small place inside so that everything could return to what it once was, as if the objects had lives of their own and refused to die, to vanish into firewood, as if they were merely convalescing and waiting patiently for their wounds and fractures to heal.

But the snow, rain, dryness and wind had cracked the varnish, tarnished the surfaces and warped the corners, and all of this took on the look of a run-of-the-mill cemetery. By keeping their furniture within arm's reach, these two old folks were mostly keeping them alive in their memories.

I walked behind the mother who was following a precise itinerary, and I saw her, when passing in front of a sideboard, take a rag from her sleeve to wipe away some dust. I stopped for a moment, struck more than I would have liked by the useless pretentiousness of this act. I was suffocating.

However, it was quite a vast garden. You could see the remains of a vegetable garden and, although alive, two emaciated apple trees. A suburban garden, similar to the one I had played in as a child, and which my parents continued to cultivate to this day. It was this impression of *déjà vu* that prevented me from breathing. The war wasn't exotic enough to be comfortable. Several neighbouring houses remained intact. Why had the bomb landed here and not elsewhere? Between chance and destiny, I never knew where to make my bed. What did it matter anyway? The bomb had already hit.

Many things can be endured. We can age until we uproot ourselves from existence like a rotten tooth. But this? How could they accept that their life story was erased by the blast from a bomb? So, on the garden's blank page, they attempted to rewrite it with the only alphabet at their disposal. This furniture and these knick-knacks formed words that they had consolidated into sentences according to the syntax of the memory that told their life story.

The mother had disappeared into the garden shed. I joined her. Silently, she took a pot of hot water from the fire and poured it into a chipped teapot. She placed it on a tray, with cups, milk and sugar, and carried it all to the dining-room table that, although lopsided, displayed its lace table runner topped with a crystal vase full of fabric flowers.

The father was out of sight, but I could hear the sound of his hammering coming from inside the house. The mother served me and then sat to sip her tea without saying a word.

As for me, what could I say? Add the son's misfortune to that of the parents'? But it had to be done. That's what I was there for.

"I want to help your son," I said.

She looked up from her cup, stared at me as if she had just noticed that I was there. She seemed faraway. So faraway. I thought of a woman in a state of shock and doubted that she would ever be able to answer me, but she ripped these words from her throat:

"He's never wanted anyone's help."

"Even as a child?"

"What can be said about one's child? All I know about him is what I wanted to see. What resembles me. What resembles his father. I know what you want to find out. You want to know about his wounds. Why do people think that parents are aware of their children's injuries? We try to make our children laugh, not cry. We learn to know what makes them happy. But we avoid their tears. I wanted to protect Viktor from sorrow, so much so that when he cried, I didn't quite know why. Sometimes you guess. At the beginning. But as time goes on, your children's grief becomes unfamiliar to you. I'm seventy years old and when I cry, my husband is confused. He doesn't cry, he swallows his tears. I don't understand. Forty-three years of marriage. I can't do anything to help him. He can't do anything to help me. Our tears are our own."

"I understand, but put yourself in the jury's shoes. What can you tell me about Viktor that would make him human, gentle and fragile?"

"I don't know my son. I don't know him anymore. I stopped knowing him once he became an adult. He became someone other than my son."

"What happened?" I asked.

"He became himself, his own person. Before that, he was an extension of my love, an offshoot of my body, an incarnation of my desire to be a mother. He was my child. Do you have children?"

"Yes, two."

"How old are they?"

"Two and four."

"You still have a little time left. But you'll see. We don't bring children into this world so that they'll remain children even though that's what we hope for. Everything we do, everything we show them, is so that they can get away from us, and that's the worst thing we can do. Because they do get away. They become their own people, they have thoughts that they keep to themselves, secrets, shadows. They develop in these shady corners, far from our sight, far from everyone's sight. I imagine that they become what they are supposed to become. We have nothing to do with it. Nothing. Rather, we are an obstacle. An obstacle!"

Her knuckles became white, her fist gripped the cup with such force that I feared it would shatter into pieces. Her voice was empty like a lament and I understood that the real drama in this woman's life wasn't the bomb, the loss of her home and her furniture, but rather the permanent solitude she shared with another. She went on:

"An obstacle! And love dictates that we step aside. Bravo love! Step aside! Leave him alone in the shadows. It's in the shadows that he became a monster. It's in the shadows that he detached himself from me, that he became a killer. Is this why I became a mother? Is this why I loved him so much? So that he could detach himself from me and become a monster? His name was Viktor. I called him Vichou. He stroked my cheek while he fed at my breast. I can tell you about that. But that's not what you're interested in . . ."

"That's not what I said."

"No, what you want to know is how one becomes a monster, and because I am his mother, you want to know my recipe!

Well I'll give it to you: Love! Give love! Give and give and give! And at the end of it all, nothing. Indifference, shame, a monster!"

I began to catch a glimpse of what young Viktor's life must have been like under the guardianship of this woman whose suffocating love demanded exclusivity. Growing up and aging was treason. Achieving the freedom to think, to feel, to act on one's own should inevitably be accompanied with a feeling of guilt that tainted everything black and cast a sort of dark veil of grief over the smallest happiness. Psychoanalysts say that the father has to be killed, but the mother? The mother is eternal, and she will haunt us forever while shedding a small silent tear because you didn't think to buy her flowers on her birthday.

How can a mother's love not be disappointed?

Meanwhile, the old woman continued:

"The child in my heart is not the man he has become. One day, he was like an open book, and the next he was closed, with the pages stuck together. He was what, twelve years old?"

I jumped. Here was something that could help me.

"What happened?"

"He had followed his older brother on a small excursion outside the city. Reckless and irresponsible!"

"No child is responsible at twelve years old."

"I was referring to Milos, his older brother. He was fifteen, almost sixteen. He let him tag along and he brought Viktor back in a broken state. One tibia, ribs, he was black and blue from contusions. But the worst part was his silence."

"He wasn't speaking?"

"Very little. He would nod his head. If I pressed him he would give brief answers to my questions. But the stories, the confidences, the loving words, they were no longer. I was so resentful. Towards Milos. It was his responsibility to look out for his little brother, and he didn't do it. He let me down and I have never forgiven him."

"How did he get hurt?"

"Viktor never told me and Milos doesn't really know. They had wanted to explore an old abandoned building. Viktor climbed a ladder and fell. I don't know much more."

"Could this partially explain what he is being faulted for now?"

"How can you expect me to know? He became taciturn, but that's not a crime. It was like a growth spurt and poof! His childhood was over. And I can say that now because I've thought about it. I've thought about it a lot since his arrest. Journalists came all the way out here. My husband chased them off with his crowbar and we saw his picture in the newspaper, menacing, with the caption 'The Monster: The Apple Doesn't Fall Far From the Tree.' No thank you. I don't want to think about that anymore. I loved that child, sir. I loved my two children more than anything in the world and this is how they thank me? I am too tired now. Look at this (she pointed to the whole garden). My husband wants to rebuild the house. He doesn't want to leave but he's been my husband for forty-three years. So I stay. I live in a metal shack, I have a son in prison and another God knows where. Do I deserve this? Is this what I deserve?"

It was not a purely rhetorical question. She truly expected an answer from me. Of course she was crazy. The kind of craziness that isn't found in medical books. The craziness of love that wants to be repaid. It wasn't a matter of being deserving. Nothing was ever a matter of being deserved, for in our own eyes, we are always the centre of the universe, whereas in other people's eyes . . .

"No, you didn't deserve that," I lied.

She seemed pleased with my answer and I must have passed some sort of test because she called out her husband's name and soon he came out of the house, wiping his hands on his pants. He came to sit and have a cup of tea with us. He had big bags under his eyes and his face had thick, rough skin with white whiskers on his chin. He wore a low-cut shirt over a scrawny, sunburned torso. A life of manual labour had left its mark and I gazed, fascinated, at his big calloused hands, knotted like roots that miraculously managed to grasp the tiny porcelain cup without reducing it into crumbs.

He followed my gaze. He put down his cup and held out his hands.

"It's the war," he said. "My hands have killed. They were taught to kill and they've wanted to kill ever since. If I let them do as they please, they would kill. They would kill you and you know it. You can tell. You can always tell these things."

"No . . ." I protested for show.

"I'm not telling tales," he said with great seriousness. "I have nothing to hide. I couldn't care less about you. You ask why my son is in this predicament and my answer is 'because of the war.' If there hadn't been a war, he wouldn't have killed. I don't know what he would have become, but he wouldn't be a killer. Put a machine gun in anyone's hands, stand them in front of someone who is going to kill them if they don't kill them first, and there you have it. It's done. You have created a murderer. So I say that it's the war that made a monster of my son and there is no need to look any further."

"Tens of thousands were part of that war, and they aren't facing a jury."

The old man went on without hearing me.

"My own war is forty years old. But every night I dream about it. I killed. I was taught to kill and I learned well. The war was over but I was still alive. And my hands (he held them out), my hands remember the sensation of a neck snapping. I can still hear the vertebrae crack."

"So your son is a victim of the war, just as those he killed? Is that what you're telling me?"

"I returned from the war with hands that desired to kill," said the old man. "But I occupied them in other ways. My hands were angry. I taught them to hold a hammer and bang nails. I contained them. For hours at a time, in the evening after work, I forced them to rest quietly in my lap. I got married, I had children. But I always had my angry hands. I always had the war in me and despite the war inside, I married and had children. Do you know why? Because I am stronger than my hands. I control my hands and not the other way around. So when you ask me if my son is a victim, I ask you: Can we be victims of our own hands? My son is my son. I wiped the boy's behind. He fell asleep in my arms. But my son is more than his hands. His hands are a part of him, he is not a part of his hands. To reach the point where hands are left to do as they please, there has to be surrender. You have to give up the fight. Power has to be surrendered, and that's what my son did, long before the war. So, is he a victim? Yes, of course. And no, not at all. Or, he decided to become a victim of the war because it was easier than keeping his hands under control. It was his decision. He bears the responsibility."

I was discouraged. If even my client's parents believed he was guilty, I had no defence to use and I was going to be eaten alive in court. Even if they thought he was innocent, what could I accomplish with these two crazy old people that wouldn't be prejudicial to him, she with her arrogant love, he with his hand stories? But I said anyway:

"Do you believe he is guilty?"

"Yes. He is guilty. But I am too. And so is my wife, and everyone around us. You are guilty too."

"I've never killed."

"But you allow thousands – millions – to be killed. People like my son, dreamers, young people who, by rebelling against authority, end up having no use for it. They're everywhere, you have them too. But it's in places like this that they become monsters, whereas in your country, they play rock music or make movies. What can dreamers dream of here, eh? Can you see the misery? Can you see the hatred? Can you see how grey it is? What is left for dreamers who have nothing to dream about? They are like empty shells. When the war arrives, their hands strangle all on their own. It's easy for you. You ask: guilty or not guilty, it's easy. But if you had lived my son's life, if you had been born here, if you had a gun in your hands and a man in your rifle's sight aiming back at you, what would you have done?"

"I repeat, your son is not accused of having accomplished his duty as a soldier, but to have gone beyond it. You cannot place the war and Rosalind on the same and equal footing."

"Rosalind! A lost girl. Girls like her die every day in city gutters and no one makes anything of it. Don't change the subject. What makes you so convinced that you wouldn't have done the same in his place? What makes you so sure? (He was almost yelling now.) You have never killed or had the opportunity to do so. You can't know and you don't want to know because if you had killed, you might have discovered the power. That idea is unbearable. You're like puritans who shower completely clothed; you don't even want to think of killing because you're afraid of enjoying it. Deep down, you know that it exists; you know that it's a possibility. You know that you're a killer and that a human life isn't as important as you'd like to think. Otherwise, you wouldn't let African children die of hunger; you would drop everything to help them. But no. You are here and for what? To defend my son? To defend a monster? We're not in a movie. The blood is real here. Death is real. My son did what he did because of the world we live in and I don't give a damn about your moral judgments that you're throwing in our faces under the pretence of helping."

"I'm not here to judge. I'm a lawyer."

"Good for you," the old man said while getting up abruptly from the table. "That way you can also hide behind your own cowardice."

He disappeared into the crumbling house from which furious hammering sounds immediately resounded. He was unleashing his hands.

The mother and I remained seated in silence. The least I could say is that it didn't go very well. The mother rose as abruptly as her husband and disappeared, as he did, into the garden shed from where I could hear her rummaging about. At last she returned, and set a tin box in front of me.

"Cookies," she said. "He loved them when he was little. Will you give them to him?"

"Wouldn't you like to give them to him yourself?"

"We went at the beginning. He didn't want to see us. I didn't even hear the sound of his voice. Tell him I love him.

Tell him I've always loved him, that I'll always love him, tell him . . ."

She swallowed a sob.

"Please."

Then, she returned to the shed, but I knew that she would not re-emerge. I took the box of cookies and weaved between the furniture, crossed the house and went out into the street.

Nothing had changed, except for the sun which was slightly lower on the horizon. On the mountains of rubble, children still played while letting out little shrieks. There were ten of them in torn clothing, unaware of their parents' struggles and choked-back sobs. They played among the ruins of their city. They were nothing but children: muddy, shaggy-haired, dreamers.

Little monsters.

I REMEMBER MY JOY

Obviously, there was no one to greet me. I inquired about the sawmill at the village hotel. A full-figured woman served me a glass of beer and told me that it was ten kilometres inside the woods. To get there, I merely had to start walking and a car or a truck would pick me up along the way.

I booked a room where I left my bags and set out on a dirt road. The weather was nice. The sun's rays played in the dancing foliage. The air was pure and fresh, and the scent of moss and mushrooms reached my nose. It felt good to walk without having anything to sell, so much so that I let the first cars pass without flagging them down.

I had donned a conservative suit and a white shirt in an effort to look presentable. In this landscape in which, behind every rock, you expected to see a bear emerge, I felt comical, out of place, awkward. Nevertheless, I was smiling. It seemed as though with each step, scales of my old life fell from my body to lose themselves in the dust of the road. Soon enough, my jacket was over my shoulder, my sleeves rolled and my shirt drenched in sweat. I had to resist the urge to head into the forest. I dreamed of living there with nothing, but what did I know about life in the woods besides what I had read in novels in which Indians were targets for cowboys? I amused myself by making a list: I would need a knife, a lighter, a shotgun or a bow. Good God! Could one really live like a savage and eat game without salt and pepper? I laughed heartily and my laugh quieted the birds.

For hours on end, in a ramshackle motorbus that made unexplained stops in the middle of nowhere, I crossed a rough countryside. From the Capital, I had to travel across the mountains in the south, to skirt the Great Forest up to the city of M. Then, I switched motorbuses to take another route, this time going around the forest to the north, and, according to my map, making a sharp turn at the foot of the mountains before leaving the province to serve its neighbour.

A child of the city, I had obviously experienced a little country. But the occasional farm visit and walks in the fields herald nothing of the solemn savagery of the ancient forest that I believed to be all around me. It looked so small, this ribbon of asphalt that led straight into the green rolling hills! This thin, fragile trench was threatened at any moment of being overrun and covered by the exuberant vegetation. I thought: Trees stood well before man did. Once upon a time, they were the masters of the world. Then, our ancestors left their cover to learn to walk, and everything became unbalanced. In some way, I was returning to the protection of the trees. I was going home.

I'm going home, I thought, as I walked towards the sawmill. I wanted to live here, to be part of this landscape. But it was rugged. The forest wasn't that of Robin Hood. There was no way to travel through it on horseback. The brambles, bushes, brush, the rotting corpses of fallen trees, the bumps and the holes, just the denseness of the trees which fought for a place in the sunshine made the terrain inhospitable, harsh and, I imagine, menacing under an overcast sky.

Behind me I heard the sound of a motor. I didn't turn to signal it and kept walking. However, after some time, I still heard the motor, idling slowly behind me. I looked over my shoulder. An old rusty pickup was following me. The driver saw me, accelerated until he reached me and peered at me through the window without saying a word.

"Hello," I said.

He didn't answer. I was certain that his piercing grey eyes could see right through to my childish dreams of Indians. He wore a heavy canvas shirt, rolled up to biceps the size of coconuts. He didn't appear to be very easygoing. I looked ridiculous. It was embarrassing. I turned towards him and held out my hand.

"My name is Viktor Rosh and I am the new cook."

He smiled slightly.

"We'll see," he said.

All of a sudden he accelerated and I was left with my hand hanging in the air, enveloped in a cloud of dust that made me cough and dirtied my suit.

The strangest thing was that I wasn't angry. I found it normal to be treated that way. I was the intruder, with my pale complexion and my polished shoes. The man was at home, in his element. But the charm was broken and I hailed a truck that loaded me in the back. Once at the sawmill, I asked to see the manager, as planned, who made me wait quite some time.

The sawmill was a vast complex of hangars, offices and temporary dwellings. Trees were cut in the forest and brought back here to be cut into all sizes of beams and boards. From there, they were loaded onto trucks and shipped to the four corners

of the country. Forest workers toiled alongside machine operators, and a whole wing took care of the administration of it
all. With its three hundred employees, the sawmill was by far
the region's largest employer, in fact the only employer, and
this had been a true saving grace ten years ago when a major
financial group from the Capital had decided to start it up.

The door opened at last. The manager walked towards me
wearing a professional smile and Italian shoes. While vigorously
shaking my hand, he told me that he insisted on personally
meeting each of his new employees. I wondered if I should
congratulate him on this feat. But upon further thought, I
kept quiet, which is likely what I was supposed to do since the
manager's speech, which was unravelling like a spool of thread
on a sewing machine, left no opportunity for me to get a word
in edgewise.

I smiled, but my smile was directed beyond the manager,
to the pretty little blonde leaning against the office doorway
and who, with her eyes and mouth, seemed to be mocking him
and his arrogant speech. She was . . . I don't know.

The manager finished with a victorious air, like a high-level
sportsman whose feat consisted of spending a few minutes in
the company of commoners without getting too dirty. Perhaps
I should have answered something, but I couldn't quite tell
what.

"Well," said the manager after a moment of hesitation, as
if this simple word was covering an old truth. He turned then
and introduced me to his secretary.

"Maria," she said, as she held out her hand.

"Viktor," I said, taking her hand as gently as possible. Her
eyes undressed me with her gaze. She emanated an indisputable
erotic power.

The manager moved towards her and, in a gesture of ownership, stroked her hip while, with his chin, he indicated a lower-ranking employee who rose from his chair as if propelled by a spring and took me in charge. The office door closed on the manager and his object, for Maria was his object and I was nothing.

The sawmill included living quarters primarily intended for administrative personnel and management, almost all natives of the Capital. Because in their eyes I was a cook from the Capital, I was offered a room, which I refused, preferring to find something in the village among the riffraff. This raised a few eyebrows.

I was given a tour of the kitchens where six pimply adolescents prepared, more or less satisfactorily, a revolting stew made of sinewy meat, overcooked vegetables and floury gravy. Since the departure of the last cook, the teens were doing their best to feed three hundred bodies, but inevitably ended up hiding their lack of taste and talent under a heap of salt and pepper. I noticed their pitiful nails, hair in the soup, and on the shelves, powdered chicken stock and canned vegetables. There was bread on the board but it was industrial, baked on racks and contained more air than crumbs. In short, it was a disaster.

I was jubilant. I could be good here. The one-eyed man in the kingdom of the blind, so to speak.

Morning and night, a canopy truck shuttled between the village and the sawmill. Following the tour of the site and the signing of working papers, I climbed aboard since apparently there was a house for rent in the village that my salary and sausage savings enabled me to consider. I was anxious to settle into my own home, to hoe my vegetable garden, to wander the woods in search of mushrooms and, who knows, even to hunt. I was going to be happy here, I decided. I gazed at my travel companions, seated on benches that followed the contours of the truck box. They were solid types, chiselled by an axe, who smoked, elbows on their knees, staring at their feet.

I wanted to engage in conversation.

"It's nice," I said to the neighbour on my right, a very tall, fairly hairy type. I found out later that his name was Rossi.

"Hmm?"

He looked at me as if he had no idea what I could possibly be talking about.

"The forest," I repeated. "It's impressive."

He turned to see the treed edge move past in a dense green fog.

"Ya," he answered, turning back to his initial position. "We keep a twenty-metre strip but behind, it's as smooth as a baby's bottom."

"Excuse me?"

"We shaved everything up this way. Clear cutting. Now the trees come from much farther away. In twenty years, there'll be nothing left."

"That's appalling."

He shrugged his shoulders.

"It's free enterprise."

He returned to staring at the floor without paying any more attention to me.

Maria haunted my nights like a lovely dream from which you never want to wake. But it was only a dream and I knew it.

Maria was a private preserve, the manager's girlfriend. The men at the sawmill would never dare initiate anything despite the region's shortage of women, which drove them crazy during a full moon. I think that this shortage of women contributed to the train of events. Pent-up sexual energy has to be spent in some way, otherwise the motor blows.

I don't believe in destiny, but benevolent fate wanted me to rent a house that would make me Maria's neighbour. She wasn't there very often. On weeknights she stayed at the saw-mill with the manager. But on weekends, when he went home to his legitimate wife and manicured children, she came to the village to take long baths or to read magazines while sipping cocktails. I remember my delight when I saw her coming home, arms full of parcels. I was seated on my balcony, sharpening my kitchen knives. I checked the blade by shaving the hair on my left forearm. Since finishing school, I have always had one bald forearm and one hairy. Knives are my tools. But when the manager's car stopped almost in front of my house, I raised my eyes and nicked my arm in surprise when I saw Maria climb out. I moved towards her, waving my hand.

"Hello!"

She looked at me, eyebrows knit, as if she didn't recognize me. Finally, a brief light of recognition spread across her face.

"Oh! Hello," she said.

"Hello," I repeated foolishly.

"You're bleeding," she said.

A wide ribbon of blood flowed from my forearm and dripped onto the ground, and I noticed that the hand that was waving still held a kitchen knife with a bloody blade.

"Um, yes," I answered.

"Little boys shouldn't be allowed to play with knives . . ."

She turned the key in the lock and disappeared into the house without even turning around.

I learned that she was secretive and shy, even perhaps ashamed of her liaison with the manager. Did she love him? I hope not. But like many others, she was trying to better her fate. It wasn't up to me to judge.

Selling your sausages, your body or your soul, it's all the same. Sometimes there's no choice. All this stuff about equality, human rights and all, it's not true. There are some who are more equal than others. I learned that. There are trenches that seem impassable, and when you still want to get across, you wind up wading in mud. There is no choice.

I say that now, but at the time I was not detached or lucid enough to draw conclusions. I was not political. At most, there was somewhat of a small grey cloud that blackened a corner of the sky, even in nice weather. The yeast of a rage that had yet to rise.

My work was not very difficult. The lumbermen's palates were as rough as their hands. The dish had to be hearty, abundant and they had to be able to soak their bread in it. For dessert, they were content with belching. You don't serve sushi to men who have just spent eight hours felling giants and dragging them through the mud. You don't garnish plates with droplets of balsamic vinegar reduction; you pile them high. You don't serve artichokes to *hungry* people.

I would have doubtlessly been happy to have filled their bellies without the sarcasm of a little repugnant man. His name was Puritz, but I called him Pruritus, and then Pustule, which stuck. He cooked for management, who surely would never deign to place their forks on the same plates as the ordinary man. To feed his dozen VIPs, Pustule had a budget that could have fed one hundred of my ogres. He had a separate kitchen, obviously, with *foie gras*, caviar and chilled champagne for special occasions – a rich person's kitchen cliché.

Pustule also had a sufficient amount of free time to make regular visits to my kitchens, dressed in white, with his hat on his mushroom-sized head. He wore small glasses behind which his eyes scrutinized you with irony. During our first meeting, I had made the mistake of telling him my story. Since then, he called me Hot Dog. I would have gladly let the air out of his hat with the tip of my knife. That was the base of his ego, a cheese *soufflé*. If I didn't like him much, he didn't like anyone. And he mocked my cooking.

It's true that there wasn't much that could be done with the stews. Meat and potatoes, chicken and potatoes. Eggs and potatoes – protein and starch, I couldn't escape it. Recipes can't be continuously improved; once it's good, a plateau is reached. So, when Pustule came to visit me and glanced around with a look of disdain before crowing over his *magrets de canards* and his Cornish hens that had been flown in, I wondered how to make him swallow his hubris.

My products were trucked in from M. or from the Capital, and they were neither stellar in terms of freshness nor quality. The vegetables were only crunchy when frozen and what was passed off to the men as butter was actually margarine. I went to see the accountant who looked after kitchen management.

"Why are we buying this?" I said to him, throwing the purchase order for the last shipment on his desk. "It's industrial crap treated with chemicals in the Capital's laboratories. This is not food."

"We've always been pleased with it."

"We can't change?"

The accountant shrugged his shoulders.

"As long as it doesn't cost more."

"Why not local beef, local potatoes, local vegetables, local milk?"

"Have you seen any cattle in the area? And as for vegetables, talk to human resources!"

I bought an old second-hand truck and took advantage of my free time to travel around the country. True, there were no cattle. However, old pastureland was evidence of their ruminant existence in this area. Here and there were the remains of long-abandoned farms, buildings in ruins, stubs of fences held up with rusty barbed wire. Hectares and hectares of land won long ago from the forest were now being reclaimed as if a catastrophe had struck human beings, big and small, from the map.

The region was poor. But what appeared to be a vast disaster zone, revealed itself, when we ventured deeper, to be more populated than I would have thought. Small farmhouses from another century sheltered indomitable elders who milked their goats for their own consumption. A barefoot woman nearing her ninetieth birthday lived all year off a small but hearty vegetable garden. Families living in tatters still held on in the hills, but two chickens and a pig hardly made them breeders, any more than a potato patch made them farmers.

I often stopped and tried to strike up a conversation. This is how I learned, from the toothless mouths of these survivors from another era, that television was responsible for the disaster.

Hypnotized by the stream of images spewing from the small screen, young people had an increasingly hard time accepting field work, said the old folks. They dreamed of big cities, money and easy women. They dreamed of shiny cars and electric appliances. They dreamed of packaged food to which you simply had to add water. They dreamed of beautiful clothing that wasn't intended to be worn to work on your knees in the earth. They dreamed of clean nails. The earth that had fed their parents, and their parents' parents, and their parents before them, that earth was no longer a noble substance, tasted to appreciate its richness and acidity, but dirt for which one was supposed to be ashamed.

And then came the war, and there were many who wanted to join simply to leave this place. When the war was over, the majority of them never returned. There were big reconstruction projects, all this money that the government infused into the system to rebuild the roads, the factories, the hospitals, the pipelines, the electrical lines, all this fake wealth that wasn't going to last, and that didn't last, but was enormously attractive to the young people. So off they went. The old peasants, stripped of the support of their progeny, had tried to maintain their crops and their livestock by doubling their efforts. But they soon gave up because who were they working for? Who were they to bequeath the fruits of their labour to if their own children weren't interested? The fields reverted to fallow land, and the fallow land to forest. In forty years, thousands of years of tradition and work ceased to exist. When the sawmill project arrived, there weren't enough men in the region and some had to be brought in from outside the area. This is what Elena told me, the woman in the vegetable garden, and Matti, who was mincing the tobacco he hung to dry from the ceiling of his overheated kitchen. These relics from another era found themselves alone with all their knowledge and experience that were destined to die along with them. I tried to collect some during my visits, but it was too little, too late. The world didn't want them. They were vanishing in silence.

It was during these outings (I had been at the sawmill for close to eight months) that I had met Manu and Jana. I had just left Elena and didn't have the heart to return to the village where every house was outfitted with a television antenna. I hit the road and plunged down small forgotten paths. Rounding a hill, I came upon a meadow and something didn't seem quite right but I couldn't put my finger on it. And then it dawned on me: the grass was low. I stopped the car, got out and leaned over the antique fencing. No doubt here, this was grazed pasture!

However, nowhere could I see a farm or dwelling, a cow or a sheep. Then I noticed, opening onto the meadow, what looked like a trail. I followed it for approximately four hundred metres. It climbed steadily, snaking between the old trees whose heavy branches hung to the ground, creating tunnels of greenery, vaults of chlorophyll through which the sun's rays penetrated at an angle. It culminated in a small prairie. Two bony cows and an old bull looked at me in a stupor, heads slightly tilted to the side. Between their ears and behind their bodies with protruding ribs, I spotted a small, lopsided house and a rickety stable. I called out:

"Is anyone here?"

No answer. I don't know why, but I imagined the mouth of a gun lodged between a frame and a window, following my slightest move like a black eye. You never know. The old folks from these parts cooked up strange ideas in the cauldron of their solitude. Every day, old Elena cooked for two and set a place at the table for her guest, her mother, with whom she talked incessantly, and who, had she still been alive, would be 120 years old.

I was scared but I moved forward, driven by arrogance. I wanted the milk from these cows. I wanted butter. I wanted meat. I wanted to squeeze Pustule between my fingers and make him ooze.

I was approaching the house. Once again, I yelled out:

"Is anyone here?"

Three children came out of the house. The two eldest, a boy and a girl, were incredibly dirty, but beneath the grime they were good-looking and slender. They looked alike and were holding hands as if they were frightened of me and found comfort in the other's presence, an assurance that they would have been stripped of had they been alone. At their feet, naked, almost clean, was a little boy approximately two years old, smiling at me with incredible sparkle while mercilessly fiddling with his minuscule willy.

"Hello," I said. "Are your parents home?"

They looked at one another. They appeared petrified, but in that exchanged look was more than just fraternal affection. The young girl bent to scoop the small child into her arms. She hugged him against her hip. I then noticed her heavy breasts, a certain lasciviousness of the action, an authority on maternal love and a slightly swollen belly.

They were there, the parents, standing in front of me.

Children.

⟨⟨⟨⟨⟩⟩⟩

They were both fifteen years old. You could say they were cousins. We never talked about it. What was done, was done. And they loved each other, they truly loved each other. They were children left to fend for themselves, who knew nothing else of the outside world than what they could see in the old magazines piled high around the house, the most recent being from the 1970s.

The mother had left them there, as she had left everything else, the house, the old wood stove, a bit of a garden, a nicked scythe for the hay, two cows and a bull. One morning, she did not wake up. Manu would soon be thirteen, Jana had just turned twelve. They had buried the mother behind the house, at the foot of a tree. They didn't tell a soul. When someone came by, they would say that the mother was in the woods. But hardly anyone ever visited these parts. Manu didn't know exactly what had happened, but he didn't have a father, his mother never mentioned it and she feared strangers, especially men. They lived in autarchy, poorly, but still. Milk, butter, wheat, eggs, chickens, potatoes, fruit from an old orchard, Manu knew all of this since birth. Jana too.

Manu couldn't remember a time when Jana wasn't there. The mother said that she had taken her in as a baby. Maybe this was true. Maybe she had bought her from a poor woman to keep her son company when the time had come. They were not brother and sister, at least the closeness of their birth dates inferred this hypothesis, but what did the dates prove? Dates can be changed. Perhaps they were siblings, go figure, but I prefer to think of them as cousins, which would explain their resemblance. This was more acceptable. It made their love more tolerable, even though it wasn't civilized, far from it, it was primitive, visceral. No flowers, no love notes, or little games. They loved one another. Period. They lived for each other; they lived one within the other.

They buried their mother as they would a dead animal, in a hole to avoid the flies. Then, they took the cows to pasture because that's what they had done every day since they had learned to walk. They didn't know that they were supposed to cry. They knew that she was dead, they felt her absence, but what does a twelve-year-old know about the formalities of grieving? Nothing. They continued to do what they had always done and time passed. A winter and a summer, then another winter and then one spring day, Jana's stomach had started to expand. They knew what was happening, they weren't stupid. They had a bull in their sight all year round, and sometimes calves were born that they would kill for meat, or that they kept to replace an old cow. They knew. So they didn't change anything, they continued as before, to cultivate their little garden, to transplant potatoes and to gather hay for the winter. They had time to finish everything before the baby came. Manu had taken it out of Jana the same way that you birth a calf. Nature does the work. He had cut the cord with his pocket knife. And now she was pregnant again.

They didn't tell me all of this right away. They took their time. They didn't know how to tell a story. They never needed to recount anything. They did everything together, they didn't need to tell each other stories, they had never learned. They knew how to talk, of course. They even knew how to read. The old woman had taught them with old children's books that their son now tortured while laughing. But they didn't tell each other stories and didn't feel the need because they completed each other perfectly, as if they formed one single entity.

They were leery of me, of course. But I could see them thinking, that first time. They were clever; they knew that their splendid isolation would have to come to an end eventually. With a second child on the way, they would need money. They didn't have a choice and would have to open themselves up slightly to the world. Just slightly.

I was asking questions about the animals over there grazing, about milk, cream and butter. I watched their twin brains operate at full speed. They were so dirty! But they were so beautiful!

I left there, the first time, with a few litres of milk, a pot of cream and a butter segment freshly churned that they had sold to me for a rather hefty price, but I would have given them double, or triple, for the pleasure of returning to see them.

I went back often after that. I bought everything I could from them for the sawmill. Obviously, the freshness of the products improved things in my kitchens. But that wasn't important. Some people go to the country for the fresh air. I went to visit them to breathe in their great love.

Manu was making a profit. He bought another cow. Things started to pick up. Other inhabitants of the area with a little land decided to work it. Beans, cucumbers, zucchini, and eggplant began to flow through my kitchen. Someone bought a pig. Others imitated him. I was soon able to serve bacon and blood sausage at breakfast.

Everyone had a small profit to make from the sawmill; but swept up by their enthusiasm, they produced more than I was able to purchase. They had to find new outlets. They sold their vegetables along the roadside, from planks sitting on trestles. They visited grocery stores and offered merchants their eggs and their meat. The population adopted these fresh products that they had been deprived of for years for whatever economical logic according to which corners can be cut in terms of quality, as long as there is no revolution.

But our revolution was the taste revolution. Our meat was not an industrial vacuum-packed product, full of antibiotics, and made up with red colouring like an old hooker hanging on to her occupation beyond the limits of reason. Our meat was on its feet one day, fed with grass and grains, and in the fridge the next.

Pustule's pathetic smile fired my enthusiasm. He had to resign himself to buying the fresh produce from the region as well. And this made him suffer. His culinary culture was an insult to the principles of sharing and celebrating: cuisine for a happy few, cuisine of money, not necessarily good, but exclusive because it was unaffordable to common mortals. Did the senior executives really appreciate the dishes prepared by Pustule? What was important wasn't the food that was eaten, but the envy of the others who couldn't afford it. A cuisine for which Pustule was the sorcerer. Such use of the culinary culture was, in my mind, as scandalous and unscrupulous as the pre-packaged one, the powdered ignorance and low-fat denial reserved for the people.

But when you reap what you yourself sowed, when you butcher the pig that you fattened, when you pierce its artery to collect its blood in an iron tub, you aren't only harvesting wheat, bread and blood sausage, you are gaining culture, dignity and pride.

But I kept going back to Manu and Jana. They were my favourites, my children. Two years after our first meeting, they owned twenty-five dairy cows, about fifty chickens and were expecting their third child. Their home was clean and clear, and everyone laughed all the time over there, as if life was a good, harmless joke. No, more specifically, as if life was a children's game, and for them, it was. They weren't quite seventeen when we started to play with cheese. Everything was a game, but a game that deserved to be played seriously. When we play cowboys and Indians, we are serious; we crawl on the ground as if real arrows are whizzing past our ears.

There hadn't been cheese in the area for a good thirty years. I was condemned to serve my guys a tasteless industrial cheese with the texture of melted plastic. However, nobody complained; it was what they were used to. People will develop a taste for shit if it's seasoned properly and if nothing is spared to market it.

In some way, I owe the cheese to Pustule as well. Once I began using products in my kitchen that weren't as fine as his, but far fresher, I thought I saw his chef's hat deflate slightly, as if someone had unexpectedly opened the oven door during the baking of a *soufflé*. But his smile quickly returned at the sight of the enormous brick of vile cheese that I was forced to serve at breakfast.

"Ah!" he simply said.

It was if he had shoved his "Ah!" down my throat. A few days later, I turned up at Manu and Jana's with books on cheese-making that I had ordered from the Capital and we began to experiment.

The first tries were disastrous. The cheese looked and tasted like chalk. Its texture and flavour varied inexplicably from one batch to the next. After a few months, we still hadn't figured out the recipe and the young couple's patience was diminishing at the same rate as their savings. To keep the experiment afloat, I invested a portion of my own nest egg. We ordered a stainless steel vat and continued to waste hectolitres of milk. And then one day, there it was. A simple cheese, firm but not too firm, that had a milky, nutty and green grass flavour. A young, perfect cheese whose recipe we hastened to write down in a leather-bound notebook.

We sold it in wheels under the name Tomme of the Great Forest. At first, the sawmill purchased the bulk of the production. But soon enough, people were showing up at the farm and grocers in the area, stuck with a store of melted plastic, obtained our permission to sell it on their shelves.

From then on, when a stranger came to our door, we presented our cheese for tasting with big smiles and irrefutable pride. When I say "we," I am referring to all area residents, because if our cheese was appealing to the taste buds, it was also good for the soul.

Of course not everything was perfect, and the work at the sawmill was very hard, but when they went home at the end of the day, the meals that their wives put on the table were tastier, and so was life for these rugged, unrefined men. It was even noted during these years, that the birth rate had increased slightly, to the point that it is no longer permitted to doubt the aphrodisiac effects of a good sausage and a hunk of raw milk cheese.

As for me, I cherished the days without theorizing about them. I was free. I had friends, more like work friends, which was no small feat. They sometimes dropped by the house for a glass of the local hooch or some vodka. We had plans. Overall, it was a rural, simple and man's life. Nothing much to do outside of work besides drinking, hunting and fishing – and, it should be noted, not always during the authorized periods.

I travelled through mountains and valleys at the wheel of my old truck. All around was the ancestral forest, except for cutting areas that only ate up a frail section, and the lean fields and pastures doggedly stolen from the trees. I enjoyed these solitary drives precisely because I was alone, and this solitude had not been imposed on me. I had chosen it in the same way that my contact with the others was not the result of a takeover, of an unfounded social obligation, but the expression of an inner need.

I often ran into Mistral during these outings. What was he doing running around the backcountry? Why wasn't he at work?

I didn't think anything of it at the time. He honked. We stopped, door to door, elbows jutting out the open windows, and we talked for a bit. He asked about my protégés and I gave him our news. How was the cheese doing? Very well. Still happy in the kitchens? I said that I was. He smiled, nodding his head, then threw out:

"That's good."

He drove off in a cloud of dust that tarnished the leaves on the trees lining the road. I realized that I had told him everything whereas he hadn't told me anything. True, I hadn't asked him anything. But it is also true that he seemed to discourage the questions even before they were asked. He was like that. Period. It was Mistral. A character.

That wasn't his real name. People called him that because of his bushy hair that looked as though it had been coiffed by the wind. He worked at the sawmill as a lumberjack but was seldom seen on the cutting sites. He was a member of union management but was never seen at union meetings. He mocked any type of authority. He came and went as he pleased, and everyone stopped talking when he approached. He was the most free and mysterious man I had ever known. Was he free because he was shrouded in mystery or mysterious because of his freedom? In any event, he was a man of power, a concealed power that was exercised outside any hierarchy or common structure. He had presence.

He was a lean man, of average height, naturally muscular and taut like the string on a bow. He was exceptionally dense which drew looks and commanded respect. He wasn't often seen at the cafeteria. Where did he eat? What did he eat? He was the type of man who could easily be imagined, cutlass in hand, eating the raw liver from a beast he had just slain. People suspected he had a life different from ours, and that was enough to rouse the imagination.

I remember it clearly. I had been overseeing the sawmill kitchens for three weeks when he came in to eat for the first time. I had prepared a provincial stew with orange rind and port. The vegetables were old and the meat was tough, but the lengthy cooking had melted the fibres and the four spices delighted the palate. I was busy correcting the seasonings when I heard one of my cooks whisper:

"It's Mistral!"

The others rushed to the window to catch a glimpse of him.

"Who is Mistral?" I asked him.

"He's the one who had the head of the last chef."

"What?"

"He didn't like his cooking and he told him. The next day, the chef left."

It was my turn to lean in to see the powerful Mistral. I recognized him instantly. It was the man who had noticed me the first day and answered, "We'll see," when I introduced myself as the new cook. He was still standing in the cafeteria, surrounded by a band of burly men who seemed to serve as bodyguards.

"How could he make the chef leave? He's not a boss."

"He's very persuasive."

Mistral came over to the counter to get his plate, just like everyone else, and then went back to his seat to eat.

I watched him as if my life depended on it (and perhaps it did!). Was he chewing hungrily or reluctantly? I couldn't say. But he was eating, and never had I seen anyone like that. It was the quintessence of the verb "to eat." It was the initial manifestation of the act that all those who have eaten since can only aspire to. There was something Greek about him; by that I mean traditional, archetypical, uncorrupted. Because eating was vital, this was how to go about it: slowly, silently, eyes almost closed to better contemplate an inner spectacle. Small, methodical bites, powerful jaws, muscles undulating under the skin of the cheeks; chewing over time, extracting every parcel of flavour and energy from the flesh; swallowing easily, flowingly; starting over until nothing was left on the plate.

He rose, carried his dirty plate towards the kitchen, and right before heading to the door, he turned to me and smiled.

In that moment, Michelin could have given me twelve stars and I wouldn't have been happier because such was the power of this man to which we all seemed to be abstractions, rough shapes, children's drawings.

I saw him often over the years. We spoke. I thought he liked me well enough, but with him nothing was certain except for this: Only he was a made man, only he was complete. He was the Man. We were merely photocopies of photocopies. Only in him could be found the brutal act of our lost humanity, that virility, that presence in the world that makes us inhabit it instead of being inhabited by it.

In short, he seemed dangerous, and this alone made him attractive. From spending time with him, I understood the worth of a man a little better, my own worth.

This didn't mean that I became his friend. He had none. He was a loner, and his scarcity alone lent weight to his presence. But he showed enough consideration in my regard that I felt privileged. Mistral's acknowledgment ensured everyone's acknowledgment. I was in.

More than six years passed. And if happiness exists on earth, I was almost there. But not quite. Because there was Maria.

If renting a house close to hers had seemed to be a good idea in the beginning, I had started to see the downsides. I was jealous, which was ridiculous because I had never admitted my feelings to her. But I watched her through the window, hidden behind the curtains, and I knew the times she came and went, I knew who came to visit and how often. There was the manager, of course. But also Pustule, who was happy as a lark and was content stocking her refrigerator with little meals to freeze. I imagine that they also leafed through fashion magazines together and had endless discussions about movie stars' cosmetic surgeries.

I was in love. A silent lover who was content to love without being loved in return. I liked loving. I loved up to the jealousy that flowed from it.

As for sex, I took care of that in cash with the two local semi-professionals who collectively responded to the name Mother. They were cheerful people, plump and widowed, who rented rooms in their big houses to employees from the sawmill who they treated like kings, fed, housed, washed and, for a small additional fee, serviced.

"It calms them," Mother #1 would say.

"It's a service to the community," would say Mother #2.

And they were right! Those years were so nice . . . With body at peace and heart almost at rest, I took pleasure in heading to the sawmill after a strong coffee that I drank standing at the window, watching for Maria.

She had become used to me. I sometimes took her to work, but most of the time the boss sent his driver, except when the wife was in the area, of course. Those days were a holiday for me, although nothing showed. Polite interaction – hello – hello – how are you – very well, thank you.

She was often pensive. I dropped her off in front of the administrative offices before continuing along to my kitchens where, for a good three hours already, the first team of my cooks assigned to breakfast duty had been bustling about.

I had to prepare lunch: 75 kilos of meat, 100 kilos of vegetables to trim, cook, season, and serve while giving each plate a small touch of colour. Teams worked until it was nearly dark, which meant that in summer we served a third meal to the starving mosquito-bitten lumberjacks and to the gunk-stained machine operators.

It was in June, I remember. I was preparing an enormous stockpot of three-meat stew (beef, lamb, pork). It was four in the afternoon when the drone of the saws came to a stop. It was rare but not exceptional. In general, it meant that there had been an accident or a breakdown. At the sawmill, fingers were lost on a regular basis, and hands, and sometimes a life. So everything stopped. Each man left his post to go and see what was happening, against warnings from the foremen whose yells fell on deaf ears, and who ended up following the crowd.

I left the kitchens, but instead of seeing a silent assembly, I saw groups of men interspersed throughout the sorting yard, gesturing and talking loudly. I walked over.

"What's going on?"

"They're closing the sawmill."

Alerted by whatever smoke signals, the teams of lumberjacks were already returning from the forest and their voices joined the others to express anger and bewilderment. All they knew was that they had been ordered to stop working. The men speculated: the most optimistic spoke of a restructuring of shifts, others of updating equipment.

"Update what, stupid? It's all new!"

But most whispered: closure, recession, and if they were whispering, it was from fear that by uttering these words aloud, they would become reality, that they would be embodied like demons during a black magic session.

Men who have always been accustomed to working hard don't know what to do with their strength when they are condemned to inactivity. They were waiting for an explanation from management, sitting on every available surface, their powerful, tanned forearms resting on their thighs. They were buzzing from unchannelled energy, their foreheads were pleated with worry, their nostrils were pinched, they smoked cigarette after cigarette and then crushed the butts under their heels in a move that betrayed an immense sense of powerlessness.

I sat in the optimist camp. It was a healthy business that turned a profit. I could see no reason for it to close.

We waited like that for almost two hours before a management spokesperson stepped out from the offices that had been locked up until that point. He wore a wide grin. He waited for all the personnel to gather around him and fall silent before explaining that the sawmill would only be shutting down for a few days. I looked for Mistral. He was nowhere to be seen.

"A team of experts representing potential investors are coming to examine our operations and assess our equipment," said the spokesman through his smile. "It's excellent news since the influx of new capital resulting from an amalgamation is a guarantee for long-term prosperity for the company and its employees. We ask for your full cooperation. Go home. Don't worry. Wait for the order to return to work which shouldn't be long in coming. By the way (his smile became the sardonic grin of a clown), these days off will not be deducted from your next paycheque; rather, you will be awarded a bonus, a demonstration of management's satisfaction with you. Now, I'm sorry, no questions, have a nice holiday and we'll see you very soon!"

The men dispersed and began leaving the sawmill. Of course they were worried. The spokesperson's speech rang untrue, and what could be expected from bosses except for strategies that, at the end of the day, benefited them and no one else? We had been capitalists long enough to understand the whole thing.

I went to the kitchens to turn off the ovens. One hundred litres of stew had stuck to the bottom of the pot and ruined the sauce. I threw the whole thing out, set the pot to soak, turned off the lights and left, locking the doors behind me.

I took advantage of the following days to set my traps and hunt small game. I preferred the woods, alone, at peace. I fled the gatherings of men in the village, drinking to fight unemployment and the fear of tomorrow. After a first day of rest spent watching television in bed, they had begun circling, pointlessly, useless. Their wives, used to prevailing during the day, chased them from the house under the pretext of dusting. But what was there to do outside and how many times could you grease a hinge before going crazy?

After five days, even the most optimistic began doubting. The next day was payday. First thing in the morning, men presented themselves at the sawmill to get their hands on their money. They came back yelling. The sawmill was deserted, and they had padlocked the entrance.

"They're gone! They're gone!"

The news spread across the region at lightning speed. Soon, there were more than two hundred of us gathered in front of the sawmill gates. Men were yelling, but at who and for what? The sawmill looked as though it had been abandoned for months. Fences were shaken, threats were uttered, and then they went home because there was nowhere else to go and nothing else to do.

I have confused memories of the days and weeks following the sawmill's closing, as if time had stopped, gluing things and people, smudging the corners, thickening tongues, shocking words. Everyone was a little stunned. Those from the unions bustled about, but incessant calls to the Capital did nothing. Management was not answering.

The situation was intolerable. The region's economy depended on the sawmill. And now the cash flow had dried out. People were living off their savings, pretty meagre for most. I was slightly better off thanks to the cheese that had provided me with fine earnings, but my reserves were not bottomless. I could stretch them with fishing and hunting and the small vegetable garden in my yard, but that wasn't the case for my suppliers for whose dependence on the sawmill I had somewhat heightened.

Manu and Jana put on brave faces, and still, night and day, continued milking their twenty-five cows whose milk they would rather give away than throw away. It was nice of them, but each litre of milk handed out worsened the haemorrhage. They were being tapped dry, literally.

Union members had notified the media, but the media prefer the general to the specific. The economic crisis had taken over the country, tension was everywhere and so was the fear of violent outbreaks, etc. They took note of our grievances and added them to the rest for statistical purposes, but sent no one to the site to witness the urgency of the situation. History seemed to want to repeat itself, they said. But knowing that you are caught in a historical glitch is no consolation.

June passed, and then July came and went in turn. We were in the middle of a heat wave – heat that was heavy as a blanket. Farther into the mountains, the forest was ablaze. The town mayor tried in vain to assemble the volunteer firefighter squad. It was the sawmill's wood. It was left to burn. For days, the sky was darkened with thick black smoke that seemed to be a better match for our state of mind than a bright summer sky. Thankfully, the wind blew from the west, and the fire stumbled over the rocky barrier high in the mountains where it quickly died of starvation.

As for me? I waited like the others. Something was going to happen. The government would intervene or the sawmill would be sold to another party, and then reopened. Something had to happen. We were like hunted animals, caught at the bottom of a ravine, motionless, frothing at the mouth, feeling the end is near but searching for the slightest chance to flee, every cell of the body irrigated by adrenaline and the instinct to survive.

Some had left the region for the Capital to join the tide of unemployed who would soon engulf them. This was not an option for me: I had been there, eaten crow and life here was preferable to living there.

Here, there was nature, deer and rabbits. And here, there was Maria.

⟨⟨⟨◦⟩⟩⟩

More than anyone else, she had been stunned by the closing of the sawmill. Her lover boss had not given her the slightest inkling. He had kissed her goodbye, saying he would see her tomorrow, and then disappeared.

Betrayed by her lover, she was equally ostracized by sawmill employees precisely because she was the boss's girl. She was no longer forgiven for her pact with the devil because the devil was gone. She was holed-up in her house, at first to be close to the telephone, then to avoid the looks from the others that burned a hole through her. When she ventured out, their silence towards her had the consistency of sputum.

Because of the heat, I kept all my windows open and I sometimes heard her cry. I knew that despite her vampy airs, she was truly wounded and stunned by the treason of a man whose love she thought was real.

Twenty or so days after the closing of the sawmill, I had rung her doorbell to offer her one of the rabbits I had trapped. She accepted it with much reticence, not crossing her threshold and barely thanking me. I didn't insist. The next time, it was a leg of deer, and Maria's smile began to appear, briefly illuminating her adorable face.

"That's much too big for me!"

She didn't know how to prepare it. I gave her a recipe.

"I'm not very good in the kitchen."

"So let me prepare it for you."

"No, thank you. It's OK, I'll figure it out. Thank you again, really."

I found myself in front of her closed door, slightly sheepish and furious with myself for having wanted to take it too fast.

I had purchased a few hens from one of my previous suppliers and every day from then on, I left two or three eggs outside her door, then cucumbers, beans, onions, and anything that grew in my garden – but never again knocking on her door, never again imposing my presence nor demanding her gratitude.

I let time go by.

One day, as I was placing a bag containing two plucked and cleaned partridges on her door handle, the door opened wide and Maria appeared, wearing a lovely yellow dress and a big smile. She stepped aside and motioned for me to come in. This is how we became friends, and a little later, lovers, but I don't want to go too fast because in the meantime, in the village, the resistance was being organized.

During the first month of the closing, I often had visits from my friends, my buddies and old suppliers who considered that because I came from the Capital and bore the title of Chef, I was more educated than them. They came to see me to hear a few kind words and to receive comfort that I was not equipped to give them. Then one day, abruptly, they stopped coming.

I suspected that my attention towards Maria didn't please everyone, but it took me some time before I reached this conclusion while my happiness of being around her filled me up.

Weeks passed without my noticing, then one day the reality of my rejection struck me dead on. I had spoken to no one but Maria for days on end.

I went to see Manu and Jana. They had recently resigned themselves to slaughtering their cows for meat, and if they still appeared just as carefree, a certain gravity sometimes veiled their eyes, reminiscent of a cloud casting a shadow over the sun.

Manu came out of the shed to greet me. He wore rubber boots and a big white bloodstained apron. He wiped his hands before shaking mine.

"Another?"

He nodded. Only about a dozen of his cows were still standing. He would not resign himself to see what had been his pride destroyed in such a way. What did he have to do with the sawmill? He had never worked there. He felt rage and powerlessness when realizing how things were so involved and interdependent. You thought you had built your house only to find out that it was merely one of many cards making up a castle on someone else's table. He exhausted his anger through work, but work isn't everything.

We talked for a while. I suspected that he was beating around the bush as well. After a while I asked:

"What's going on, Manu?

He turned red and stammered. I insisted.

"Manu, is it me?"

"I have nothing to do with it, I swear. I was against it."

"Against what?"

"The vote."

"What vote? Who voted? Why a vote?"

"I can't."

"Aren't you a free man?"

He held my gaze for a moment. I could hear him thinking. I had given birth to Manu, in a manner of speaking.

"So, tell me what's going on. Is it because of Maria?"

He nodded.

"They were afraid that by letting you in on things, you
would tell her about it."

"Who?"

"Mistral, mostly. But many others as well."

"Well, wait. First, I am capable of keeping a secret. Second,
Maria is not a spy for the enemy. She's been dumped and she
is in as much shit as you and me. And third, what are you plot-
ting?"

"Come," said Manu.

I followed him to the kitchen where he took out a bottle
of grain alcohol, called frizz in the region because it was potent
enough to take the frizz out of an African's hair. Manu poured
two big glasses and held one out to me.

"I'm sorry," he said. "I should have warned you."

Everything had started with a little something Mistral had
let drop during an impromptu booze party with a handful of
men on the brink of despair.

"I don't know what's not working here," Mistral had said,
sober because he never drank. "The sawmill is still here. You
are still here. The trees are still here . . ."

The idea had spread without Mistral having to do anything
more. He was content with planting the seed: the sense of
urgency had made it sprout.

"Nationalize" the sawmill! Form a cooperative and sell the
wood ourselves – outside the country if we had to. The men
were turning the idea over in their hands as if it were a curious
but desirable object. Aided by alcohol, the obstacles facing the

realization of this project seemed increasingly surmountable. They went to see the union, which jumped on the opportunity to demonstrate their usefulness and to take command of something. They began to hold meetings, organize committees, and develop a plan.

"And of course we were counting on you for the cooking," said Manu.

"That's too kind. And when would I have been told?"

"Well, at the last minute. You know, if they found out about it over there, it could make trouble. We have nothing to lose, but Maria . . ."

I left Manu, promising to keep the secret. I felt hurt to have been kept in the dark, even though I didn't let it show. The love and confidence of others are very volatile. I was angry with them for being angry with me. I mistrusted their mistrust.

This quarantine drew me even closer to Maria. I knew now what she felt, and without knowing the cause, she felt that I knew.

We became lovers very naturally, like two beings huddled against one another during the storm that crackles on roofs like the electricity of an angry sky. I had prepared supper and we ate together. Afterwards, she asked me to stay. I wouldn't have made a move. She took my hand. I swallowed hard. We stayed like that for what seemed to me to be several minutes, but no doubt it was the density of that moment that was considerable, rather than its duration. We both knew that it was rife with consequences. There would be no going back. Then, without letting go of my hand, she came closer and rested her head against my chest. She had no one in the world but me, and I thought I was indestructible. Her head against my chest was what I had always been missing; at that exact moment, I was convinced of it. All my life, this feeling of incompleteness, this emptiness in me, had just been filled, her head against my chest, her hand in mine, and soon her mouth against mine. I was indestructible because I was finally complete. What had always been missing had just been restored to me and I felt an immense, incredible feeling of gratitude. Maria, I said her name, Maria; she quieted me with a kiss. Maria, Maria, I was full of her and she was full of me.

What made me happy:

Her smile. How she seemed to light up when she saw me! Her entire body radiated a light destined only for me, I thought.

Her modesty. She sometimes had the reactions of a young girl, hid her body after lovemaking and refused to let me kiss her or hold her hand in public. We were not married, she would say. Her home was not my home. Not right away, let's take the time to do things right, she would say.

Her abandon. When I managed, in the secrecy of our retreat, to break down the barriers of her modesty, she would give in to the bouts of love with an abandon and energy that sometimes left me stunned and infinitely grateful.

Her body. Both compact and elastic. Her firm breasts overflowed from my hands and her pink nipples hardened at the slightest touch. Her pubic fleece was red and silky. The scent of her genitals, faintly bitter, swelled my head. Her narrow vagina seemed tailored to me and when I penetrated it, it was as if I was going home.

But during this time, the conspirators' project was going full steam ahead. Manu only spoke of it to me in whispers. I had little interest in it anyway; I had other fish to fry.

"It's coming soon," Manu told me.

"Oh! When?"

"Three days, but . . ."

"Yes, yes. Shush. Not a peep. Good luck."

But I told Maria everything because you can't keep from one part of your soul what the other already knows.

The following day, the telephone lines were cut off throughout the entire region. The day after that, it was the electricity. On the third day, at dawn, I was awoken by a convoy of military trucks crossing the village and from which sections detached and took up position along the road. The bulk of the troops set up along the periphery of the sawmill. The conspiracy had failed before it even existed. The power had unleashed its dogs.

People came out of their houses and, clutching their agitated children against them, anxiously watched this parade of men in iron helmets. They knew that their lives would be forever changed.

I dressed hastily to find Maria, who slept so soundly that she may not have heard a thing. Her door was wide open. I imagined the worst. The soldiers were not choirboys. I called out her name. Silence. I entered the house. There was no trace of violence, but there was no trace of Maria either. In her bedroom, clothes were strewn on the floor. The closet was half-empty of its contents.

She was gone. Whore. Bitch. Courtesan.

I dropped to my knees. And I screamed. In rage, in despair. I screamed her name.

THE IMPORTANT THING
IS TO COMMUNICATE

"What's that?"

"A box of cookies."

"May I?"

"Go ahead."

"They're disgusting!" yelled Cevitjc after having tasted one.

"That's what the Monster seemed to think."

"He talked to you?"

"A grimace was enough. They're his mother's cookies. She told me that he loved them. He didn't even open the box. He smelled them through the lid and started to scowl as if his teeth were being filed. How could a mother be so wrong?"

"You're asking the wrong person: mine is perfect! I forgot, here's the final file of the charge."

"Bad surprises?"

"It could be worse," said Cevitjc shrugging his shoulders.

"It's not the first time that he's been silent," I said after a moment.

"Meaning?"

"When he was twelve years old, following an accident, he stopped speaking altogether."

"And?"

"Could the trauma from that experience explain the train of events?"

"And the fact that at the age of six, he forgot to brush his teeth! He's tired of childhood boo-boos. Can't you come up with anything else?"

"It works for me."

"Because collectively you've remained children."

"Really? And you haven't?"

"We aren't playing war. We've lived it. But that's not the question."

"No."

"What did you really learn about our man by meeting his parents?"

"Both of them are half mad, but I suppose you could say that about most parents when they are judged from their children's perspective. Under the circumstances, their madness is somewhat normal. It's a little off-putting."

"Nothing useful then?"

"No, nothing except for that accident when he was twelve which I would like to examine more closely despite your sarcastic remarks. I would need to speak to his brother, Milos Rosh."

"From what I know, he fled the country many years ago. The police were looking for him. He wouldn't make a very credible witness for us."

"What did he do?"

"Political unrest. In this country that is like a powder magazine, those who rise for a cause are locked up pretty fast."

"And what cause did he rise for?"

"Peace. Yes, I know, it's paradoxical."

"I would still like to speak to him, if possible."

"I'll ask Josef to find him for you."

"Josef?"

"Don't underestimate him. He's very resourceful. You'd be surprised. He was one of the biggest fraud artists of recent decades."

"Counterfeit money?"

"Paintings. He paints like an old master. And when he's not at his easel, he's surfing the Internet. A very peculiar guy. Secretive, but efficient. He's worked for me since I got him a non-suit."

"How did you manage that?"

"Who would believe that a career military man could have the sensitivity to reproduce a Titian or a Delacroix? All I had to do was exhibit his military file, filled with blood and gunpowder, and tell them that they had the wrong man. Josef plays the idiot to a T. Even here, judges tend to believe that culture and intelligence are incompatible with violence and testosterone."

"Culture versus barbarism . . ."

"But it's a load of crap! Take the Monster . . ."

"What about the Monster?"

"The culinary arts. A chef! The balance of flavours, scents and textures! Respect for meat! This didn't stop him from cheerfully killing his fellow men. Happily for us, he didn't go as far as to serve them for lunch, covered in sauce and accompanied by vegetables . . ."

"Another reason to dig further. When the killing isn't based on ignorance or instinct, there has to be a reason somewhere."

"And if there isn't?"

. . .

"Well?"

"I guess we'll have to make one up."

- *News Update, Regional Channel*
  (Black Bear Inn, 6 pm)

An announcer in a blue suit, shoulder-length hair framing her carefully powdered oval face. Behind her is a photo of François Chevalier taken as he left the offices of Mr. Cevitjc.

Announcer: New developments in the Monster story. Viktor Rosh, accused of war crimes and whose trial will get underway in ten days, will be defended by a representative from Lawyers Without Borders, Mr. François Chevalier. The organization, recognized for the radical positions it assumes, has taken its share of criticism over recent years. The prosecutor's office is in an uproar that a foreign organization is interfering in the internal matters of a sovereign country. The prosecutor in charge, Mr. Gorlund . . .

Mr. Gorlund, in gown, on the steps of the court house: And now they want to defend terrorists? Imagine we went to their countries to attempt to free serial killers and psychopaths! How would they react, I ask you? With indignation! And it is with indignation that we denounce this intrusion in our perfectly legal and democratic judicial process.

Announcer: Mr. Chevalier was unavailable for comment. Economics. The gross domestic product increased by 0.3 percent this quarter, which seems to confirm the . . .

- *Telephone Conversation*
  (Black Bear Inn, 8 pm)

". . ."

"Hello? Hello?"

"..."

"HELLO?"

"It's me."

"Oh."

"Oh?"

"Well it's . . . Are you OK?"

"No."

"What's wrong?"

"..."

"What's wrong? (A pause) WHAT IS WRONG? An accident, what, WHAT?"

"Arthur."

"What? WHAT?"

"He's . . ."

"Flo, what is going on? What happened to Arthur?"

"Nothing."

"WHAT?"

"Nothing happened to him. He's asleep. He's sniffling a little. I think he's caught a cold and he's woken up crying three times now. I . . ."

"You scared me. Why did you scare me like that? I thought there had been an accident, that he was . . . that he was dead."

"He could have been."

"Why could he have been?"

"What would it have done to you if he had died?"

"Don't say that."

"It could have happened. There could have been an accident, and what would you have known? Nothing."

"Flo!"

"Nothing. You wouldn't have known anything. Do you know what day it is? It's two days later. You were supposed to call us

when you arrived. You promised. The children were waiting by the telephone. Mind you, they didn't particularly feel like it. But I thought it was a good idea, waiting to hear the voice of their father who is so far away. But no voice. Do you know what Arthur said?"

"What did he say?"

"He said: You can't count on Daddy."

"Oh, Flo . . ."

"He said it. He's four years old, François, and he already understands everything."

"Listen, I'm so sorry that I didn't call you earlier, but I'm up to my neck in shit over here and . . ."

"I couldn't care less that you didn't call us. You see, I don't care. It's over."

" . . ."

" . . ."

"What's over?"

"I can't stand waiting for you anymore. I waited for you so often. But now, I can't take it anymore. I have to save myself. I'm afraid for me. Do you know what I was thinking earlier? When Arthur woke up for the third time? I went to see him, I took him in my arms, I comforted him, I put him back in his bed, and I tucked him in. I couldn't take it anymore. I was tired. Do you know what I was thinking? I regretted having children. It's your fault. It's because of you that I thought that. I hate you. I can't take it anymore. You're not here, you're never here. And even when you're here, you're not."

"I love you."

"I know that's what you think."

"But it's true!"

"Loving like that goes nowhere. Have you been drinking?"

"Uh . . ."

"You have been drinking. Who am I talking to?"

"It's François."

"No, it's the other guy. I don't want to talk to the other guy. I didn't fall in love with the other guy. I didn't have children with the other guy. What have you done with François?"

"I'm coming home, right now, wait for me. I'm dropping everything here and I'm coming."

"No. I've been waiting for you for too long. I don't want to wait anymore. Don't come back."

"I want to come back."

"And drop your client? You're a child, François, and I already have two."

". . ."

"I have to think of myself."

"What are you going to do? Find yourself a man?"

"You don't understand a thing. I don't want another man. Not at all. I'm not going to do anything. I'm going to do as I always do. Only now, I'm making your absence official. I've stopped waiting for you. I'm not waiting for you any longer."

"I'll change."

"I don't believe you."

". . ."

". . ."

"I'm still going to come home one of these days."

"We'll see."

"You'll see."

"That's right."

"I love you."

". . ."

". . ."

"..."

"Good night."

(Dial tone)

• *Inside Monologue*
  (Black Bear Inn, 3:42 am)

Oh my God, oh my God, OH MY GOD! What's happened? What have I done? Not even able to talk to her. Not able to say what? I love you? What is that? I had my cock in my hand when she called. I was masturbating. I was masturbating in a hotel room while watching naked actresses in a bad porn movie on television. Oh my God! But I don't believe in God, I don't believe in anything. I don't believe in anyone.

What is my life? I'm not comfortable anywhere. I don't know how to behave anymore. Once upon a time I did. It seems I knew how. The miniature mini-bar bottles. Tiny plastic bottles of vodka, gin, whisky and rum. A hangover with a plastic-coated tongue. I dreamed my life, my life is the dream of a drunk. Perhaps my memories are the delusions of a drunk. A plastic memory. I dreamed my life, I didn't live it. And what if it never happened? How could I be sure? I should lie on a couch and unravel all of this under the watchful eye of an old bearded monomaniac.

Psychotherapy, psychoanalysis, Swedish massage, chiropraxis, anti-anxiety pills, jogging, osteopathy, camping, acupuncture, musicotherapy, vitamins A, B, C, D, E, royal jelly, spirulina, grapefruit, climbing, voodoo, archery, birth chart, palmistry, market indices, yoga, aromatherapy, luminotherapy, floatation tanks, primal scream, hypnosis, animal therapy, fast-ing, Kama Sutra, volunteering, Compostelle, gardening and abstinence.

How? How do you end up with this feeling of being permanently split in two? It's as if part of me is watching me exist while commenting on my every move, on my every thought. My very own little sports journalist, on the catwalk of my brain, calling me every name in the book and demanding that I be traded to another club. I shrivel up under my own gaze, and look for a hole in which to bury myself.

What happened to my dreams, my ambitions? Who gave me this body, this life? It's impossible, I can't be more than eighteen years old, I don't know a thing about life, I'm not ready and I've never been ready! I don't know what to do. I pretend to know, but I don't. Who gave me this memory?

I couldn't have lived all of this, love stories, a marriage, a house, children, and more cars than I can count. It's impossible that I experienced all of that. Someone planted these memories in me, they're fabricated, I'm not old enough.

One day, someone will come to take me by the hand and lead me home. Someone who, after having stroked my hair, will give me the time to grow up. It's not my fault, Flo, I'm not ready.

She wants to leave me!

She wants to leave me?

She wants to leave me.

To leave me. To leave me all alone.

Of course I drink. Who wouldn't drink in my shoes? Of course I drink too much. There they are, the plastic cadavers, a fortune in mini-bar expenses, and for what? A few hours of forgetting? But when you wake up, you remember everything, or, if there's a blank, you imagine the worst. You could kill someone in one of those blanks. I'm not saying that I'm capable. But it's possible. How many times have I not remembered driving my car? I drank to feel alive, to overcome my shyness, to become someone other than myself. Now, I drink to forget that I drink. Tomorrow, I'll drink to forget that I drink to forget that I drink.

I have just enough energy left for work, and then some. I spend my weekends on the living-room couch watching stupidity on television while Florence takes the children to the park, the zoo, a party, the movies, to visit her parents. As soon as they're out the door, I breathe a sigh of relief. I can finally make room for the suffering of my sick nerves and doze in spurts while waiting for it to pass.

That's not the worst. The worst is the hours locked in a murky bubble of alcohol and mini-bar noises, the last comforting place on earth, where one controls their own descent into Hell. You man the controls, sure, like a pilot in a plane. It's not a free fall, it's a full-out nosedive. Everything is under control, finally.

Oh Flo! I'm dragging you with me, a passenger in a relationship that isn't, or that was not destined to be. But were we destined for this? When I met you, you were radiant, you soaked up the rain as you did the sun and you opened up like a flower in a perpetual spring. Not always happy, no, that's impossible. But you were capable of happiness. You watched it like a cat, ready to pounce when it came out of its hole. Even the wait was a pleasure. Our two children: two joys who appeared out of nowhere to come and live with us for a few years. As for me, I only knew how to worry. Since the beginning of our union, I have lived off the happiness that I borrowed from you. And now it's time to pay, although I have nothing left.

Two children and me, it's too much for you. Your face has closed. Now, a worried fold crosses your forehead. I stole your youth like a vampire steals the blood from its victims for nourishment. You understood. So you've turned your back on me. You have reserved your strength, your blood and your laughter for our children. We barely speak. I know, I was coming home late and drunk more and more often. I feel your anger, Florence, all the way over here, right into the bed at the Black Bear Inn.

I come home drunk. I rush to bed in order to avoid your hurtful look. I go to bed, I pretend to sleep. I don't ask about anything. But I listen. I recognize your anger towards me in your footsteps. You walk briskly on your heels, and the floor resounds like a drum skin. You make noise. You noisily manifest your disapproval, your humiliation, your distress, your desire to hurt me, to avenge the hurt that I'm causing you. But you are too well educated. You don't believe in the benefits of violence. So you bang the plates, the cups, you handle things roughly, as if they were me. You have to let go of this rage, get it out of you; it tenses your muscles, constricts your lungs; it chokes you.

I don't do anything. I wait for it to blow over. I have come to prefer fiction to indifference; it's so much more comfortable. But I listen, I take it. The plates bang together, the knick-knacks are shaken. Each step, each shake is inflicted on me. What good is talking? You and I have developed a dialogue – not between deaf people, but between blind people. We don't see each other, but we hear the tremors, the blows, the cracking that accompany the crevasses that appear in our foundation.

I do nothing. I am weak. I am made of weak material. It's cracking where I am. So I don't move. I do nothing. Inertia is the only strength that I am left with.

You were my strength. You who wanted things, who desired, who dreamed, who drew blueprints, who projected yourself into the future – who projected us into the future. Without you, I stay glued in the present, in the mud of the present that is sucking me in.

And when you finally come to bed, your anger calmed slightly, I always pretend to be asleep. There will be no tender gestures, we've forgotten how. I listen to your breathing slow, your breath quiet. I can only hope to sleep myself. We lie side by side without touching, love depleted, and both knowing that tomorrow won't be a new day, but the same day, until the point when something gives beyond all hope.

And it has happened. Did it happen? Deep down wasn't I wishing for it, way deep down? Why don't I feel relieved? I did everything so that this would happen, so now I'm happy, right? I should be jumping for joy, I should be celebrating. Waiter! Champagne! Pop the cork and raise my glass way up high and drink . . . to what? Eh? To what?

To what?

What do I toast?

• *E-mail*
(from Fchevalier55@hotmail.com to floflocheval@youhou.com, 8 am)

Florence,

I have such vivid memories of how happy I was in my parents' yard, in winter, armed with a broomstick, I played "seal hunter." It could be me now. What I mean is, I still feel as though that's still me now. My years accumulate without adding up. I remember having stars in my eyes and strength coursing through my body. The future was unfolding in front of me. The movie of my life recorded on virgin film, and me, shaking with impatience before diving in. I'm not a whole. But the thought of losing you is unbearable. I must learn to count. I must learn to count on myself.

I am still, and will always be, the little boy hunting seal between the two apple trees in the snow-filled backyard. And I'll never be armed with anything other than a measly broomstick.

But I love you. I love you all.

François.

• *Message*

(Black Bear Inn reception, 9 am)

You can write to the brother at the following e-mail address: Mrosh99@hotmail.com

Happy to have been of service,
Josef

• *E-mail*

(from Fchevalier55@hotmail.com to Mrosh99@hotmail.com, 9:15 am)

Dear Mr. Rosh,

As you may not be aware, your brother is currently in prison. He is accused of war crimes for which he may have to pay a higher price than is fair in the absence of an adequate defence. I am one of his attorneys and your brother is very much alone before adversity. I need your help. He needs your help.

I fear that the trauma of war has shaken him too hard. For now, he refuses to talk. Large parts of his life and personality are inaccessible to us. Therefore, we need to access them to prepare a defence strategy. Could you answer a few questions that I believe are essential to mount your brother's psychological profile? We could then collaborate more closely to ensure that Viktor has the best chances at an acquittal.

1. What type of child was he?

2. What type of an adult did he become?

3. Can you remember the slightest traumatic event that could be used in his defence? Your parents told me of a fall in which he was injured during a nighttime outing with you; could you provide me with details?

4. Could you make yourself available to testify on your brother's behalf? (I learned of certain legal restrictions that could prevent you from doing so; could you please clarify these restrictions?)

Thank you for your attention to this matter,

François Chevalier, Attorney

• *Telephone Conversation*
(Black Bear Inn, 10:38 am)

"What's going on?"

"What are you talking about?"

"The indictment."

"And what?"

"Rosalind isn't there anymore."

"That's correct."

"You think that's normal?"

"*I told you that it could be worse.*"

"I don't understand."

"*It's not up to you to understand.*"

"He's no longer accused of the worst crime that he could have committed? Do you find that logical? Something is being hidden and we have to know why."

"*No doubt the prosecutors thought that Rosalind does not make an ideal witness. She isn't exactly lily-white, you know. Difficult to like.*"

"The victim's likeability has nothing to do with the severity of the crime."

"*Wait a minute! Don't forget who you are: lawyer for the defence. Be happy that they removed that thorn from our side. Without Rosalind, we have a chance to spare our client some long years in detention.*"

"I know, I know. Only, I don't understand. I find that suspicious. It doesn't please me. How is he a monster without Rosalind?"

"*He killed many others. You saw his arrest photo. He really looked like a ferocious beast! Take my advice: Forget Rosalind.*"

"That's what everyone tells me."

"*Everyone can't be wrong.*"

"Really?"

• *E-mail*

(from Mrosh99@hotmail.com to Fchevalier55@hotmail.com, 11:50 am)

Mr. Chevalier,

I am writing to you from Rwanda, my adoptive country. Coming from a country at war, I chose to live in another country where people don't know peace, at least not how we define it. I swapped a machine gun for a machete. But at least in Rwanda, ignorance and acculturation can be held accountable for the genocide, whereas there . . .

Of course I am aware of my brother's situation. I own a computer, which works, as you can see. Africa is not the black hole of the planet, although you may think so. As for my brother, if I left my country, it is precisely to avoid finding myself in his position. I despise my country with a passion. I despise its traditions. I despise its future. I despise its people. Any sane person should emigrate. Those who stay are responsible for themselves, and that goes for my brother as well. Let him rot in jail; at least there he can only hurt himself.

I work two hundred kilometres from Kigali, in a refugee camp which has not emptied since what they pre-emptively call "the end of the war." Here, half the children have had an arm hacked off with a machete by other children from the enemy army. An army of rags. Hate is tenacious, it feeds on the empty bellies of men and fattens itself on their famine. We end up by finding it normal to see two families kill each other for a bag of rice. The war lords control the region's economy and get rich to the detriment of the population. Those carrying out the orders can only dream of the scraps that fall from the tables of the affluent.

The people from my country don't have that excuse. They have a full belly, refrigerators, cars. So why have they killed one another? Because they wanted to. I don't pity them at all. I blame them.

But for having shared with my brother, as a child, a room with two beds, and for having loved the innocence that we shared, I will answer your questions.

1. What type of child was he?

He was an ordinary child, I don't know what else to say. Our family was ordinary. A little curly-haired guy, he liked books, stories about children lost in the woods, witches and owls. Our father worked and our mother stayed home. We had friends, children's games, children's dreams, children's fears, that's all. Nothing other than normal. Normal for my country. Without our knowledge, we were infected with the hate virus. Our world was split in two for obscure reasons of language and religion, and money – never forget money – because language and religion are first and foremost means to procure it. There were us, and them. We learned that very fast. Us – our own people. Them – the others. Our parents didn't have a warlike spiel, but when an entire country prefers division to unity, children pay the price. Hate simmered in us. And if it is true that children are naturally cruel, how lucky we were to have been born there other than somewhere else!

2. What type of adult did he become?

I left the country when my brother was barely twenty years old. I hadn't seen him in two years. All to say is that I didn't know him much as an adult. I approved of his passion for cooking, although I could also see a hopeless quality that left me confused. I am leery of monomaniacs. Captains of industry work twenty hours a day to build their empires, inventors of engineering who forget to eat, movie stars ready to do anything to break through, subjecting their bodies to the scalpel to render them compliant to a false ideal . . . They are the ones perpetuating the false, but grand, idea that we can all be rich and famous if only we truly wanted it, with all our might and with all our will. The other side of this discourse is that the poor and miserable are responsible for their poverty and misery because they are lazy.

There was a little of that in my brother; a little of that exclusive passion that slowly cut off the others. I believe that in the kitchens of the Institute, he found a standard of organization that reassured him, a strict order in the world to oppose the chaos of humans. You know exactly what your role is in a kitchen. There is no room for vagueness. And each one dreams to climb the ranks instead of questioning the ladder at which he sits at the bottom.

That said, my brother was also a scared, timorous individual, not a go-getter. More the type to take rather than give orders. All in all a good soldier, but with fantasies of being a colonel. As far as I know.

Adolescence separated us. I was a militant, a protester; I marched in the streets brandishing signs. I had deep convictions. My brother was boning up on Mediterranean cuisine and the cod almanac. He lived in the defined. But at least he was well fed.

3. Can you remember the slightest traumatic event that could be used in his defence? Your parents told me of a fall in which he was injured during a nighttime outing with you; could you provide me with some details?

If you exclude the fact of being born, I cannot see what trauma my brother could have suffered from, and that could not have been enough to make him a monster. Or we are all monsters, and maybe you should first investigate that a little more!

As for his fall . . . It's funny, when I read your letter the first time, I had no idea what you were talking about. And then, all of a sudden, it all came back to me, clear and precise, although slightly shrouded in nostalgia. It was summer. A summer of bike rides and cold drinks under a scorching sun. With friends, we conversed seriously, we had plans for the future, we talked of our respective chances to become astronauts or race car drivers, skippers or rock singers. Girls still scared us but we were a few months away from becoming bolder. It was delicious but it was a lie. We were heading straight for the deception of adulthood, when suddenly the women and men around you stop speaking to you as a baby and in one fell swoop, reveal everything that up until now they had protected you from: duplicity, the contortions of life in society, the dreadful obligation to earn a living, the total absence of pity in a world that reveres money and sacrifices men out of cupidity. I would soon learn of that horror. But not yet. Not that summer.

Viktor followed me everywhere. He was still small but he loved wearing my clothes that hung on him like a flag without wind. I took him willingly with me. He wasn't a bother. He was a good little brother who adored me. He lifted his big eyes with overly long eyelashes to me and I knew that with one move of the head, I could make him melt into tears. I didn't like to make him cry so I invited him to tag along, and he would run at me like a happy dog, turning circles around me, taking five steps for each one of mine.

That summer, we got into the habit of going on night excursions, unbeknownst to our parents. It was our way of living dangerously: riding our bikes to an abandoned building that we would explore with a flashlight, and finishing on the roof, the five of us sharing a scandalous cigarette stolen from one of our fathers. We were so innocent!

Two of those friends from those days have since died; one in the army in which he enlisted *for the adrenaline*, the other during a somewhat forceful police *interrogation*.

That night, we had planned a daring outing, very far from our usual territory, outside the city limits, almost in the country. We noticed it during a school fieldtrip to a model farm, not far off the main road, its dome barely rising above the treeline. It was an old abandoned observatory, judging by its dilapidated state and the old rusted gate closing the overgrown road leading up to it.

We debated it for a long time. On bikes, we had to count over an hour of travel time. We were going to stay overnight. But summer was coming to an end and school would soon start again. It would be the end of sleeping in, free time, improvising. Our parents' attention would once again turn to us and render us powerless. It was now or never.

Viktor was obviously aware of our plans. But he was still too small to follow us, his legs were too short and he couldn't spend the night outside, awake, he who would fall asleep in our father's lap during the evening TV shows!

But he insisted, he moaned, he cried, he turned circles on himself on his tiptoes to show how much he had grown. He was selling himself with everything he had and I let myself bend. I brought a blanket to wrap him in when he inevitably fell asleep by the fire.

We pedalled slowly so that he could keep up the pace. We had placed pillows under our sheets meant to fool our watchful parents. The city was quiet, it was magic. We had to cross the unending faubourgs, all those sleeping houses sheltering families like ours. Then the houses grew farther apart, there were more trees and small fields. We began to see farm buildings, and then nothing. The countryside. No lighting either. We were riding on bad asphalt that seemed to absorb the faint gleam of the stars. I could feel that Viktor was scared and I reassured him as best as I could, but I was scared too. In the darkness lurked unknown shapes, the grass whirred without reason, on the edge of the woods, pairs of eyes glinted then disappeared abruptly.

We arrived at last. Actually, it was easy for us to get around the rusty gate on our bicycles. We followed the road overgrown with brush that gently climbed up to the top of the hill and we arrived at the foot of the observatory.

It was an ancient and traditional construction, the work of some sky-crazy individual no doubt, who had dedicated all his savings to erect this three-storey tower using inexpensive materials, wood and painted sheet metal. We let our bikes drop and craned our necks to contemplate the summit.

"There's no telescope," I said, "not in all this time."

"But maybe there is one," whispered Viktor.

I stroked his hair.

"Sure. Maybe."

But there wasn't one. The first two floors had no doubt served as a home for the sky-crazed guy, but the rooms were dirty and stripped of anything of interest. The third was completely empty except for a three-metre-high platform to which was screwed what must have been the base of the telescope in the observatory's glory days. There was really very little to see and we were slightly disappointed. The smallest abandoned factory concealed scrap treasures.

We went outside to prepare a fire. A friend had stolen a few bottles of beer from his father; there were lots of cigarettes. The night wouldn't be lost because we could still talk about the future.

Viktor asked my permission to stay and forage through the lower rooms. I didn't want him to smoke or drink so I let him go and warned him to be careful.

I was sure that he was. He was a good little guy, nice, obedient. It was an accident, nothing more. Right?

We all had a pile of dead branches that we threw on the fire for the sheer pleasure of seeing a shower of sparks. The beer was going to our heads nicely and the cigarettes numbed our bodies. The conversation had reached the stage at which each, lost in his thoughts, emerged at times to issue a great truth that we all rallied around before falling back into silence. Silence . . . I meditated on the silence. All this silence. I jumped up yelling: Viktor! How long had he been gone? How long had it been since I had heard him? I yelled again.

I delved into the observatory yelling his name. He was not on the first or the second floors. I found him on the third. He was at the foot of the platform, lying on his back in a pool of blood. I approached. His eyes were open. I thought he was dead. I yelled his name again. He blinked his eyes and turned his head towards me.

"Don't move!" I told him. "I'm going to get help."

Get help! At three o'clock in the morning, out in the sticks. On a bike. At fifteen.

I mounted my bike and pedalled and cried. I said "Wait for me, Viktor. Wait for me, I'm coming."

I found a farm and rang the door until someone opened it. I bawled as I explained the accident. They called an ambulance, and then a man held out a telephone to me so that I could call my parents. I told them everything, apologizing, crying, yelling that I wanted to go back right away, then I gave them directions and hung up. The farmer had me get into his truck and we took the road back to the observatory. My friends had stayed with Viktor, terrified, sponging the blood with the blanket.

The paramedics arrived soon thereafter and asked us to move back. I looked up and on the platform I saw the telescope. No doubt it had been hidden below somewhere. Viktor had found it and carried it up there and placed it in its base. Then he fell.

My father arrived as the ambulance was leaving for the hospital. He didn't say a word to me. He took me by the arm and sat me on the seat next to him. I wanted to mention my bicycle but I guessed by his gaze and his tense jaw that it was better that I remain quiet. I haven't had a bicycle since. Is my old bike still rusting in front of the farm near the observatory?

We spent the night at the hospital. Viktor had been lucky. Fractures, a concussion, but nothing too serious. A cast and rest. There would be no after-effects, said the doctor.

But there are always after-effects. My friends and I took the road to school again, but devoted our free time to more conventional activities. We had become serious, already little men, with the fears of men, and the divergences of men. That autumn, I began to take an interest in politics.

At home, under my mother's inordinate attention, Viktor pointlessly dragged out a convalescence that had made him sullen. Did he think that I had let him fall? My own guilt prevented me from asking him. Maybe he thought that he had let me down. The result is that we no longer spoke to one another. In the long run, all the love that had bound us together was swept under this rug of silence. As for my parents . . . Since you have met them, you know what I think of them.

There you are. From then on, we followed separate paths, and with time, we became little more than strangers, and that's enough of this story.

4. Could you make yourself available to testify on your brother's behalf? (I learned of certain legal restrictions that could prevent you from doing so; could you please clarify these restrictions?)

The legal restrictions, as you call them, are perfectly real and prevent me from returning to the country if I was inclined to entertain the idea, which is unlikely.

I am a pacifist. However, in my country, pacifists are hunted. And the pacifists, in spite of themselves, resort to force to make themselves heard. This was the case for me, and I regret it. I killed a man. That is the irrationality to which my country pushed me. In the name of peace, I killed a man. I won't go into the details. Suffice to say that violence is contagious to the point that it can contaminate the idea of peace. It is that contagion that I escaped, not justice. My brother should have done the same.

I disown my country and I disown those who inhabit it. Here I have thousands of children who depend on me to eat.

Their existence is hell. My brother will be housed and fed for the rest of his days. That is a privilege that many envy him.

And so, Mr. Chevalier, if I have answered your questions, I hold you no less responsible for a part of the harm afflicting our planet. Here, there, you and your kind revel in your humanitarian efforts and your peacekeepers, but your remedies are often worse than the harm.

Previously, in my country, we did business amongst ourselves. In all it was a private affair: our murders, our injustices, our trivialities, our consuming passions and our ancestral hatred. Our remorse too. And our real grief.

Our pain was our own. All that has changed. Globalization, television reports, peacekeepers, the this without borders, the those without borders, the International Tribunal for the Prosecution of War Crimes . . . The eye of the world, resting on us, judging us, has divested us of everything. There is nothing left now but you. Your compassion. Your pity.

Of course, we were and we are aggressive, bloodthirsty and a danger to ourselves, but what is left for us now? The feeling of constantly being watched? Constantly caught at fault, with our hand in the cookie jar? Infantilized by you.

When we judged ourselves, we knew what we were dealing with, but you! You think that you are doing good, but it is true of my country as it is for Rwanda, you have taken away our responsibility for our actions. By judging us, instead of letting us judge ourselves, you have taken away what is most precious to us, although it was repulsive in the opinion of many: our identity.

What is hatred between two sibling nations if not a family tie cementing its history? You take away the cement by objectifying us. You have transformed what was a private tragedy into a global spectacle; you applied your own theory of the staging to our explosions. We became actors in your theatre, puppets of your arrogant compassion.

Perhaps we were better off during the war before you intervened. At least it was our war, our hatred, our problem to solve. Before, in my country, there was always a winning camp and a losing camp. That's been over since you've been there. Without even having waged it, you have won our war. And for the first time in my country's history, we are all losers.

You want to save us? Go away. Leave us to destroy ourselves. Let us suffer. Once we have hurt enough, once we have killed enough women and children, maybe we will resign ourselves to learning how to live.

But until then, I refuse to be a clown in your circus.

Milos Rosh

THE SLEEPER AWAKENS

Okay, we're not going to waste too much time on this. Amputees often complain of pain in their phantom limb that cannot be eased. With Maria gone, I had pain in her and there was nothing I could do. I know that I spent a few days dulling myself with frizz, but the alcohol numbed nothing, rather it pushed me to shed bigger tears, to sob more violently, to howl without restraint.

Love is strongest. Love can move mountains. Love. The power of love . . . I kicked myself for having believed in it, but at the same time, I resented Maria for not believing. I oscillated between being disgusted with love and disgusted with myself who hadn't known how to love enough for two. Reduced ambivalence. In fact, my panicked soul was searching for a way out, anything, a button to press so that the pain of loving without being loved in return would cease. But that type of button doesn't exist, or it did, and it was the front door bell that Maria's finger would have pressed to announce her return. That's what I was watching for, in fact, while turning circles in my small house. I cursed Maria and I wished for her to return. I jeered love and I dreamed that it would flourish again.

Only fatigue, I think, can lead you to end these contradictions. The crying stops because your tear glands have been emptied. The howling stops because your voice is hoarse. The searching stops because you are completely lost. The body's stiffness drowns in lactic acid, and no matter how much you would like to continue howling love's betrayal in the night, there comes a time when you have to sleep. And it is in waking, hours later, that you understand that you won't die from this. And even that seems unfair.

I was not nice to look at. I hung around my house like a vagrant. I slept everywhere except in my bed. I ate food straight from the can. I have no idea what I could possibly have been doing with those days. They went by without leaving a trace other than the beard on my face and the bags under my eyes. When, after some time, reason began to pierce through the pain like a crocus through the snow, when some life flowed back in my veins, when the solitude became too heavy to shoulder – when Maria's image began to blur around the edges (as if my vision of love had been nearsighted) – I realized that I didn't dare leave my house.

After all, I had betrayed. Out of love, I had betrayed Manu's trust and that of my community. I made no illusion for myself: I was responsible for the military presence and the sawmill's occupation. Out of love, I had sold out friendship. Out of love? Not even. How was I going to face this?

There didn't seem to be any other choice than to leave the region, but to go where? This country was stupid, and we dragged its story like a ball and chain around the ankle. Emigrate? I had a trade, and people everywhere had to eat. But I was a coward. I avoided the windows for fear that I would be seen, and when one morning I heard knocking at my door, I held my breath and didn't answer. The knocking went on for a long time and then it stopped. I noticed that I was drenched in sweat, terrified and panting. I went to my room, threw myself on the bed and buried my head in the pillow. If the house had had a basement, I would have buried myself there while letting myself die from starvation. I heard someone clear their throat.

It was Manu. He was leaning on the door frame. He was smiling. Tears formed in the corner of my eyes and rolled down my cheeks. But they weren't bad tears, not tears of pain or sadness. I was crying faced with his smile, the smile on the face of a friend.

"What's new?" he asked, coming over to sit on the bed.

"You know," I answered, wiping my face with the corner of a sheet.

"Ya."

He touched my shoulder.

"It wouldn't have worked anyway."

"Why do you say that?"

Manu looked at me, taken aback, and then burst into laughter.

"I was talking about the sawmill! You don't know? The whole country is paralyzed. We would never have managed to get the wood out of the region. In a way, she saved us a few days of useless work, your Maria."

Was he sincere? No matter, I thanked him with a trace of a smile, but I didn't have the courage to go any further.

"Listen," he said again, "no one is mad at you. It's me they're upset with! I'm the one who told you everything. The others understand. She got into your head, that girl, she knows what she's doing. I should have known. I took a few punches, nothing serious. And besides, Mistral doesn't allow anyone to talk badly about you."

"Really?"

"He's not the only one. And it's not your fault if we're up shit creek. It's those pigs, it's their fault," he said, designating the outside world with his thumb. "Come on, we're going for a walk."

"We can?"

"We haven't done anything wrong! We didn't have the time!" said Manu, laughing. "Legally, they can't do anything. They satisfy themselves by watching us out of the corner of their eye. They look really bored."

"Make some coffee, I'll be right there."

I showered and shaved. I put my pillowcases and sheets in the hamper, then put on clean clothes and went down to the kitchen.

"Manu . . ." I began.

"Well, say," he interrupted me, "you drink Nescafé now? What is the world coming to? Come on, sit down and drink this shit."

We drank coffee in silence. I felt better under Manu's amused, and at the same time protective, eye.

Suddenly, my stomach let out a long series of gurgling noises in protest against the abuse in a can that I had inflicted on it.

"I'm hungry," I said.

"Come on," answered Manu.

He dragged me outside and I followed him with slight reticence. The strong military presence didn't seem to bother him. He got used to it, I suppose, as we get used to everything. But for me, it was new. They patrolled in pairs, and I couldn't help but feel guilty in front of them, but guilty of what? They made me want to hug the walls, jump the fence and hide in the woods. I felt their potential danger. Their simple existence was an invitation to disaster. This is what sets an army apart: it places automatic weapons in the hands of children whose training essentially consists in mainly not thinking.

But Manu was enjoying himself. He was right in a way: at least things were clear. No more sawmill, no more livestock, culture, good cheese. No more peace. No more complexities of peace, taxes, laws and regulations. After months of oppressive wait, it was a relief. There was a certain fever in the air, a revolutionary drunkenness. When there is nothing left to lose, there is freedom. And while Manu babbled like an overexcited child, I began to feel the effects of this drunkenness.

Even the women on the balconies were sweeping the floors with a pretentious arrogance, as though pursuing daily activities had taken on a sort of heroic quality. Nothing like facing an enemy to brighten the colours and give things back the taste of the first time. Fists in my pockets, I crossed a village under siege that seemed to have never been better since the glory days of the sawmill. People greeted one another in strong voices and made exaggerated gestures with their hands. It was contagious, as though our smiles were weapons and our carelessness, time bombs.

The soldiers weren't fooled. They grimaced, hands around the grip of their firearms, which encouraged us to provoke them slightly more. Instead of steering clear of them, passersby went straight for the patrols as though they didn't exist, forcing the soldiers to let them by – or open fire. But why fire on an unarmed passerby who, nose in the air, pretends to be contemplating the sky? They must have received strict orders, but this wouldn't prevent them from becoming increasingly nervous. So, in turn, they stuck out their chests and walked with their legs spread like parodies of John Wayne in cowboy movies. It was the battle of appearances; no lives were at stake yet, only egos being measured, like a penis contest in a boys' locker room.

Manu took me to eat a sandwich at the hotel, which was packed, but people drank tea or water because they had no more money. They seemed pleased to see me, greeted me with such wide smiles that I ended up believing them. For a moment, I forgot that I was devastated. I smiled in return. I ate heartily and the owner offered me a beer that I turned down with pleasure. I felt better. I put my arm around Manu's shoulders, and he was tactful enough to pretend that he hadn't noticed.

It was a type of convalescence. For three consecutive days, Manu came to get me at tea time for a walk without an admitted purpose. He told me about the village gossip and commented with a certain fierceness, which surprised me, on the recent political developments. He spat on the Capital and those running the country. I was floored. This child from the fields and the woods had integrated civilization just to criticize it? But it was difficult to defend the State's decisions and the country's situation was deteriorating to a point where the issue was becoming too foreseeable. Manu dreamed of fighting. I understood why. When I met him he had nothing, therefore he had nothing to lose. But since then . . . It was a bit my fault. I had raised him, so to speak, only to let him fall from greater heights. Perhaps he was nostalgic for his past life, but it was impossible to go back, just like it is impossible to forget the taste of chocolate.

I tried to put things in perspective but he was spurring me on. He had a heap of arguments on the tip of his tongue that left me thinking. No doubt the setting was right; I desperately needed to transform my pain into anger, my powerlessness into frustration. That is how, slowly, I agreed to become a victim.

Maria had not left because she didn't love me, but because those who had taken advantage of her had rendered her incapable of feeling real emotions. The sawmill's manager made her a thing, and things are incapable of love. Each soldier on patrol was an excrescence of that man and all those who attempted to reify us.

In the chaos of my thoughts, in the swamps of powerlessness where I had been wading since Maria's departure, these considerations had something profoundly reassuring: my weakness was non-existent, it was an illusion maintained from above to prevent me from acting. Throughout my walks with Manu, I almost came to believe that I had never lived my own life, but that in fact I was playing the role that had been assigned to me in a script written by others. Everything I didn't have, everything I hadn't experienced, all my ideas, each of my desires, and even the content of my dreams, were conditioned by those who wanted to keep the power rather than share it. What they did not want to give had to be taken, said Manu. But I didn't agree. Violence was not a solution. My brother had driven that in to me.

"Then what?" asked Manu. "Die of starvation? Let my people die? Give in and live off crumbs?"

This boy, barely a man, explained all of this to me with great seriousness, and if I listened attentively, I sometimes laughed to myself that he was using words whose meanings were unknown to him ten years ago, belonging to a universe that he didn't even suspect existed. I ran a fatherly hand through his hair.

"Where are you getting all of this?"

"You'll have to understand that I have to keep secrets now," he said as he fixed his hair with all the seriousness of a young revolutionary.

I pretended to laugh it off, angered within, but what could I do?

Life seemed to go on as before, but in austerity. One evening, Manu invited me to his house to eat with Jana and the children. The soup was too thin and the bread was stale, but it was good not to talk politics for a few hours. Despite the clothes with frayed sleeves and the shoes with worn soles, I felt as though I was returning to the fold. The children were so happy to see me that they were overexcited. They screamed as they jumped up and down and spun like tops until they were dizzy. One after the other, and then all three at once, they climbed into my lap and played for a while at inserting their index fingers in my ears and then in my nostrils. At dessert (half of a wrinkled apple per child), the eldest, Andreï, looked at me in silence, his small forehead pleated by the effort of thought.

"What's wrong, little man?"

"Why did you do that stupid thing?"

"Who told you that I did something stupid?"

Andreï shrugged his shoulders and kept quiet.

"Everyone does stupid things," Manu explained to his son.

"If no one ever did stupid things, the world would be a very boring place," added Jana.

"When you do something stupid, the most important thing is not to do it again," I said looking Manu straight in the eyes.

"OK," he said.

"And when we forgive, we forgive," I continued.

"OK."

"We wipe the slate clean and start over. We trust."

"That's right," said Manu.

"Otherwise, you shouldn't bother."

"Bother doing what?" asked Andreï.

"Bother loving," answered Jana, leaning over to kiss him.

"Can I have another apple?" asked Andreï.

"There aren't any more, my love."

"I'm still hungry!"

"But there are things that can't be forgiven," said Manu.

"That's true," I answered.

"The children's hunger, for example."

"Yes."

"We can't forgive the children's hunger."

"Yes."

"We have to fight it."

"I understand."

"Using all possible means!"

". . ."

"Using all possible means."

"Yes," I finally said. "Yes, I understand."

"Understanding does not replace a meal. Understanding doesn't stick to your ribs. There is no protein in understanding."

"OK Manu."

"Understanding is not enough," he said again.

I leaned back in my chair and closed my eyes. There comes a time when you have to choose a side. I opened my eyes.

"What can I do?" I asked.

Manu came to get me at the usual time but quickly took me outside the village. We took the tar road for a bit then cut over and vanished into the forest. Through an inextricable network of small trails known only to hunters, we disappeared into the woods. Like all poachers, I was very familiar with this region and I knew that we would soon happen on a fairly large clearing where I usually set snares. The idea of a stew was not unappealing.

We travelled at a good clip, like men who are used to outdoor living, familiar with the forest and the mountains bordering it. I walked in silence, attentive to nature's meaningful whispers in my ear. It was soothing. When we came out into the clearing, instead of a few hares wearing iron neckties, I saw a dozen men from the region, guns strapped, sitting on stumps, smoking in silence and greeting me with nods of their heads.

I knew them all; I had fed most of them, drank with some of them, and hunted with others. They were strong workers, lean men, gnarled, roughly shaved, with unclear pasts. Nevertheless, they were ordinary men. I knew who had children, who had alcohol problems, and who had kidney problems. Regular men who were gathered there, armed, hidden in the woods and silent.

I sat on a rotten branch to wait with them. Wait for what? Wait for my destiny, I guess. There was nothing else to do: be with them, share their lives, their battle. We were already in full battle; it was impossible to remain impartial. My fate had been bound to theirs for far too long now, since my first milk order, the first potato harvest. Since my first soup served at the cantina.

Suddenly, in a whirl of leaves, the clearing filled with men with painted faces pointing the black mouths of their automatic weapons at us.

"Not a move," ordered a voice that I thought I recognized.

And then, everyone began to laugh and I identified the voice. It was Mistral's.

Dressed head to toe in fatigues, he wore grenades in a bandolier and several magazines on his belt. He was magnificent, a lord of war. He was also laughing, circulating among the men and doling out praise. Finally, he stood in front of me.

"Hello Chef," he said without embracing me.

"Hello."

"They came for her in the middle of the night, you know."

"I figured."

"One car, two men. She had packed her suitcases."

"I know."

"You told her for us."

It wasn't an accusation, just a simple statement. But I would have preferred that he smiled.

"Yes."

"You shouldn't have, Chef. She's a whore."

"Yes."

"Not a whore for you. You don't realize."

"No."

"You should never have told her our business."

"I know, I'm sorry."

I was. Mistral's face brightened.

"In the end, it spared us a lot of trouble. We wouldn't have held for two days before they still would have come to dislodge us. There would have been deaths and it wouldn't have been pretty."

"Perhaps."

"But wait! I'm not saying you were right, Chef."

He stared at me for a moment, jaw clenched.

"Don't start up again, Chef."

"OK."

He paused again, turned half way to the others who were listening avidly.

"Men work better when they are well fed, right Chef?"

I waited.

"And they fight better when they are well fed. Right?"

"Right."

"Right?"

It was my turn to look him straight in the eyes. Mistral was smiling.

"Yes," I said, "Yes."

And it was a done deal. Just like that. One simple stuttered syllable: yes, yes, and I belonged to the militia. Without further thought, without a contract or prior notice, I had become a cook-soldier. I was going to fight for a cause – and any treason would be punished by death.

It was like a late-night dream, you know? Just before you wake up? You're still asleep but you know that you're asleep. You're dreaming, but you know that it's just a dream.

Throughout the weeks preceding the start of our action, several times I had the diffuse impression of being a character in someone else's dream. I saw the dream through reality and reality through the dream. I attended clandestine meetings, training sessions, handled explosives with the carelessness of a dream, waiting for someone somewhere to wake up. But who was the Sleeper?

I knew that I was in Mistral's dream and that Mistral was the dreamed-up character of another. But who did this other character belong to? And how far back did this dream chain go? Was it endless? Did anything else exist besides these fantastical projections? Was someone going to open their eyes and put an end to all of this?

But no one was waking up. Through I don't know what secret channels arrived weekly deliveries of weapons and communication equipment, right down to military clothing, barely worn but unmatched, combat boots and even socks. The government army was beginning to get nervous. I couldn't put my finger on it, but it felt like something was going on.

What was going on here was going on everywhere, said Mistral. The opposition that the power was trying to muzzle had gone underground. Patience, he said. When we were strong enough . . .

Mistral was like a fish who discovers water as an adult and who can't get over finally understanding the usefulness of its gills. He was made for this. He threw grenades as though he had always thrown grenades, in a full, wide motion of the arm and body. The projectile was propelled twenty metres in the air before landing exactly in the centre of the target (an old truck tire) less than a second before exploding.

His natural charisma made Mistral a perfect leader, and through military training, the violence that had always existed within him found an ideal, controlled and productive outlet. For several years, his bedside reading (the only book he had ever owned) was an old shredded copy of *The Art of War* by Sun Tzu, from which he liked to read us passages after having made us crawl through the mud. One of them went something like this:

The act of war is based on lies and duplicity. Deceiving the enemy is the only truth.

He who is strong must appear weak. He who is weak will appear to be strong.

He who is far will appear to be near. He who is close will appear to be far.

Etc.

He was exulting, in his own way. We sometimes caught him smiling or congratulating us after a particularly well-executed exercise. His pleasure was infectious. We were preparing for war like Boy Scouts at summer camp, pranksters and virile.

Manu was in heaven. In a small training camp that we had set up in the middle of the forest, he learned how to handle the radio and laughed like a child when uttering coded phrases that he pronounced with a low voice to be more like a spy. His young body, brimming with strength, was being spent through the crazy trials to which Mistral subjected us in order to prepare us for what was coming.

Between Mistral and Manu, I let myself be carried away. It's true that firing a grease gun at a cardboard target can give you a certain sense of power, but it is also true that you can feel empathy for the cardboard as long as you put yourself in its place. But it was best not to talk about that.

In the middle of autumn, the military occupation became more aggressive. After pillaging them to distract the troops, they set fire to a few pitiful farms. Simple soldiers, beardless and smiling, had practised their aim on the last panic-stricken chickens of old Elena, who, despite her old age, had run, tearfully, from one explosion of feathers to another to scrape the flesh off the ground and save something from which to make a last soup from the catastrophe. Then, she resigned herself to seek refuge in the village after being proud all her life for never having asked anyone for anything. A few weeks later, an embolism took her.

Our men, faced with such actions, stamped their feet impatiently and screamed for vengeance. After all, they were a mere one hundred soldiers covering a huge territory that we had the advantage of knowing in detail. But Mistral tempered the mood:

"Patience. They're provoking us. They want us to leave the woods. They've taken the initiative. Answering is playing their game."

Mistral wasn't the only one preaching patience. Commander Cousteau advocated it too each time he came on inspection. We called him that in jest, because we were civilians disguised as soldiers and in memory of nights in front of the television from our youth. We were obviously unaware of his real name. He was Mistral's immediate superior and, as such, coordinated all the guerrilla units in the region. He always arrived unannounced. He was a calm, tall and large man, who would have been gentle if he hadn't been merciless. He was stubbornly committed to turning our band of unrefined lumberjacks into an elite unit, respectful of the military hierarchy. He surfaced, two or three times a month, supervised the training, uttered a good word to each of us, then shut himself away with Mistral for hours to discuss I don't know what military strategy intended to secure total victory for us.

When he came out of his secret meetings, Mistral was all worked up. The effect he had on us, the commander had on him. Each of his visits fired up Mistral who in turn fired us up.

Patience and lashes of the whip took effect. At the end of autumn, we managed to resemble something warlike.

The nature of the terrain and the scarcity of our heavy equipment prevented the militia from establishing itself as a model battalion marching in step towards the enemy. Our only artillery consisted of two grenade launchers and a single mortar. Our forces were scattered in small, very mobile companies. As far as I knew, there were six others training in secret, as we were, in the region. Commander Cousteau was coordinating all the operations. Some fifty men at the beginning of the war; one hundred and fifty men and women towards the middle of the war; a handful at the end.

I clearly remember the day when the Sleeper opened his eyes. It was the ninth of November. The air was crisp and the ground was strewn with leaves. The village was still asleep, shivering under the blankets. The military authorities had reduced by half the firewood that families could go out to cut down on the company's land. The problem was that, by government decree, the entire forest belonged to the company, and winter was not necessarily going to last half as long. So, wood was conserved and people shivered in the households of a village nestled in the heart of an immense supply of combustible material.

Hunger was becoming more and more pressing. There were no more supplies or money, and nothing in the stores. The military authorities had seized all the hunting weapons they could find. Even if most households had stashed a weapon, infinite precautions had to be taken and a distance of about thirty kilometres before even beginning to think about hunting. But the game wasn't going to allow itself to fall any easier because we were hungry. It did as it pleased, disregarding our rumbling stomachs.

Children with protruding ribs set snares everywhere (iron wire was not yet forbidden), but hares were scarce. All that was left was pilfering. And the only ones left to pilfer from were the military men.

That day, Andreï may have had a craving for sugar. Or a craving for chocolate. Something to melt in the mouth with closed eyes. For weeks now, he had known the location of the cantinas and the habits of their keepers. Who would be suspicious of a nine-year-old boy with lips so red that they looked stained from strawberry syrup?

Every day, the camp crawled with children fascinated by weapons and uniforms. They giggled during reviews and, from afar, attempted to do the rank and file making fun of attention. Down from the hills with his father who had meetings in the village, Andreï was the only child roaming around at that time of the morning.

I remember the scene very clearly. I was at home on the porch. I was sharpening my knives again. I only had to turn my head to the left in order to see, straight ahead, down the road, approximately three hundred metres away, the government army camp. Perhaps the officers had received orders that day. Perhaps the increasing tension of war had worn down the nerves of the simple soldiers? Perhaps.

I didn't see Andreï enter the camp. I wasn't paying attention. I was sharpening my knives. Like a gust of wind, he had stopped in to see me, ran up the three steps to the porch, and kissed me before leaving just as quickly. I remember the coolness of his lips on my close-shaven cheek, a feeling that lasted a minute or two, long after Andreï disappeared from my sight and I went back to my blades.

The wind was blowing, carrying the smells of bacon from the camp to my quivering nostrils. The wind blew strong and long, without letting up.

There was a security parameter around the camp. We often made fun of it. Full of holes like Swiss cheese. Children wove through to filch under the watchful eyes of the infantrymen who scolded them like older brothers – basically, having fun. It was the impunity of childhood, at least up to that point.

I am sharpening my knives. Suddenly, carried on the wind come bursts of voices, shreds of yelling. I lift my head and turn towards the camp. Running towards me, two hundred metres away, is Andreï with a package under his arm. One hundred metres behind him, an orderly shoulders his rifle and takes aim. A sergeant leans towards him and yells at him. The fragments of this bawling outreach me, confused and piecemeal. I hear this word:

"Fire!"

Andreï hears it too, no doubt. I see his frightened face, his little legs running, he sees me from afar and lifts his head.

The sergeant yells at the soldier who does not want to fire. The soldier yells:

"Halt! Halt!"

But Andreï keeps running. I leap down to the street and run towards Andreï, arms flailing and yelling:

"Stop! Stop!"

But the wind! The words barely out of my mouth are pushed back by the damn wind. Andreï doesn't hear me. If only he could hear me! He sees me, he thinks I am calling him, he comes closer and the fear on his face slowly disappears. The closer he gets to me, the safer he feels. He is smiling now. In his arms, against his skinny chest, is a sack of sugar. Suddenly, Andreï stops, surprised. His eyes open wide. The sound of the discharge follows, slightly delayed, the same trajectory as the bullet. It reaches his ears and then mine. I run towards him. The sack of sugar falls on the pavement and bursts open from the impact. Andreï sways. He doesn't fall. He places a knee, then a hand, in the sugar. I run to him and arrive just in time to catch his head before it hits the ground. I kneel and place his head on my thighs. I scream:

"Help!"

I howl:

"Help!"

I whisper:

"Andreï."

His eyes are open, he looks at me, he sees me upside down. His lips are red. His face is white. His long lashes bat. A single tear wells in the corner of his left eye. I scream for help again. I look right. People are coming out of their houses but hesitate to come forward. I look left. The sergeant is gone. The soldier who fired stayed at his post, rifle in bandolier, shoulders heaving as though he was sobbing. But he looks away.

I see Andreï's lips move. I lean over, stroking his hair.

"I . . . I did something stupid," he whispers.

I have no answer. I have no time to find one. His gaze fixates, and a last breath escapes from his mouth. His child's body becomes heavy.

On the pavement, blood mixes with sugar.

The Sleeper awoke, the dream ended in a last tearing of white sails. He opened his eyes on a nightmare. Reality is no more logical than the dream. Reality signifies nothing, it tells nothing, it tumbles, it falls; it hurdles down the slope of time like an avalanche of events, objects and people. Everything gets caught up, everything breaks, everything is lost. For nothing. To follow the slope. Because that's the way it is.

I hadn't moved a muscle when Manu finally arrived to take the body of his son from my arms. He wasn't crying. I painstakingly rose, legs numb. My knees cracked in the silence.

There was nothing to say. The body was so light, Manu didn't need my help to carry him. So I escorted them, useless, to the truck. Manu put his son down in the passenger seat and fastened the seatbelt. He walked around the vehicle, slid in and started the engine without looking at me. Long after the truck had disappeared from my sight, I heard the sound of its motor, carried on the damn wind.

The burial took place two days later in the old cemetery, before a handful of people. The others were afraid. No eulogy. No prayers. A single scream, brief, quickly choked by a fist between the teeth, when the first shovelful of earth hit the lid of the coffin like a drum hit. It was Jana. The first mother's scream of the war that was beginning.

⊙⊙⊙⊙

In December, we ruled the region. We had pushed back the government army to the county seat of the province.

The government troops, some one hundred poor men, never had clearly identified enemies. We sprang from everywhere: houses, roofs, woods and cars. Our numbers were lower but we had hate. We were not defending a territory on the orders of our superiors in the name of abstract economic interests. We fought to take back our homes, our lives and our dead.

Commander Cousteau had decided to attack at dawn. When we opened fire, more than half the soldiers were still in their underwear with a toothbrush in their mouths.

Within minutes, it was over. Few men had managed to escape by jeep. The others lay where our fire had mowed them down. I didn't have time to take it all in, everything happened too fast.

After Andreï's death, Manu had argued for immediate action. Mistral had calmed him, then Cousteau.

"Soon," they said.

Throughout the country, hundreds, thousands of groups such as ours waited for the signal for insurrection.

It was exciting, it has to be said. Despite the agony, the grief. Having an enemy is exhilarating. The clash of two armies traces a clear front-line in a world up until this point confused, complex and incomprehensible. Suddenly, there is me and him.

Us and them. Their pain, our well-being. The enemy's presence justifies my existence, my means of action. I don't take up arms because I want to, but because he gives me no choice. I no longer act, I react. I am no longer responsible for my actions, the enemy is. The enemy asked for it. The enemy is my objective, my foil, my excuse, my justification. The enemy gives me a purpose. It is my relationship with the enemy that suspends all the usual rules of procedure. It is my hatred for him that irrigates my body with adrenaline and makes me a little more than a man: stronger, more courageous, unbeatable, more concentrated.

Of course there is fear. In the days preceding our action, fear came first. Fear of dying, of being wounded. Fear of being a coward. And what if my legs gave way beneath me? What would happen if I couldn't resist the urge to flee and I was found hidden in a closet, whimpering like a little girl? We didn't talk about that. At least I didn't talk about it with anyone. I kept my fears to myself, my fear of being afraid. We said things like:

"I'm going to rip off their balls."

Or:

"They're going to get it up the ass."

But the truth is, none of us had ever killed anyone and we had to get used to the idea that we had to play with the enemy like a little cat, tease it, tickle it, manhandle it a bit until it bares its teeth, shows its claws and starts to growl. Cousteau and Mistral agreed. They told Manu:

"They can't be forgiven for what they did to your son. I know you're hurting, but that's useless. They mock your pain. Your pain makes them laugh. Give your pain the time to turn into hatred. They'll be afraid of hatred. Sharpen your hatred like a knife, and with it you'll slit their throats, for your son, for our sons, for all of our lives that they have wrecked."

"When?" asked Manu.

"Soon."

This warlike rhetoric was fed from the source of true agony, real guilt, a real sense of powerlessness, but promised to transform the agony, guilt and powerlessness into a power just as real. The power of vengeance.

Manu didn't have to wait very long. "Blunders" like those that had caused his son's death were multiplying throughout the country, and even though television and radio belonged to friends of those in power, you didn't have to be very sly to deduct, from the circumlocutions, that the mounting blunders formed a tsunami that threatened to swallow the country.

Manu had sent his wife and children to a neighbouring village and all the fathers in the company wanted to do the same. Cousteau had dissuaded them.

"Emptying the village tells the army that we are preparing to attack. However, if the children continue to play in the streets, the army will be reassured. We want them to be reassured."

"I don't want my children to serve as shields," said Rossi, the giant teddy bear.

"They aren't shields. They are warriors, the same as you."

"They're children!"

"Look what happened to Andreï! He was but a child as well, and what is our children's future if we don't regain our freedom and our dignity? Famine? A bullet in the back? Slavery? Today you want to shelter them but tomorrow there will be no shelter. We will fight everywhere, and our wives and children will fight as well, in their own way. And their way of fighting, today, is not to flee, but to stay here and continue as before. They are not shields, Rossi, they are a smokescreen."

That is how the women and children stayed. On D-Day, just before dawn, I crossed the kitchen of a village house I had never visited. A woman waited for me, a pot of steaming coffee in her hand. Not long ago, she had leafed through magazines while answering the telephone in the sales office of the sawmill.

I took position at the kitchen window that looked out onto the road, my submachine gun resting across the sink.

"Thank you for the coffee."

"Good luck," said the woman, and then she gathered her three children and led them to a room in the back where they would be relatively sheltered from stray bullets.

I watched them move away, took a sip of coffee, placed the cup on the counter, grabbed my weapon and directed my attention to the road. I waited. It was an effort not to put my index finger on the trigger, but it went back there on its own, tirelessly, trembling impatiently.

I remember myself, as a boy, at the public swimming pool. I was scared stiff of the three-metre springboard although I dreamed of it. I saw myself flying. I imagined myself effortlessly climbing the ladder and walking confidently to the end of the board, springing and jumping very high, then bouncing and shooting skyward. I saw myself with arms outstretched, chest out and eyes closed, slicing through the air and falling, straight on, and breaking the water's surface like a pointy knife. I saw myself. It was easy. I just had to close my eyes.

It was another matter when I kept my eyes open. I was so determined, I wanted it so badly. But halfway up the ladder, already, I felt fear taking over. When I placed my foot on the board, I knew I wouldn't make it. I tried, though, but it was no longer a question of will. It was the fear of jeers that propelled me forward. Two-thirds of the way down the board, the fear of being mocked was stronger than the fear of empty space.

I advanced as though in a minefield, grasping the handrails with all my might and I could hear my friends' laughter and razzing in the distance. Looking down, I could see the bottom of the pool, so far away, so incredibly far away! I moved forward by a toe, then two, and reached the exact point of balance between the fear of emptiness and ridicule. I couldn't move. I was petrified. I clung with two hands, and each time someone was sent to help me down.

Without wasting time to look for my towel, I disappeared into the locker room to quickly get dressed and run home to shut myself in my room.

I couldn't understand. Sure, I cried, I was hurt, I felt ashamed. But most of all, I was enraged by the visions behind my eyelids, showing me executing the perfect swan dive – I was enraged because these visions did not correspond to reality. I was enraged because I was capable, in all evidence I was capable because I could see myself doing it. I felt the wind, I instinctively understood the curve of flight and the hardness of water. How could my spirit know what the body was incapable of accomplishing? My body was a coward. I was imprisoned in a cowardly body and I was convinced I would die from it.

It was the three-metre springboard that I thought of while looking out the kitchen window, finger on the trigger. In a way, at that moment I had reached the exact point of balance between the desire to fight and the fear of being a coward.

Through the window, just above the sink, I saw a segment of road that I was to spray with bullets if the government troops were to take it in an attempt to flee. From the first shots, I was to shatter the window with the butt of my weapon, then be ready to shoot on sight. I decided to open the window without breaking it and wait.

Only no one came by.

Heavy gunfire had exploded in the direction of the camp, but the portion of the road before me had remained deserted. The shots began to stagger when I heard the sound of a horn grow near. A covered jeep, driving slowly, came into my field of vision. I made out the bloodied face of the driver who was slumped over the steering wheel. His dead pupils were turned towards me. The vehicle slowly left the road and finished its drive against a tree. The light impact was enough to slide the driver off the steering wheel thereby releasing the horn. To be sure, I fired three bullets at the jeep. Nothing happened. Soon after, the last shots ceased from the camp. It was over. My first clash of arms. Had I proved my courage? No. No more than I had proved my cowardice. I had proof of nothing.

I heard crying behind me. I turned around. The woman hugged a little girl with brown curls who was sobbing gently.

"Is it over?" asked the woman.

"I think so."

But I knew that it had just begun.

I bent down to pick up the three cartridge cases that had rolled onto the kitchen floor and I tossed them in my hand. They were still warm. I moved closer to give them to the child.

Between two sobs, she closed her small fist around my present then, lifting her face towards me, she smiled faintly.

Manu had set himself on the body of the sergeant who had ordered that Andreï be gunned down. Using a knife, boots and fists, he had beaten the corpse into a pulp of bloody flesh and crushed bone. The deformed head had been driven into the ground up to its ears from having been trodden on. When I arrived, there were about ten of them watching him, standing in a half-circle behind him, keeping a respectful distance.

Kneeling in front of the body, Manu hit while crying, reciting the name of his son like an incantation. Perhaps he was expecting him to come back to life. But exhaustion was gaining on him to no avail. I moved forward and placed my hand on his shoulder. He stopped hitting immediately as though he had only been waiting for that: a hand on his shoulder, a friend to whisper his name,

"Manu."

The bulk of the troop made it through without fighting. Some fifteen dead, about twenty wounded, most only slightly. On our side, our only casualty had slit a buttock climbing over barbed wire to get to his post. His injury embarrassed him less than the fact of having an exposed ass during the entire operation.

"I felt . . . vulnerable."

Even Manu managed to laugh. Nonetheless, a medic had to sew up his rear end.

"Could you do my pants while you're at it, Doctor?" asked the one who from then on was known only as Stitch.

While Stitch recovered from his emotions and went on a search for pants his size, we assembled the prisoners to load them into the trucks. Mistral had interrogated some of them. What he learned didn't serve us. About ten heavily armed men were to escort the prisoners to the border of the neighbouring province where some of our allies would take them in hand. The men designated, the trucks departed, we sacked the camp in a joyous atmosphere worthy of a sporting rally. What could be broken was broken. What could be stolen was stolen. What could be soiled with urine or feces was as well.

I commandeered the cantina and the kitchens. The food supplies had to be preserved and I didn't have the heart to participate in the celebration because I hadn't taken part in the assault. It was my comrades' victory, not mine, and I was perhaps a coward.

With the food supplies retrieved from the enemy, I promised them a memorable banquet. I recruited a few volunteers to help me in the kitchens and valiantly set to the task of preparing the victory feast. But all day handling the knife on the cutting board while I sliced the meat, I knew that I had to kill an enemy to finally belong to my kind.

The day following the victory, in the dissipating fog of alcohol, while the blood pounded in slow heavy blows in our ears and our distended stomachs resonated with the gurgles of a catastrophic digestion, Mistral ordered us to pack up because it was time for us to disappear into nature.

Government retaliation couldn't be far off, and our under-equipped forces couldn't stand up to the armoured vehicles and the light artillery of a professional army. The only way to be effective, held Mistral, was to use guerrilla tactics. Hit and then disappear, hit and then disappear.

"Disappear where?"

"There," said Mistral, designating the forest.

"There?"

"Our fortress."

No one knew the forest better than we did. Over thousands of square kilometres, cutting and prospecting paths had been traced, some of which, to avoid the pitfalls of the topography, ended in a marsh or terminated, without warning, at the foot of a cliff. It was a labyrinth that the forest workers had dug with their hands, in the living matter of the trees and the decaying humus. Shelters made of boards, prospectors' cabins and hunting camps had popped up everywhere over the years in which the forest had been at once a source of income, a playground and a continent to explore. If immense parcels of land had been cleared, even bigger ones appeared to be an inextricable clutter of branches and needles, rocks and thickets. Under the cover of the trees, the army's helicopters couldn't locate us. Within the intricate crossroads, the government troops could only lose themselves and become stuck. In our forest, we were invincible.

On a fine cold and clear December morning, after the men's wrenching goodbyes to their families, in a caravan of light duty vehicles taken from the enemy, we delved into the forest. As for me, I had no one to say goodbye to and, at the time of departure, I felt none of the heart pinching experienced by those who were losing something. The winter was going to be long.

"Once all the supplies are used up, all we'll have to eat is what we can steal, trap or hunt," Mistral had said.

"That's nothing new," I answered.

I almost felt lighthearted and I wasn't alone. Several men whistled while the forest closed its brown and green arms around us. Had we not spent our entire lives preparing to lead this existence? The allure of fishing and hunting, the love of rugged nature, the taste for well-sharpened knives and axes . . . Were we still human enough to live off nature, in nature, or were we perverted to the point that we couldn't survive without a coffee machine, microwave oven, a shingle roof and an electric-ignition engine?

It was snowing that day, first in soft, light flakes that hesitated as if suspended in the air before resigning themselves to land on the ground. Then the snow became heavier, denser, erasing our tracks, muffling our noises while we dug, like a human axe, into the flesh of the forest, deeper and deeper, to its secret heart.

We stayed in the forest for close to four weeks and our main occupation consisted in looking for a little warmth while avoiding the government patrols launched to find us. Until further notice, we were to avoid conflict at all cost. Helicopters crossed the sky at low altitudes which was the reason we were forbidden to leave the cover of the trees. We lived like tracked animals, and once our supplies ran out, we had to feed ourselves with meat that was raw or barely cooked on a fire made of dry grass. We were incredibly dirty; our clothes were stiff with mud and filth, our faces hidden by beards. We took turns sleeping on the two straw mattresses belonging to a small hunting camp, otherwise on the beds of dead leaves and pine branches under hastily built shelters. Fifty woodsmen, already welded by a trial by fire, were now subjected to a trial by cold.

Survive? Oh! We were capable, no question. But why? For what purpose? What were we waiting for?

I had long asked myself if Commander Cousteau hadn't willingly preserved this situation in order to allow us to develop and feed our rage. The result was that at the end of those four weeks, we had progressively rid ourselves of the attributes of civilization; we dreamed of action and the celebration of victory, because brute energy is rewarded brutally.

In the meantime, we made fires whose smoke we had to disperse by waving pine branches above the flames. The exercise warmed more than the fire – and the real cold weather was still to come! The men, usually particularly eager to prove their virility, slept closely nestled against each other, like teaspoons in a kitchen drawer, without a single joke on the topic ever being made.

So when the order came to move out, these same men jumped to their feet, scratched their balls through their mitts and let out beastly grunts leaving no doubt as to their true warrior nature. Better death than spooning.

I say "the men," but I include myself. At last I was trying to include myself. The question of my courage was always hanging. I conducted myself like the others, I laughed at their jokes, I accepted their thanks after the frugal meals, I hunted with them, I listened attentively as they talked of their childhoods, romantic escapades and dream cars. I looked like one of them, I was accepted as one of them, but I wasn't and I was very much aware of it.

When it was time to leave, I added my grunts to theirs. I hit the road in their company, weapon in hand and fear in my gut.

I was scared of being scared.

I won't go into the details of the operation. They are in your files. Suffice to say that we were to intercept a convoy of weapons on the southern road that was destined for the garrison in the city of M. Turns out that it was a trap.

A two-day forced march led us to the road on which we took up position on each side after having mined a few segments. Then we waited, hidden by the trees or buried in the snow.

Once again, I found myself on the springboard, trying to calm my racing heartbeat. Underneath my gloves, my clammy hands could feel my weapon slide from my grip. But this time, no one was going to come to help me get down.

That summer, I didn't return to the pool for a whole month. I remember a hot, sticky summer. Every fold of my body filled with sweat as soon as I stepped outside. But I was afraid of my fear and I wanted to stay far away from the three-metre springboard.

One evening, my brother woke me from my slumber by whispering:

"Come."

"Where?"

"I said, come."

I dressed in silence and climbed through the window. He sometimes took me with him on his nocturnal expeditions, and I thought that we were going to meet his friends to smoke on the roof of an abandoned building. But there were no friends and he was taking me to the swimming pool.

"No," I said.

"Come on," he insisted, pulling me by the arm.

We climbed the fence and I followed my brother to the foot of the diving board.

"Don't look at the bottom," he said after lighting a cigarette and taking a deep drag on it.

"What?"

"The bottom, don't look at it. When you dive off the springboard, you are three metres from the water, that's what counts. But the bottom is six metres away. So if you look at the bottom, you'll feel as though you're diving from a much higher place."

"Three metres is still high."

"Well, how tall are you? A metre twenty-five?"

"One twenty-eight."

"It's not even three times your height and you're little. Three metres is three times nothing."

I wasn't convinced. But my brother convinced me to climb the ladder with him, fully clothed, just to take a look. I held his hand very tightly.

"Look," he said. "You can't see the bottom."

It was true. You couldn't see the bottom, but rather the reflections of the moon undulating on the water's surface, so close that I felt as though I could almost touch them by reaching out my hand.

"Do you think you can do it?" asked my brother.

"Yes, I think so."

So, on a night lit by a full moon, I undressed at the top of a three-metre springboard, and I walked along the board with a hopeful heart. It was dark and it was as if my eyes were closed.

I could see myself diving. And I did it. I hopped at the end of the board and I dove. I fell like a brick, stomach first, and I made the best and most painful belly-flop a diver could fear. When I emerged from the water, I was still howling in pain. I don't know quite how I managed to swim to the edge, panting and eyes red from the chlorine and tears. My brother was waiting for me, crouching, a smile on his lips.

"You see, easy as pie," he said to me, hand outstretched.

"It's as easy as pie," I repeated under my breath, while in the distance I could hear the racket of the approaching convoy.

No joke. Since then, I could never be bothered to perform a dive worthy of that name.

Don't look at the bottom, I told myself as the first covered trucks came around the bend.

When the first mines exploded, the entire convoy stopped. Suddenly, the tarps over the trucks spread apart and from them spewed soldiers by the hundreds who immediately deployed to capture and exterminate us.

Don't look at the bottom, I told myself, whatever you do, don't look at the bottom. And I began shooting.

WHAT'S WRONG
WITH THAT?

I woke early that morning in my room in the Black Bear Inn, prey of a hangover due as much to the excess of alcohol from the day before as to the countless unanswered questions that were violently knocking about in the bony cavity intended to protect my brain. In the meantime, I had set to work with a certain enthusiasm, confident despite the circumstances of having to win back Florence's love. I had also written her a nice e-mail to soften her up.

This extraordinary recklessness (I probably still had alcohol in my blood) extended all the way to the Monster's cause, whose trial I could already see myself winning. Armed with a pot of coffee, I attacked the file of charges. The absence of Rosalind and the murder of her child by Viktor Rosh had me perplexed. A telephone call to Cevitjc had been no help to me. Suddenly (no doubt the alcohol was beginning to wear off), future perspectives seemed gloomier. I now doubted the power of conviction of my letter to Florence. I doubted my merits as a lawyer. I doubted my merits as a human being. Like a deflating balloon, my spirit was collapsing on itself. Reality, from the end of a needle, was titillating my neurons.

I regained some hope when I received Josef's message. I sat myself down at the computer to write to the Monster's brother, convinced that I was on to a good thing there.

When, three hours later, the good thing blew up in my face, I was nothing more than a miserable Westerner, useless and unhappy. Discouragement took me by the hand and led me to the contents of the mini-bar that no chambermaid had had the chance to restock so far. It wasn't yet 1 pm, but Operation Anaesthetic could begin while, all around, the universe as we know it was caving in on itself for a Big Crunch that was aimed at me. Unless of course it was an acute attack of paranoia, in which case a good dose of whisky was also prescribed.

So, let's take inventory, I thought to myself as I filled my glass.

My wife is leaving me.

My client won't talk to me.

My client's attorney is hiding something from me.

My client's brother sees me as a murderer.

My client's country sees me as an invader.

Why in heaven's name is Rosalind's story no longer recorded in the indictment?

I roamed the room in briefs and socks, glass in hand. Through the drawn curtains, I could make out a bright sun, and suddenly I wanted light; I wanted to be bathed in light. I opened the curtains and my eyes to the blinding sun. I was burning my retinas; I could feel the rays spearing me through the window, warming my skin. I finally closed my eyelids and through their skin the world had become orange. I stayed there for some time, surprised to enjoy it so much. All surprised that enjoyment still existed.

Go figure. Under the benevolent effects of the light, I could feel my strength returning. Oh! Three times nothing. But there was light. I experienced a long shiver, as though my body was shaking. Without opening my eyes, I felt my way to a plant and emptied the contents of my glass into the potted earth. How could I explain the hope? I wasn't kidding myself; the sun had only temporarily quenched my thirst. But what do you do when everything is lost? I had no desire to die. On the contrary, something inside me rebelled; a healthy anger shook my neurons by reactivating them. I mentally rolled up my sleeves. On the blank page of my future, I sketched the itinerary of my return to the land of the living.

If a cloud had veiled the sun, or worse, if it had rained that day, nothing would have happened and what followed may have been merely a continuation of the past. And if I had abruptly drawn the curtains instead of opening my eyes to see the crowd of journalists at the hotel's entrance, I would no doubt have abandoned the whole thing, packed my bags and returned home to try to glue back together the pieces of my family and career.

But I opened my eyes and I could clearly see the crowd of journalists cooling its heels on the sidewalk across from the hotel. Two or three mobile TV units were parked any which way, blocking half the traffic. Scared that they would notice me, I backed up two steps and then called down to the front desk, which confirmed my fears.

They were there for me. A dozen interview requests for the written press, radio and television, not counting the photographers.

Judging from the previous day's news reports, they weren't there to follow legal proceedings, but to overplay a so-called

political affront by a wealthy country on one that was less for-
tunate. I was outraged. This time, I had no intention of agreeing to the bad-guy role that they wanted me to play: the one
thing I was sure of was my good faith in this whole affair.

I tried to reach Cevitjc but he was in court that day.

"So give me Josef's telephone number please," I asked his
secretary.

"Oh no! No one calls him! He'll call you in ten minutes."

I took a shower and sure enough the telephone rang right
after. Josef already knew the journalists were staking out the
hotel. He agreed to my request and I listened to his recom-
mendations. We hung up at the same time.

An hour later, I slithered down the back staircase, travel bag
in hand, sunglasses covering my eyes. I wore one of those
expensive designer safari outfits popular with advertising agency
directors to take on the plebeians behind the wheel of their
Jaguars. I had bought it on a whim, never intending to wear it.
Now it was helping to camouflage my appearance as a lawyer.

The Russian Mafia's 4x4 waited for me in the alley behind
the hotel. At the wheel, Josef the Garden Dwarf was smiling
at me maliciously.

"Let's go," I said, settling in next to him.

"Go where?"

"Let's follow the Monster's tracks."

Josef paused, tilted his head to the side and squinted. He
sat up in his seat and put the vehicle into first gear.

"The Great Forest then," he said.

And for the remainder of the trip, neither of us said a word.

We took the northern road, which in fact headed northwest. At first it was a straight road along which stretched villages that were so distended it became impossible to tell where one began and the other ended. At first flat, the countryside undulated and then climbed aimlessly towards the mountain chain that protruded on the horizon before launching its peaks in an assault on the clouds.

Such was the setting of the Monster's war. Nothing was stranger than to imagine, in this scenery, the thundering of the mortars and the crashing of the fire, but it is true that war on such a scale leaves few traces in nature. The passing of a few springs are generally sufficient to heal all wounds. Men's flesh is another story, and the wound inflicted on one individual is enough to make several generations suffer. I thought of the Monster's parents. I thought of the children he never had. This made me think of my own. I shook my head and chased away this painful thought. I was not ready to deal with it yet.

I had all of the reports and the files on my client with me. If Viktor Rosh didn't want to talk to me, too bad for him, but there were others who could clear things up for me, tell me his story and that of this war that he hadn't waged all on his own. I suspected that there were monsters in every village and that what my client was accused of, with close exception, didn't deserve the hounding he was being subjected to.

Once again, my mind drifted back to Rosalind. Once I had read the account, I shivered all over in horror. If evil existed somewhere on this Earth, it was there, in this gratuitous and murderous act for which my client was guilty. But why, I wondered again, why was the prosecution of this action no longer mentioned in his charge sheet? Why leave out the pure horror that would doubtlessly have led to the heaviest sentence for my client?

The rest dealt with simple facts of war. Violence and blood, indifference towards the suffering of others, hatred and stubbornness, sure. But without Rosalind, how did the Monster distinguish himself from the other militiamen who had fought as well? Or yet everyone had to be judged and Cevitjc hadn't finished paying for a vacation on the Côte d'Azur.

We travelled in silence and I looked out the window at a countryside that was not completely unfamiliar to me. It looked somewhat like mine, like that of my homeland. Forest-covered hills and mountains, deciduous leaves and conifers, streams and torrents. I could have been at home if not for the presence of men and the signs of their lunacy. Deep down, hadn't I thrown myself into the pursuit of this countryside? As if, by confronting its colours, smells and textures, by following in the Monster's footsteps, by travelling across the paths of his personal war, I could arrive at an intimate knowledge of his reasons for being and acting.

I knew it was a delusion. I couldn't put myself in anyone else's skin, and no one could put themselves in mine. We were eternally condemned to isolated senses, caught in our network of nerves like the prey of a spider that will never reveal itself. Only brief illuminations could cast light on our solitude: an outstretched hand, a smile, a caress. Love. In Florence's eyes, I had seen the hope of escape, the possibility of escaping and joining her to face, together, the spider's traps. But that was long ago.

The innocent faces of my children looking up at me had also been like an open door to their souls, expanding my prison. But I had looked away and the door had closed, leaving me alone and miserable. I had engineered my own solitude. I had spun the web myself. I was the spider and I was the prey. This had gone on long enough.

"We're coming up on the village," Josef said.

A village that looked just like the others that we had already crossed: simple houses made of boards, disseminated along the road, at first spread apart from one another, then closing rank until they were stuck together around a square, a bistro and a hotel. On either side, gravel roads dug out with ruts and ravines due to the rains. One led to the sawmill, and as for the others, God only knows where.

Josef had slowed the vehicle, waiting for a sign from me. He stopped at the village exit, at the foot of a steep slope snaking into the dense forest.

I hesitated. We had driven for three hours, the afternoon coming to a close, and I didn't have the energy to tackle my research. But the thought of sitting in the bistro with nothing to do but down drinks until sleep took over repulsed me. I wasn't thirsty, which was new, and this apathy left me idle.

I took the files and leafed through them distractedly, searching for I don't know what, the beginning of an idea. Josef came to my rescue.

"Less than an hour from here, towards the mountains, there is a very nice observatory."

He looked at me. I didn't answer.

"The Chef fought there during the war. It was pretty bloody."

Sure, I remembered now. The militiamen had attacked the observatory at the top of which the government army had set up a communications antenna. The commando unit the Monster belonged to had become famous by not taking any prisoners. But a wounded man had survived to tell the story after having escaped into the woods. He was one of the main witnesses for the prosecution.

An observatory, I thought. Did this mean something? Was history repeating itself or was it merely a coincidence? As for me, I had never stepped foot in an observatory, but the Monster, he had shed blood in two of them.

"Why not?" I said to Josef, who promptly engaged the clutch.

We drove for a little over an hour. The closer we got to the mountains, the more the forest became wild, enhanced, torn with rocks and violent torrents. A rugged, old landscape that was wrinkled with shadows. In there is where the Monster dove, got lost, alone like an ogre who distances himself to resist the temptation of eating children. He didn't snatch the booty of war to escape abroad and exist under an alias as a millionaire, no. Not him. I tried to imagine his state of mind at the moment of renunciation, when he turned his back on the war and civilization, when he dove into the forest, alone, never to come out. Hadn't he turned his back on himself? Wasn't he running away from a part of himself, his culpability?

The observatory was located on the western border of a mountain chain. Mount Antique was detached like a premature child, solitary, separated from others by a freak of geology that made the site ideal for an observatory: easily accessible, at an adequate altitude and surrounded by hundreds and hundreds of kilometres of uninhabited forest.

"You're playing tour guide?" I asked Josef.

"Of course."

The observatory had been rebuilt, Josef began, at the beginning of the century by a transitional government that wanted to validate its own grandeur. A committee of handsomely paid experts had selected the site, another had imported the marble from Italy and a third had organized a contest for architects, the winner of which would later be revealed as the cousin of the minister in charge. But despite the repeated scandals and through a miracle that no one could explain, the final result had surprised the fiercest critics of the government.

A single problem remained: no university in the country trained astronomers. Consequently, from the day of its inauguration, the observatory became a splendid monument of uselessness arising from land in the middle of nowhere, a bastard child of the criminal union between megalomania and systematic corruption.

Since then, the observatory had only served a handful of students wishing to pursue their studies abroad, and the only stars that could be observed were the rare movie stars who had come to film outside scenes for period pieces.

We arrived at the foot of the mountain. The road turned quite abruptly to the left in order to avoid the foothills of the mountain chain and then went on to serve the neighbouring province located to the north. To our right, a dirt road twisted steeply upwards along the eastern flank of Mount Antique. Josef switched into second, hit the gas, and we began the ascent as the wide tires of our vehicle sprayed a shower of disturbed stones behind it.

As soon as they were inaugurated, the observatory's installations had, in scientific terms, revealed themselves as obsolete because pompous had been preferred over efficient and splendour over utility. But for these same reasons, its museum-related value was significant and this perhaps explained the three wars that had passed it over, practically sparing it. In many regards, it must have revealed itself to its designers as it appeared to the

Monster and as I saw it, at the detour of a final bend, when it rose from behind a curtain of trees: a white sugar pastry placed atop the mountain by the delicate hand of a giant gourmet.

Josef braked at the entrance to a gravel esplanade bordered with trees, and killed the motor. For a few moments, we gazed at the observatory in silence.

"It's beautiful," he finally said with the voice of a proud owner.

"It's more than beautiful," I said. "It's magic."

In the crystal purity of the air at this altitude, in this green setting that uncurled its scrolls all the way to the horizon, the observatory lifted its white dome like a palm extended to the azure, the gesture, noble and yet doomed for failure, of a humanity wanting to speak to the gods.

Despite the stupidity and folly that had contributed to its birth, or perhaps because of them, the white arrogance of the observatory that was carved out on the blue of the sky seemed as fragile as a dinosaur's eggshell. The observatory resembled a hollowed-out witness from a distant period in which an extinct race of giants walked the Earth. In the end, it was a monument of our frailty.

"It's the only church that counts us all among its faithful," said Josef.

We got out of the car to walk around the esplanade. We were alone. Tufts of grass grew through the gravel. The wild ivy threw itself in a vain assault on the white marble and fell in a vegetal clutter like wavelets breaking on a coral reef. Here, the Monster had killed.

I tried to imagine the din of the firing, the scalding mouths of the weapons spitting smoke and steel, the cries of the wounded, the confusion of the senses – impossible to escape, no matter where one turned, the frenzy of the men and one's own. As I approached, I could see on the observatory walls traces of the bullets' impacts, like as many insect bites on its stone skin. Each of these bullets, I thought, was destined to kill. There were no quarters. Why? However much I looked around, saturated myself in the soul of the place, followed in the Monster's footsteps, I couldn't understand.

"No. I don't understand," I said out loud.

"Do you want to try to understand?" asked Josef.

I stared at him, intrigued.

"Yes."

"Are you sure?"

"What are you trying to say?"

"Wait here."

He raced off towards the car, opened the door and leaned in to grab something from the back seat. He stood up, closed the door and came back to me, still trotting, brandishing his enormous black matte pistol like a relay baton.

I stepped back.

"No . . ." he said, breathless. "It's . . . for you," he finished, holding it out to me.

"I've never . . ."

"How . . . do you expect . . . to try to understand if you . . . have never . . ."

I held out my hand. He laid the weapon in it. I was surprised at its weight, its denseness. Generations and generations of designers had worked so that its grip would perfectly mould the palm of my hand, that its shapes would be a natural extension of the line of my arm and that the trigger would fall under the index finger like one falls in love. This was human genius at work. And I was against it.

I was against it like being against vice and sin. I denounced it from the pulpit, I dreamed of it at night. My sense of reason was against it. I was against the use of violence as the ultimate recourse in settling conflicts within society. But this was an adult decision, whereas I had spent my childhood playing cowboys and Indians, sculpting rifles out of wood scraps and, later on, pelting, with small shots, anything that moved in the fields and woods in my native suburb, including the thigh of a young neighbour who had run home howling despite the lack of severity of his wound, so much so that my father had confiscated my weapon until I had matured.

"Try it," said Josef.

But more than twenty-five years of mental restrictions made me hesitate. I remembered how seriously we had played war. I tried to imagine myself: forty-something, a lawyer without borders, at the deserted summit of an isolated mountain, firing his weapon unnecessarily for the simple pleasure of going "bang, bang."

"Listen," scolded Josef. "How do you expect to understand what happened here if you can't even be bothered to fire a single shot without driving yourself nuts with moral considerations? And you want to put yourself in the shoes of an assassin?"

I didn't let him finish his sentence. I stretched out my arm, aimed at the wide trunk of a century-old walnut tree fifty paces away and fired.

"Nice shot," said Josef. "Dead centre."

I didn't allow myself to smile. I tossed up the weapon, which spun three times, giving off flashes, then caught it by the barrel, held it out to Josef and said:

"Are you happy now?"

John Wayne couldn't have done it better.

Josef burst out laughing, and I cracked up as well. My God! It had been so long!

Josef placed the pistol in his pocket, took me by the arm and we continued our stroll. For several minutes, we would burst out laughing, and then the giggles grew further apart to yield entirely to silence.

The sun was disappearing behind the horizon. Even the birds were quiet at this hour when day becomes night, as if the world flipped at once into another dimension. I knew very well what I felt when I fired the shot. Pleasure. Power. Pride. The desire to start over. I knew. I had always known.

The stars began to appear in a royal blue sky, and as we passed in front of the observatory door, I asked Josef:

"Can we go inside?"

"There's nothing left in there. Or there are too many things . . ."

I waited. Soon he spoke again.

"We don't know exactly who is responsible, who's idea it was, but that night, after collecting all the fallen bodies belonging to the government army, wounded and dead, the militiamen piled them inside the observatory and set fire to the hundred-year-old wainscoting that covered the walls, as well as to the twelve thousand books in the library. Everything burned, the dead and the living, and if the dome didn't crack from the heat, it's because someone left the telescope's skylight open through which escaped the screams of the dying, the smoke, the flames and billions of sparks. Funny, isn't it? That night, instead of gazing at the stars, the observatory was creating them."

I looked at Josef whose eyes were lifted towards the sky sparkling with stars.

"The observatory became a mausoleum," he went on. "There's been talk of making it a true monument to the dead, with official ceremonies and a velvet rope, formal speeches and military fanfare. A nice photo opportunity for the country's leaders . . . So, as you can see," he said, looking me straight in the eyes this time, "all this won't have been for nothing."

He turned his back on me abruptly and headed for the car. I let him get ahead of me, then followed and got in while the engine was already running. We tore down the road at top speed. The lights from the car bounced against the foliage as though we were travelling through a tunnel of vegetation that threatened to swallow us at any moment. It was only when we met the main road that we relaxed a little.

"I knew him, you know."

"Who?"

"He wasn't a monster yet. They called him Chef."

"Cevitjc didn't tell me that."

"Cevitjc didn't ask me."

"And?"

"And nothing. Everyone in the region knew him. I sometimes went to bum a meal at the sawmill. It was better than in most of the restaurants in the city."

"That's it?"

"What do you want me to tell you? He was a regular guy."

"He was?"

"Obviously, he isn't anymore. The war changed him as it changed us all."

"What did it change in you?"

"It was so long ago! I don't know anymore . . . I was so young that it had nothing to change, I think. The war created me. I was eleven when my first war broke out. My parents were killed early on and I joined my brothers in the militia. I was small, thin and agile. I was assigned to sabotage operations. In my free time, I juggled with sticks of dynamite! At thirteen, I drank and smoked like a man! And that's nothing. We had a good time, my brothers and I. You won't believe me but those were great years! No school but adventure, big fireworks . . . We moved all the time, we often slept under the stars, we poached food, took what we wanted . . ."

"And the danger?"

"It was part of the game, I accepted the rules. My two brothers died in combat. I mourned them, and then I avenged them. I was wounded several times. I was proud of my scars."

"That's no life."

"It was mine until I was sixteen years old. Only one I knew."

"Then what happened?"

"Peace. How dull! With the war, I knew what to expect. But peace didn't keep its promises. You had to wonder if it was worth fighting to end up with that! Falling into line, wearing down my butt on school chairs, finding work? Painfully earning your pittance by submitting and shutting your trap, and for what? To buy a house and the furniture to put in it on credit? That's not freedom – that's buying your own prison! Twenty whole years before you can tell the bank to fuck off! And, from one day to the next, to hell with friendships and every man for himself? No, I didn't like peace. It was too hypocritical for me."

"What did you do?"

"My two best friends and I lied about our ages and enlisted in the army. It was easy; there was no more civil register or ID cards. And we were tough."

"So you swapped the monotony of peace for blind obedience and marches!"

"Go ahead and laugh, but I had talent and my talent was useless outside the army. Besides, there was always a rebellion to crush or a terrorist to track. The rules are less rigid on a campaign. And you know, war never really stops: it happily regains its strength. So I fought once again. Only that time, we were better equipped and it was slightly more comfortable. However, that didn't prevent us from losing!

"You think that's funny?"

"I had become a professional soldier, not a young idealist on crusade. The army picked itself up, sort of dusted itself off with the top of its cap and swore allegiance to the new bosses."

"You switched sides!"

"I continued to practice my profession until my retirement because that's what I was: a soldier."

"That's a sad story."

"I experienced great times and great friendships."

"What became of your friends?"

"They were killed."

"Ah!"

"But, Mr. Chevalier, if they hadn't been soldiers, they would probably be dead anyway!"

Below appeared the first lights which indicated that we were approaching the village.

"Mr. Chevalier?"

"Yes?"

"Be careful."

"What do you mean?"

"I'm afraid that you aren't really aware of what you've gotten yourself into."

"Can you be more specific please?"

"I told you. War never stops, it regains its strength. Commander Cousteau is dead but Mistral is still around. He is believed to be responsible for dozens of attacks. Many of those you are going to meet served under him, and others fought against him and continue to do so."

"Am I in danger?"

"Not really. But . . . how can I say this? The role you've come here to play is perhaps not the one for which you were hired."

"Josef, you have to be more specific."

"I know," he contented himself with saying.

Thereupon, we arrived at the village and for the rest of the evening I was unsuccessful at getting him to say another word on the matter.

The hotel could only be called such because of the improper use of plywood boards that divided a low-ceilinged attic into six minute rooms. The place was a licensed beverage establishment that never emptied, except between four and eight o'clock in the morning, no doubt to rinse out the glasses before the next rush.

As soon as it opened, the ground floor would fill with sturdy workers who ate breakfasts of beer and pickled eggs before clocking in at the sawmill. Sitting in pairs, nose in their glasses, they emitted nothing but brief whispers interrupted by suspension points.

This low, melancholic morning hum was a strong contrast to the general hubbub of a practically unbearable volume that had greeted us the night before when we had come to inquire about a room upon our return from the observatory.

The night was already quite far along, and so were the barrels and the clients. The strong smell of alcohol sprang at me like a familiar animal and my first reflex was to grab a glass so I could kiss it on the mouth. Then I noticed that, one at a time, all eyes were turning towards me and the noise volume lowered a notch each time until it was at a level almost equivalent to silence.

"How does it feel being a celebrity, Mr. Chevalier?" asked Josef in such a loud voice that it was as though he was in a play on an outdoor stage.

And no doubt it was a play, in fact it was a small skit intended to diffuse a potentially explosive situation.

My mind was working at top speed, looking for the right answer.

It makes me thirsty? I thought. *This calls for a round? Stop exaggerating, Josef? My wife doesn't share the same opinion?* No.

"It scares me," I finally answered, in all sincerity.

A few laughs greeted my answer, then, as if I had passed a test without knowing the subject or the question, the looks turned away from me and the conversations slowly resumed, swelling to a racket. The indifference they found again was a comfortable cocoon into which I slipped to put back, standing at the counter and one after the other, three tall glasses of mineral water.

"Not bad," I said to Josef, who smiled as he watched me.

"For water, yes."

It was morning and the coffee tasted like water. The night before, I had preferred to go up to bed than face an evening without drinking among an inebriated crowd that was talking too loud. I had to cross the entire room to get to the staircase and that's when I noticed a significant proportion of amputees among the patrons. Here and there were missing arms, hands, lots of fingers, and more rarely feet and legs.

"Did many of them fight?" I asked Josef the next day.

"Why do you ask that?"

I explained and he burst out laughing.

"You don't get it!"

I frowned.

"They didn't fight?"

"Yes, but that doesn't explain everything."

"What explains it then?"

"Who is the main employer, if not the only employer, in the region?"

"Ah! The sawmill."

"For a finger, they are allowed a week off. For two fingers, ten days. Each additional finger adds a day but be careful: more than five fingers means you aren't useful anymore and you lose your job. You have a better chance if you lose an arm: below the elbow means a month's salary. Above the elbow gets you a month and a half."

"And for a leg?"

"The legs are from the war."

"A pension?"

"*Nada.*"

"Compensation?"

"Nothing."

"A rehabilitation program?"

"*Niet.*"

"Relocation?"

"*Non.*"

"So they just throw them away?"

"Like old socks."

"It's pretty inhuman," I said.

Josef just nodded his head while scanning the room with his eyes. He leaned towards me to whisper:

"Around here, you consider yourself really lucky to have work. It hadn't even been a month since the war was over and the sawmill reopened. It filled all of its positions that week. As though nothing had happened. Except for one thing: reduced salaries. The company, you understand, had lost so much . . . It had to rebuild one way or another. Apart from a few grumbles, no one protested. They learned their lesson. Until the next time."

He took the time to take a gulp of coffee before continuing:

"Temples, churches, mosques, public buildings, schools and even nursery schools were subjected to vandalism, arson and destruction during the war. Not the sawmill. The sawmill was never damaged throughout the entire war. Do you know why?"

He took his time. I waited.

"You've got to eat. Before, during and after the war, you always have to eat. The army didn't destroy the sawmill because it belonged to the people whose interests it was defending. The militiamen didn't destroy the sawmill because in actual fact, they dreamed that it would be handed to them by right after the victory. When you dig a little, behind all conflicts, there is always a question of making a living. It's just that there are different levels of ambition."

He was nodding his head, his eyes staring into emptiness.

"People want to improve their fate," he continued. "All misfortune stems from there. We take up arms to make the world a better place! And we become inhuman from dreaming of a bit more humanity. Can you see where this has led them (he swept the room with his eyes)? They are back where they started from, and even a little less better off. And they mourn their brothers and sisters, their parents and their children. And they mourn their dream . . ."

Suddenly, he grabbed my arm, his fingers sinking into my flesh with all his old soldier strength.

"Do you know how the war will finally disappear?" he asked me. And in his eyes, there was not an ounce of humour, nothing sparkled. Two black holes absorbing the light.

"I don't know."

"War will disappear once there is not one person left on Earth to dream of a better life."

I took a haunted trip with Josef along the small roads of the land of the Great Forest. I wanted to see and I saw. I wanted to meet and I met. On the dirt roads, on the bumpy paths, on the trail of the Monster before he had become that, I backtracked, windows down, the wind on my face and tears in my eyes.

I first noticed what I had expected to see: the calcined beams from the retaliations, the kilometre-markers turned on their sides, the charred houses; the telephone and electrical lines hung every which way on precarious supports and hanging to the ground; an overpopulated cemetery, half of whose gravestones appeared new under the bouquets of flowers wilting on the ground; shell-craters overrun by grass. A plagued countryside.

Josef drove slowly to allow me the time to take a good look. A small red-brick building had a perky look to it and I turned my head when we passed it. The side wall had fallen, revealing a clutter of student desks and torn books inside. A blackboard displayed a chalk drawing of a naked hangman with an enormous appendage.

"In a place where there is no future, there are no children," stated Josef.

No children. Or so few that they seemed out of place when, by chance, I happened to catch a glimpse of one out of the corner of my eye. They didn't stray from their homes and hid whenever we came close to them. They had been taught well.

Josef answered my questions in a neutral voice, stripped of all passion and feeling; a voice bare to the bone – a toneless voice.

"They didn't all return," he said. "Some died, others are in prison. Several emigrated. But most of them went looking elsewhere for a little hope, in the big cities, in M. or the Capital. They went to feed the flood of unemployed without stipends. They live with a family member, sleep twelve in a room and spend the entire day outside looking for work or something to eat."

The region showed signs that hinted at a form of violence more insidious than that of weapons. Abandoned houses already warped from freezing and thawing, peeling paint and missing windows. Rusty abandoned cars with concrete blocks for tires. Everywhere was filth and garbage like gored corpses, the insulting whiteness of plastic bags hung on tree branches by the wind. And then suddenly, the new foundations of a house for which three workers were busying themselves pouring cement, like a note of hope, something new built to last in an abandoned setting.

"The vanquishers," Josef let out.

There would be more houses like that one. In time, a new population would replace the old one. A school would be rebuilt for the children of the vanquishers, and perhaps they would accept a few rejects from the vanquished who, to avoid being mocked, would end up converting or abandoning their studies. There were tons of opportunities here. Those who had money bought the land and work of others for mouthfuls of bread. They had come from elsewhere to start over in a big way. It was the inverted exodus of the conquered.

At times, Josef would stop the car and gesture for me to get out and follow him. We knocked on doors to meet up with the elders and talk about the Monster. I saw faces who flat out hesitated to open up. Sometimes we had to insist and I left that to Josef. I preferred to look over his shoulder at the inside of the houses, the furniture's shredded velvet, the floor in need of varnish, the lamps shut off and the indispensable television set pouring forth flows of staged happiness into the void.

I wasn't learning much and that left me cold. They had known Viktor, but they knew nothing about the Monster. They mistrusted me because I was justice and justice had never done anything for them. Sometimes one sentence, one word gave me a glimpse of living, breathing beings. An older woman led me to understand that she had welcomed Viktor into her bed and that he had been awkward. A man, too old to work, proudly showed me the crumpled label of a regional cheese that the Chef had helped to design. A man who had fought alongside Viktor Rosh at the beginning of the war compared him to a cat that transformed into a tiger. He didn't want to talk about his war, but that didn't stop him from proudly showing us his scars among which was a roughly sewn-up gash on his buttock that looked like it mistook itself for a zipper. Then, he chased us out of his house, screaming obscenities and threatening our lives. Afterwards, he met us at the car to cordially shake our hands and wish us a safe trip.

Later, a couple of invalids offered us tea and from a drawer took out a family photo album that contained no trace of the Monster. But it took half an hour to understand that they had not known him – half an hour to understand that sometimes solitude is heavier than anything.

I forced myself to keep my eyes open. I fought against the inevitable desire to flee this place that was draining the life out of me. I had already fled too often. And by dint of looking truth in the face, I saw that everything was not always completely lost. Through freshly turned plots peeped the tender green stems of flowers that had yet to open. An old truck tire swung from the end of a new rope attached to the branch of a very old oak. A goat's muzzle jutted between two boards of a pen. Freshly washed sheets snapped in the wind in the yard of a repainted house. Two teenagers, a boy and a girl, held their bicycles by the handlebars and as they talked, leaned into one another. Their free hands timidly sought each other by their fingertips, like butterflies.

Yes, there was still life here. Time and forgetting made the best fertilizer. Under the scabs, wounds would scar if they were given the time and the opportunity.

Near the village, an underground water-pumping station was still smoking from a recent explosion.

"Mistral and his men," said Josef. "The war never ends," he repeated. "It's regaining its strength."

Now you had to boil water when you were thirsty. This was another annoyance to add to an already long list.

"Who is benefiting from this?" I asked.

"No one," answered Josef. "But it doesn't really bother Mistral and it really bothers the local authorities."

We had returned to our starting point in front of the hotel at the centre of a village that had seemed abandoned. We looked at the empty square.

"Almost all of them are at the sawmill," said Josef.

And I knew that we had to go there, but not right away. In an hour or two. I hadn't finished digesting all of this. I was thirsty. It was a reflex. But I knew that I wouldn't have a drink. Not now. Maybe never again.

What was most striking was the noise. In the sounding box of the vast hangars, the screeching of the saws fed on itself and became denser until it became a quasi-solid matter that escaped through the doors and windows, spreading outside.

I was like Darwin disembarking on the Galapagos Islands. In a moment of clarity, I understood why the people in the bar felt they had to yell. They were deaf.

Among the sixty some workers busy in and around the cutting hangars, none wore ear cups – except for one, sporting two additional helmets, and who was heading straight for us. He did not look like a worker. He was a young man, prematurely bald, wearing a light grey suit and who, as he approached, looked at me as if from far away through incredibly thick glasses.

"The welcoming committee?" I yelled to Josef.

"I told you they'd be waiting for us!" he yelled back.

I had obviously been unaware of the fame I had acquired in the region, in spite of myself. My plan was to linger awhile in the area, taking in the surroundings and maybe glean a few bits of information before introducing myself to the management. But it was management that came to me.

"Mr. Chevalier, we were expecting you earlier," I thought I read on the lips of the short-sighted man.

Josef and I put on the ear cups that he held out to us. As soon as I did, I noticed that I had a headache and that I was in a bad mood.

"Let's get out of here," I yelled at Josef, who fell right into step, leaving the short-sighted guy behind who was blinking and had to run to catch up to us at the end of the yard.

At that distance, the noise became bearable. I removed my headgear and tactlessly threw it at the little man who caught it but fumbled and missed the one that Josef had thrown at him more forcefully a quarter of a second later. The first one dropped as he tried to catch the second. In a final effort to save at least one of them from a deathly fall, the little man bent over a bit too much and found himself kneeling in the dust. I tried in vain to stifle the laugh that was tickling the back of my throat.

"Great," he said, getting up. "I'm only doing my job."

His words hit me like a slap. He was right, of course. I took the ear cups from him while he dusted off his pants.

"I'm terribly sorry," I said.

I had behaved like a ruffian. Why, I wondered. But I knew why. I had seen enough misery today to feel as though I had stepped into the Devil's den. As if the sawmill was the only one responsible for the region's problems and that each of the management's representatives was a keeper of the doors of hell. But nothing was ever that simple and I had given in to a bad mood that was pointless.

"Forgive me," I said with complete sincerity.

The little near-sighted man looked at me and shrugged his shoulders.

"It's OK," he said.

He thanked me with a smile so juvenile that you would have thought that his hair had grown back in one shot. He was what, twenty-five years old? With his bottle-bottom glasses, I could easily imagine the misery that he must have been subjected to in the schoolyard, and I felt even worse for having behaved like a big heartless brute.

"François Chevalier," I said, extending my hand.

"Jules," he answered, extending his. "I have a family name but everyone calls me Jules. In fact, everyone calls me 'My Jules' and I think I like that," he added with a shy smile.

"Well then My Jules, what do you say we get to work?"

"Let's go!" he said, and his face lit up like a lantern, from the inside.

My Jules took us around the entire facility. It was very informative and perfectly devastating for my client, who seemed to have left only bad memories behind here. If My Jules had not personally known Viktor Rosh, he had heard a lot about him and he excused himself as he told us his account of the stories that all painted the portrait of a man who was envious, quarrelsome, ambitious and petty, if not perfectly dishonest.

To serve the expedition, My Jules introduced us to a department manager with a very big belly who was initialling paperwork while putting on airs. He declared that the Monster was a monster who believed he was superior to everyone.

"What makes you say that?" I asked him.

"Well, it's that . . ." answered big belly. "You can feel those things. And he never spoke to me. Rude."

"Hang him!" I whispered to Josef.

Deceit hung in the air. It had to be expected. Viktor's picture had been in all the newspapers, and the people from the region, already worn out from the war and from peace, had been hurt that they could be associated with the monstrous crimes for which he had been accused. Since he was a Monster, logic would dictate that he had always been one. Memory was selective and from the past retained only the elements to explain the present.

I learned that the Monster:

1. Required "gifts" from his kitchen suppliers;
2. Was a bitter enemy of the accounting department because of unexplained cost overruns;
3. Had a reprehensible attitude towards certain female staff members;
4. Was quick-tempered, manic-depressive, sexually ambivalent and suffered from a compulsive nature.

My Jules dragged us through all the departments so I could collect from the employees an impressive variety of unpleasant comments that didn't hold water once submitted for examination. Therefore:

1. All department managers required "gifts" from suppliers.

2. The accounting department was the bitter enemy of all those who spent company money instead of letting it sit in the safe even though it was to feed the staff.

3. The reprehensible attitude towards female staff members seemed to be summed up by a noticed indifference in the face of advances made by a handful of secretaries out for a good time during a small party thrown by the administration department. It seems that this same indifference was enough to qualify my client as "sexually ambivalent."

4. His temper and manic depression could not be illustrated with any probative example other than he sometimes raised his voice to be heard in a place full of deaf people and otherwise he was rather subdued. His compulsive nature was explained by the compulsion to wash his hands a good ten times a day which, for a cook, seemed like a pretty good idea to me.

Before meeting the manager, we toured the kitchens where Viktor Rosh had reigned for more than seven years.

We crossed the yard and just before entering the building, My Jules pointed out a huge rusty pot.

"That's what he made on his last day in the kitchen."

I bent down to look inside. Dry and brownish, an old crust of unidentifiable substance lined the bottom.

"Are you kidding me?" I asked My Jules.

"Of course not," he answered, blinking so wildly that my anger dissipated immediately.

Inside, the chef who had replaced the Chef placed on the counter the thick bundle of purchase orders he was attempting to sort, and then, turning towards My Jules, bellowed:

"Get out of here!"

My Jules's eyelids fluttered as he bit his upper lip. His gaze moved from the chef to me, and then from me to the chef.

"I'll wait for you in the yard," he said.

Then he turned on his heels and disappeared.

"I can't stand him," said the chef. "Listen," he went on, "I don't like talking badly about colleagues and in any event, I didn't know Viktor Rosh. All I can tell you is that I've never seen a site kitchen in which the clientele is sophisticated enough to come to me after a meal to discuss my choice of sauce. So the Monster must have done something right at some point in his life. That's all I can tell you . . ."

"I knew him."

I turned around. A pimple-faced sous-chef, not yet twenty years old, smiled at me from behind a row of skillets that hung head first on hooks from the ceiling.

"What more can you tell me?"

"Not much. I was fourteen when he hired me as a dishwasher. My father was a boozer who no longer worked. My mother took off with another man when I was six months old. I'd been doing stupid things since I was eight. He taught me a trade. As for the rest . . . When the sawmill closed, I left the region to live with an uncle. I lived the war over there."

"What do you think of the charges brought against him?"

"I don't know. It's terrible. But I saw others."

"Is there anything you can tell me in my client's defence?"

He thought for a moment.

"His lamb navarin. But I don't think that will impress the jury."

"A jury, no," I said, thoughtful. "But a judge, maybe."

"I'm sorry."

"Don't worry about it."

"Are you going to see him?"

"Yes."

"Tell him that Martin says hello."

"He'll be happy to hear that," I lied, and then left the kitchens.

We joined My Jules again who guided us to the main administrative building, then inside, up to the manager's door. The thickness of the carpet indicated that the end was in sight.

"I'm leaving them in your hands," said My Jules to the secretary who was guarding the manager's door with all the stiffness of her hairspray.

She nodded her head in our direction without moving a hair.

"The manager will see you in a couple of minutes."

"Goodbye, Mr. Chevalier," said My Jules, extending his hand.

"Goodbye, My Jules. It was my pleasure. And again, sorry about before."

"It's nothing. Goodbye."

I let myself fall into an armchair. During our entire tour, Josef had stayed one step behind me without uttering the slightest comment, which was unlike him. I thought that, like me, he felt bad about the way we had treated My Jules and that he was paying penance by hanging back. But once he sunk into the chair beside me, I saw that he was sporting his usual giant-elf grin and that he was looking at me as though he had an ace up his sleeve.

"What?" I sighed.

"The manager's name is Gerhart Bolchick. He has held this job for over fifteen years and, in many ways, he is the true governor of the region. An elegant man who would be more at home in the Capital if it wasn't for the fact that his wife rules it and she is the one with the money and the contacts. Oh! And by the way, do you know what My Jules' name is? Jules Bolchick."

"He's the manager's son?"

"His nephew. Don't ever trust appearances. He's a rat," he said with an air of satisfaction.

"It's a little late to warn me," I complained.

"No, I don't think so," answered a smiling Josef. "In fact, I believe it's exactly the right moment."

At that instant, the door leading into the manager's office opened and a slender man – in his fifties with brown hair and eyes, wearing an expensive suit that I assumed was Italian – the smiling manager signalled for us to enter.

I was boiling with rage. I had wasted my time following a trapped route. I had apologized three times over to a kid who had taken me on a ride and who had carelessly manipulated me.

Nonetheless, I donned my best smile as, in front of a huge cherrywood desk with sleek lines, I settled into the comfortable armchair the manager pointed to after he warmly shook my hand.

Two-faced bastard, I thought.

"What can I do for you?" he asked.

"Answer a few questions, that's it," I said in an affable tone.

"That's the least I can do. Go ahead."

"What's with the act?" I asked.

"I don't know what you . . ." began the manager.

"Come on. Between gentlemen," I cut him off.

"Of course, between gentlemen . . ."

"Between gentlemen nothing!" I yelled at him. "What gives you the right to waste my time?"

That felt good. It wouldn't get me anywhere, it wouldn't help my cause, it could even make trouble for me, but it felt good.

The manager had jumped out of his chair as if he had been sitting on a spring. He walked around his huge modern office to press the intercom button while casting worried looks in the direction of a closed door behind the bar that I hadn't noticed until then.

"Magdalene? Magdalene? Please call security," the manager said.

But I wasn't finished quite yet.

"What do you have against my client?"

"He's a criminal."

"A war criminal, not a common criminal. Why do you want to do him harm?"

The manager looked nervously at Josef.

"He's a terrorist. Everything he preaches goes against my work and my life! He belongs in prison."

"You know him well?"

". . ."

"Answer me. Do you know him well?"

"I pride myself on knowing all of my employees," he answered.

I knew that in fact this was just boasting.

"What was the nature of your relationship?" I asked him.

"He hated me," let out the manager, as the door opened to let in a pair of massive young men.

The manager gestured to Josef and me with his chin. The pair of massive young men split in two. I felt a hand as broad as a racquet slide under my arm and lift me from my seat.

"Why?" I asked the manager. "Why did he hate you?"

I can give him this much: he could have not answered. But while the tips of my toes grazed the carpet without disturbing it, just before I was nicely but firmly accompanied to the property limits, turning my head, I saw the image of the manager who was taking an expensive cigar from an expensive humidor and who said these words:

"Because I am me . . . He hated me because of who I am, and he was only himself."

Then, I was thrown out.

We waited for the arrival of the forestry workers at the bistro. They came here every day to knock a few back after work before heading home. I had taken a shower in a plastic cabin that was so narrow that it was almost impossible to bend down to pick up the soap if, unfortunately, it happened to drop. With the caution that characterized him in every way, Josef had preferred to abstain and proceeded to an internal cleaning by downing vodka.

The men began to return from work, perched on trucks and crammed into the shells of pickup trucks. They were numerous, several dozen, filthy and proud of it, covered in gunk and resin, and their hair powdered with sawdust. We let them settle in and then, with my money, Josef bought a round for the house before going over to talk to them.

He brought four who had known Viktor Rosh back to my table. Not only had they worked with him at the sawmill, but they had also fought alongside him.

"But only at the beginning," said a man named Rossi, a huge middle-aged fellow with the eyes of a girl. "As soon as I felt that we weren't going to win, I went to join my family to wait it out. So we weren't there for the whole Rosalind story. We didn't see anything and we don't know if it's true."

"But is it plausible?"

They looked at one another. They knew who I was, and not trusting me, they instinctively chose defence to accusation.

"Don't know," a guy named Franz finally said.

"It's too bad, but there were many incidents like that," put in a third whom the others called Karim.

"When the war stops," added Vlad, the fourth, "everything should be forgotten. Otherwise, there's no point in making peace."

"What was he like before the war?"

They exchanged smiles as they looked at each other.

"He wanted so much," said Franz.

"He wanted what?"

"To be part of the gang. Go hunting, knock a few back, that kind of thing . . ."

"What stopped him?"

"Nothing," said Rossi. "But he was an intellectual. OK, he worked with his hands. But cutting down pine trees and slicing carrots is not the same."

"You looked down on him?"

"No, that's not it," said Vlad. "Mostly, he made us smile. He came from the city. He was a little awkward. Not a bad guy but . . ."

"But?"

"Dreamers aren't always very comfortable with reality."

"Did the war change him somehow?"

"It was as if he had been waiting for it his entire life," said Rossi. "As if he enjoyed it."

"Easy for him," interrupted Karim. "He didn't have a wife or children."

"He had his two lovers!" exclaimed Vlad.

"Lovers?"

"In a manner of speaking. Manu and Mistral. Those three never stopped pushing one another like kids playing dirty tricks. Manu admired the Chef who admired Mistral who was completely nuts. It could only end badly. Unless they won, of course."

"They were reckless?"

"That's not it," said Rossi. "At least not the Chef . . . You know, it happens sometimes in sports, when someone performs well above their normal capabilities. A kind of state of grace. Do you know what I mean?"

I nodded my head.

"Well, that's it. The rest of the time, he was the same Chef as before, slightly clumsy, poorly adjusted, who did too much or not enough. But in the heat of the action, when bullets were flying from everywhere and we were up to here in shit, he entered into somewhat of a state of grace . . . In those moments, he was the best among us, and by far. Better than Mistral. But . . . towards the end, just before I left, when it was pretty clear that we were never going to win, he became . . . nasty. Even with me. He told me he would rather put a bullet in my back than let me leave. I believed him. I left anyway, but I waited for him to be away on a mission."

"Why was he like that?"

"He didn't want the war to end. He didn't want to become the Chef again, a man like the others and perhaps even less."

"Unless they had won," said Franz. "Maybe he could have accepted peace if we had won."

"Why?"

"He could have had what he wanted. He would have been a hero. And he would have had Maria."

"Maria?"

"The manager's mistress. The Chef was crazy about her. Maria liked him too, but she was a boss's girl. So, he would have really liked to have won the war to become the boss."

"This Maria, she knows the Chef well?"

"At least more intimately than we do! Just ask her."

"She's here?"

"Somewhat, yes."

"Where?"

"The manager hides her in his office because his wife is in the region," Rossi cleared up. "He has a fully equipped apartment over there, with a big bed and bathroom bigger than my kitchen. Before, she pretended to work but now it's not worth it. Besides, he knows we would give that whore a hard time if he let her out. She sold us out. We should have killed her."

"What stopped you?"

"The Chef. He would have killed us if we had even touched a hair on her head."

"He can't touch you now," I said.

"Hey!" cried Karim. "He could still get out of prison. Isn't that why you're here?"

I was asking myself that very question. I thanked the men by offering them another drink. We clinked glasses. I had something. It seemed to me that for the first time my investigation was progressing.

I wished them luck. They wished me nothing at all. Rossi appeared thoughtful. Just before going to join his buddies, he leaned towards me to offer me the results of his cogitations.

"Maria," he said, "is the kind of woman who you don't know if you should slap or fuck."

Then, after a pause:

"Perhaps both."

THE FEAST OF THE DEAD

It was still winter. We were still in the forest, in bad shape, hiding. There had been departures that weren't called desertions just yet. There was talk of moving towards M., but the order hadn't come. We were hungry. The men were bored. Not me, the others.

Mistral came to see me and took me aside.

"They could use a little party, Chef, a feast, something."

"Snow cones flavoured with sock juice, tapenade of pine cones with resin vinegar, leg of birch on a bed of its leaves, and for dessert, lichen mousse. What do you think?"

"Very funny. I'm serious."

"So am I. What do you expect me to do?"

"Figure something out. Otherwise, within ten days, only you and I will be left here and they will all have taken off. Take Manu, take the men that you want (he paused dramatically). I know that you can do it."

I nodded my head in agreement. He patted my shoulder and turned around to carry on with his duties as captain, whatever those were.

Mistral had confidence in me. Now, he trusted me. Since the convoy attack, he trusted me. I had killed some twenty that day. Mistral would say: the Day of the Tiger. The day on which the tiger within me awakened.

Since that day, I had confidence in myself as well.

The idea of preparing a feast for the troop didn't appeal to me one bit. But going off to steal some supplies, that was a great idea. With a little luck, there would be some action. But there were two problems:

Go where? In the region, the only ones with sufficient supplies of food were the government troops. I could see myself having a hard time entering their camp to steal, and I could see myself having an even worse time getting out with a side of beef on my shoulder and bottles of booze under my arm.

How was I going to get back? If it was relatively easy to exit the Great Forest by travelling light, it was completely wishful thinking to believe that you could come back loaded down by two or three hundred kilos of necessary food across twenty-five kilometres of invisible paths, covered in places by a good metre-and-a-half of treacherous, powdery snow.

I pondered my plan for a while, and then went to see Mistral with Manu.

"We have to ask the men to make snowshoes," I said.

"Snowshoes?"

"Snowshoes and sleighs. Don't worry!" I said as I saw Mistral about to protest. "They won't have to go very far."

I explained my plan to them.

"It's doable," said Mistral.

"Oh yes!" added Manu.

There were still a few details left to settle. The most important was the drop point, but Mistral knew the forest better than anyone and his suggestions were all excellent. We agreed on a meeting place and within the next hour we headed out for the Capital, unarmed and in civilian clothing.

The old man was deeply moved. He had lost a lot of weight and his eyes seemed bigger than I had remembered. He didn't scare me anymore, my old master, but I think he no longer scared anyone. He didn't preside over the kitchens of his own restaurant anymore, leaving that task to the younger ones. He was happy greeting his clientele and chatting them up. With age he had become sentimental, or perhaps it was from seeing me after all this time that had that effect on him. He called me "my boy."

It took us two days to reach the Capital. First on foot, then hitchhiking among the cars, overloaded with furniture and trinkets, which were fleeing the city of M. following the news of a probable attack. Arriving downtown on a Tuesday, I didn't have the feeling of going back in time. I knew the streets, the architecture, but it's not the same when you come back as the enemy. The last time, I was nothing: a hot dog vendor. Now, I was an enemy. I was dangerous. Danger has nothing to do with weapons.

We walked to the restaurant. I hoped that it was still there, otherwise we would have to improvise. But it was still there, not as prosperous as before, the front could have used a fresh coat of paint and when I entered I noticed that the dining room had been made smaller by putting up a wall that hadn't been there during my time.

I told Manu to wait for me on the sidewalk. My old master was sitting at the bar going over the night's reservations, his back to me. I called his name softly. He turned around and looked at me, frowning. I said my name. His face cleared and he climbed down from his stool with difficulty to take me in his arms. Then, he stood back to get a better look at me, and I could see that his eyes were teary.

I was happy to see him again. He asked a slew of questions about my life, and I told him a slew of lies that made him happy. I embellished the truth. I told him about my hot dog adventures while he laughed. I told him that I had sold my business because I had moved to M. in order to open a small restaurant that was doing well. He seemed pleased. I told him that I had come to the Capital to wait for the trouble to pass. That's when I remembered Manu and I went to get him from the sidewalk.

It was the first time he had set foot in a big city. It was the height that impressed him. Nothing under four storeys. And the noise! And the numbers! The number of people scared him somewhat. I took his arm and introduced him to my old master, saying that he was a friend, which was true. It's always better when there's some truth.

My old master sat us at a table and served us a drink while we waited for supper time. All afternoon and all evening, he sat and rose to tend to his duties before returning to sit with us. We ate and drank a lot. Perhaps once or twice during the evening, I wondered if the Great Forest still existed, if somehow it belonged to another plain of existence. As if my entire life was reduced to a snap of the fingers. Those impressions only lasted a few seconds, but I felt as though they could have lasted if I had let them. I understood that nothing had its own reality, a little like those infants who think, confusedly, that their look creates the world – and when they close their eyes, everything returns to nothingness.

There was some truth there. Or then realities exist in parallel universes and we are able to jump from one to the other.

We spent a nice evening and with a little concentration, I managed to not lose sight of the reason why we were there. We were on dessert when my old master asked where we were spending the night. I answered that we hadn't dealt with that little problem yet. As it was already late, he invited us to his place. That way, we would have the time to find a room somewhere the following day. Manu and I thanked him.

I had a very full belly and a head that was spinning a bit with all the wine we had consumed. Manu was smoking a cigar with a dreamy air, but I knew that this was just a front, that all this food, the good wine and the smoke of his cigar reminded him of Andreï, reminded him that this reality only existed because of Andreï's dead body.

I asked my old master if he still went to the airport to pick up his merchandise on Wednesdays. He said yes. I told him that I would be happy to go with him, for old times' sake. He answered that he would be thrilled but that we would have to get up early.

The most important part was done. After that, I could let myself go a little and enjoy all of this until bedtime.

The Capital's restaurant owners used small transport planes to import fresh products, rare items, fish and even, since the beginning of the war, meat. Just before leaving my old master's apartment above the restaurant, I took a kitchen knife from a drawer, but Manu told me to leave it and he took out a nine-millimetre automatic pistol from under his jacket. It was stupid, I had said no weapons, and if we had been searched . . . OK, we hadn't been searched and we were going to need the pistol.

My old master had us get into his truck. He had been going to the airport every week for thirty years so he was allowed to pass with a wave. After that, it was simple. I knocked him out. We boarded the plane and told the pilot to take off while we held a gun to his temple. We hadn't needed to repeat our instructions.

Once we passed the mountains, we told him to descend and to fly just above the treeline. When we recognized the terrain, we gave him more specific instructions. Finally, we flew over a large clearing, white with snow. I told him to circle the clearing and while Manu stayed with him, I went to the cargo hold. There were hundreds of crates with stencilled words. I opened the door. The wind was icy. I took the crates and threw them out of the plane, into the open, one after the other.

We made four or five passes above the clearing that was now dotted with wooden crates. I could see that some had cracked open but for the most part, the deep snow had absorbed the impact. I returned to the cockpit to find Manu. I asked the pilot if there were parachutes. There was only one.

"That's annoying," I said.

The pilot tried to negotiate but I wasn't listening to him. I was thinking. I told myself that we could fly over the clearing once more at tree-top level and Manu and I could jump. The snow would break our fall. But the pilot knew our position and it wasn't a good idea to let him live. No, we had to jump with a parachute, which we had never done. I told the pilot to gain altitude. I strapped on the parachute and with the rope ends, I attached Manu to me. At a thousand feet, I told the pilot to pass over the clearing again while maintaining a steady heading on the city of M.

I took the pistol from Manu's hands. Right before we flew over the clearing, I put a bullet in the back of the pilot's head. Then I closed my eyes and jumped with Manu attached to me like a child in a harness.

As soon as I could, I pulled the cord. The parachute opened without a hitch but we were heavy. I could feel the wind. We landed right at the edge of the clearing. Twenty metres further, we would have run into the trees. When we got up, the men came out of the woods. They were walking funny with their makeshift snowshoes. They pulled sleighs made of branches with ice-covered runners. They shrieked like children as they approached the crates. From one end of the clearing to the other, they exchanged information by yelling out the contents of the crates. I knew that there was everything. It took several minutes to organize it all.

The plane had continued its course for some time, and then disappeared from the sky without us hearing the crash, probably about fifty kilometres away. We were at ease.

We returned to camp surrounded by a festive atmosphere. There were oysters on the menu that night.

I was a hero.

Apart from the occasional skirmish that consisted in harassing the government troops rather than attacking them, the rest of the winter unfolded incident-free. Other men, and even women, joined us and the laughter became more subdued because this meant that the offensive would be starting shortly.

Then came spring. We waded through mud. I watched Manu try to write long letters to his Jana that he couldn't send. He laboured over the paper since he barely knew how to write. He knew even less about describing love which had always been something natural for him that didn't require words. He dedicated many hours to his missives, chewing the end of his pencil. Then he put them away in his bag. There were lots of them. He never rested when in action, assassinating his son's assassins. But when he leaned over the sheet of paper, his forehead wrinkled, and a small pout distorted his mouth. I remembered, he already had it when I met him for the first time, still a child and already a father.

Towards the middle of April, the order came to take to the road.

Things went fast from here on in. The order of events escapes me. Memories overlap. I close my eyes so that the images become clear. I remember the fear. I was scared. You had to be dead not to be scared. It was a strange sensation. It's completely ridiculous to rush towards the enemy, towards enemy fire. And yet, it wasn't ridiculous. In war, there is logic that can't be found during peace time.

I remember Mistral ordering us to travel light and I remember this scene. All the men and women going through their bags and tossing into the snow everything they had to leave behind: books, cameras, blankets stiff with dirt, pornographic magazines, war trophies (helmets, military belts, medals, costume jewellery), records, all sizes of used batteries, mess kits, socks with holes, disposable razors, a music box with a cracked top. I only kept a German kitchen knife, carefully sharpened. I fashioned a sheath out of leather from a boot taken from the enemy. I wore it at my waist. On my warrior gear, this black handle adorned with a red logo, balanced to slice leeks, caught the eye like a ridiculous detail. I knew that with it I could be recognized. The knife was my signature. I was the Chef. Hell's cook. The blurred, undefined contours of Me in times of war compelled us to these redefinitions. I became another, an avatar of myself better adapted to the new situation. Rossi was the crazy Italian who, in the moment of attack, bellowed the few words that he still knew of his ancestral language.

Cousteau was the Strategist. Mistral, Anger. Manu was the Avenger of the son. There was no joy left in him. He made a thick stack of all his letters and tucked them away in a pocket against his heart, and threw away the rest of his possessions that couldn't be used to kill. We were heavy with ammunition, knives, grenades and weapons. At our feet lay the last remnants of our former personalities, as though we had shed translucent skins that fell from us, retaining our shape but not our essence.

All of our forces converged towards the city of M. This was to be the opposition's first major victory. Other companies coming from elsewhere and which we knew nothing about were also heading to M. to take over the city. It was essential to maintain the element of surprise, to advance under cover until the last minute.

The Great Forest unravelled into thickets up until the first faubourgs. We lay on the ground as we waited for the signal. I looked at my companions. Their faces were expressionless. A part of our brains blocked out, preventing our consciences from realizing that some of us were going to die.

The attack was perfectly coordinated and, beset on three fronts, the garrison didn't know where to direct its artillery. At the outset, our losses were fairly severe, but we ran towards the enemy as if we were driven by a torrent of adrenaline. Under those circumstances, courage is chemical.

We penetrated the city pretty quickly and we moved towards the centre where the bulk of the opposing infantry was concentrated.

The further we progressed, the more the air thickened with smoke and bullets. After entire neighbourhoods were abandoned to us, the government army defended the houses in the centre, one by one. Each building was a trap. Each doorway was a bunker. I felt as though I was butting against a perfectly transparent plastic film that didn't stop my movements, but slowed them. I could see the imminent moment in which our advance would be stopped, in which we would get stuck in urban trench warfare as costly as it was absurd. The objective of invading the city was suddenly reduced to taking a candy store or a flower stand. Our ambitions were reduced to a portion of sidewalk, to a building floor held by a sharp-shooter. But as small as they may be, these objectives completely filled our field of vision. They took on an importance that someone observing from above could never understand. That piece of sidewalk and that candy store were everything to us because they represented life or death. In this brutal magnification of our vision, the rest of the world was relegated to a haze, to a larval state of existence, shapeless and patient, waiting for a sign in order to materialize.

Showers of metal. Explosions of concrete and glass. Bits of torn flesh. Blood. Organs spread beyond the open abdomens. I said earlier that it was like moving against a plastic film. I should have said: like in rotting flesh. Maggots in a revolting corpse.

I kept Manu on my left, Mistral on my right, within hailing distance. We communicated in dry barks. We still lacked ammunition that had to be brought up from the back – but where was the back? There was only the front, a few metres to gain for the price of blood. There were no trees, no forest, no hills. It wasn't our world and this went on for three days. I remember the sunlight playing with particles of dust. I remember catching a quick glimpse of the face of a young boy, behind a window. He was wearing a uniform too big for him and armed with a gun that was too heavy and falling from his hands. I remember his beardless, pale face and his thin lips that formed a silent "o" when I hit him in the chest. I remember a stray cat caught in the crossfire. When it passed by meowing, there was a moment of silence, a few seconds stolen from the war by surprise. Then the cat ran off and the shots started up again from all angles.

I remember a sleep as heavy as a bag of cement. My back was pressed against a wall that came to a corner and from where I was being hit with shrapnel. After two days of combat and dust in my eyes, my eyelids were the texture of sand. I had closed my eyes to clear my vision and fell asleep as I was while receiving fire. This lasted a few minutes but when I woke it was as if I had spent the night in a comfortable bed beneath a down cover.

I remember the faces of my companions, of this breakdown of expressions that reduced one's vocabulary to nothing. No hope, but no despair either, and nothing in-between, as if emotions had fled, had left this inhospitable place.

After three days, reinforcements arrived. Not ours. We had almost won the battle. We had taken the neighbourhoods, the houses, the centre; we held the city except for the airport, which would fall soon. Then came big air carriers which, once on the ground, regurgitated fresh troops and light armoured vehicles.

We fled through the streets we had conquered step by step. Around Mistral, the company's solid nucleus remained pretty much intact; approximately ten of the hundred or so that we had been. Instinctively, without consulting us, we backtracked to regain the shelter of the forest.

During this retreat is when Manu was injured. A bullet, shot from behind, cut across the joint in his leg and exited through the front, shooting a geyser of pieces of patella and bits of ligament. The pain took hold of his traits like a powerful fist closes over a lump of clay. I threw him over my shoulder and ran for cover.

Manu moaned in pain and when I placed him on the ground once we had cleared the treeline, I could examine the gaping hole with shredded walls marking the bullet's exit point. There was nothing left to reconstruct. It would have been wiser to abandon him in plain view so that the army medics could tend to him under proper sanitary conditions, but my whole being protested against that idea. While I thought, Manu lost consciousness. I stroked his hair.

I saw our people appear one by one, hesitant, finger on the trigger, filthy, bloody. They came out of the shadows like extinguished ghosts, phantoms of phantoms, and you had to look twice at them to recognize the normal human beings that they had once been. They crumbled around us to finally rest on the pine needle–covered ground whose healthy aroma vaguely reminded us of something. Mistral fell down beside me. He glanced over at Manu's wound and no doubt came to the same conclusion as I did.

"We have to leave him here."

"No way."

"The journey is too long for him. He'll die of blood loss."

"Not if he gets a transfusion."

He let out a little dry laugh that rang comically beneath the branches.

"Blood," he said, "we shed a lot of it, but we didn't bring it with us."

I didn't answer. I continued to stroke Manu's head as he moaned in his unconscious state. However, his knee, reduced to nothing, continued to bleed. I removed my shirt to tear off strips and bandage the wound. A feeling of powerlessness that I hadn't felt during the battle crept through me. It's so much easier to kill than it is to heal. My talents were worthless in the face of Manu's suffering. I had an idea.

"What if we went to the lake?"

Mistral looked at me thoughtfully. I knew how his mind worked. He assessed, weighed, thought strategically.

"Not a bad idea," he said.

Northwest of M., on the northern marshes of the Great Forest, surrounded by ancient mountains smoothed by time, there was, there still is, a fairly vast lake with deep, clear waters. The well-to-do city dwellers had built luxurious summer homes there. With time and a growing number of summer visitors, a small village was born, comprised of merchants and service suppliers who had seen there was a market there: baker, fishmonger, newsstand. A small medical clinic was built a few years earlier to treat the ills of the vacationers, the blisters from sunburns, the badminton players' sprains, and the elderly gentlemen's constipations.

A clinic.

Even if the village emptied in the fall not to come back to life until the very start of summer, the facilities remained all year long. The clinic was there, its instruments, its medications and even its blood supplies should be there too. Mistral was right. It wasn't a bad idea at all. Enough cars and trucks had been abandoned on the roads to provide us with means of transportation. By travelling at night with all the lights off, it was doable.

Proud combatants flee from sunlight. They crawl and advance with curved backs. Defeat condemns them to a life of never walking upright. Helicopters circle above the city of M., stirring the darkness with their luminous blades. But we're already far away, in the darkness.

Manu moans, sighs, suffers. His skin is the consistency and colour of wax. We constructed a stretcher out of two pairs of pants, a belt and two wooden poles. We travelled a few kilometres on foot before meeting a secondary road. We looked for vehicles; most were damaged and the others were out of fuel. The region seems deserted; the inhabitants have either fled or are holed up in their homes, in the dark. They are as afraid of the army as they are of us. They are afraid of the war as they would be of a hurricane. Natural disasters.

We finally find a small electrician's van in working condition. Eight of us cram in, crouched against the walls, with Manu lying in the centre. The others will join us as soon as they can.

We travel in darkness. The foliage comes off on nothing. In the absence of houses and kilometre markers, everything is dark on dark. White doesn't exist in the forest. Where is the road? There's no moon. No stars. We travel by ear, very cautiously. When the tires bite the shoulder gravel, Mistral straightens out the wheel. Only the gentle hiss of rubber against asphalt lets us know that we are staying on the road. Deprived of our sense of sight, time acquired a liquid quality, as though we were floating in highly salted water, carried by an invisible current.

This seems to go on for hours. And it does. Manu doesn't wake up anymore. His breathing is reduced to a slight trace. How can he survive on so little oxygen?

Something against our cheeks alerts us to a change. A humid caress. On the right, there are no more echoes. The trees have disappeared, replaced by the lake's plane surface. I hear a distant lapping. At the speed of a walking man, the van crosses the deserted village of building fronts decorated like they were part of a theatre set. Everything here points to summer, carelessness, the pleasures of sailing and of a beach ball. Searching for the clinic, I sweep my flashlight across the brightly painted signs. No houses: stores, restaurants, boutiques. This is not a place to live. It's a construction of spirit, an illusionary negation of misery, inequality and suffering. It's an illusion maintained for a high price for rich people whose big summer houses monopolize the shores of the lake. I wouldn't be surprised if the façades were just that, façades, simple painted wood panels held up with planks.

We finally find the clinic resembling a Swiss chalet. Mistral deploys the men while I break the lock. Is there really no one here? It's hard to believe that the place has been completely abandoned.

Behind the façade's gingerbread, the clinic is modern, functional and anonymous. We carry Manu inside then, weapon in hand, I explore every recess. The entrance. The reception area. Then a hallway where two doors open on the right and one on the left. I open the first door on the left. It's an exam room, clean and so white that it seems to throb in the darkness. I open the door on the right. It's a lavish consultation office. The back

wall is covered in diplomas. I pause in front of the last door. I
think I hear something. I wait. I smile. I open the door carefully. A man is snoring softly. He is lying on the couch in what
appears to be a common room with a refrigerator and coffee
machine. I approach. He doesn't wake up. I shake him. He
protests in his slumber, then opens his eyes wide, grabs his blanket and holds it up against himself as though it were a shield.
He says:

"Oh my God!"

"Is there a doctor in?"

"Oh my God!"

"Is there a doctor in?"

"No. Only during the summer."

"A nurse?"

"Er . . . no."

"Why er?"

"I'm a nurse. I mean, almost."

"Come with me."

I drag him by the arm to the reception area where we had
put down the stretcher.

"Oh my God!" repeated the nurse when he saw Manu's
knee.

"Help me."

We carried Manu to the exam room.

"Light," I said.

From a cupboard he took a powerful lamp hooked up to a
car battery. The light jumped out, cruel. I have to close my eyes
for a moment. When I open them, Manu's wound appears to
me in an explosion of colours: red, yellow, black, white from
exploded bone, pink, brown, violet. I struggle to avert my eyes.
It's as if I'm seeing for the first time. But I take hold of myself.

"What's your name?"

"Theo."

"Theo, take care of him."

He sees my expression and doesn't dare to yell "Oh my God!" again. He opens a drawer and takes out a pair of scissors. He cuts away Manu's pants and leans over the wound. When he straightens up, his forehead is covered in sweat. At that moment, Mistral makes his entrance. He questions me with a look. I shrug my shoulders.

"There's nothing I can do," says Theo.

He is afraid of my reaction. He is afraid of me. That's good.

"You're going to do something."

"But I'm not a doctor. I haven't even finished nursing school."

"He's going to die if you don't do something," I said while pointing to Manu. "And if he dies, you die too."

Theo chewed his lip. His eyes jump from Manu's knee to me.

"He's lost a lot of blood."

"Give him some."

"But I don't have any!"

"What?"

"We don't keep supplies here. Only a bit of plasma. The refrigerators need electricity."

Suddenly, fatigue was felt. I sway. Mistral comes over and holds me up.

"You did what you could," he says to me.

"No."

"We'll take him somewhere where the army will find him. It's his only chance."

"No."

I close my eyes. I breathe. I open them again. I walk towards Manu.

"Take mine," I tell Theo.

"Your what?"

"My blood."

"Are you the same blood type?"

"He's my son."

"That doesn't mean anything."

"Take my blood and give it to him! And then take care of him."

To Mistral:

"He has to rest. Find a place and some rations."

"And what about him?" he asks, pointing to Theo with his thumb.

"He comes with us to tend to Manu."

"Your blood could kill him, you know."

"It won't kill him."

To Theo:

"Take what you need."

I was set up for the transfusion. When the needle pricks my arm, I close my eyes so that all my strength, all my hope and all my love flow through my blood. I concentrate. With my heart, I push the blood into the tube. After some time, I lose consciousness.

I felt as though something terrible had happened. A few seconds before I opened my eyes, I was sure of it. I was going to wake up alone, and there would be nothing but darkness, total, absolute, eternal devouring obscurity. I opened my eyes. Leaning over me was a face covered with whiskers and with very kind eyes. It was Rossi.

I wanted to speak. I was only able to let out a moan.

"Gently," said Rossi. "They almost emptied you."

On Rossi's face was the answer to a question that I could not formulate, that I didn't want to formulate.

Then Rossi smiled. He turned his head. I followed his eyes.

On a bed beside mine, Manu was resting, motionless. Theo was sitting at his bedside. I raised my eyebrows in a mute question.

"He's sleeping," he said.

"I didn't kill him," I articulated with difficulty.

"You're the same type. If you hadn't been, he would have died within minutes. (He looked at me with reproach.) You aren't his father."

"Now I am."

Then I closed my eyes. I would sleep now.

I slept, dreamless, for nearly thirty hours. When I finally woke, I was very hungry and thirsty. I sat up and threw back the blankets. Then I turned towards Manu. We were alone in the room. His hair had been washed. His face seemed peaceful. His chest lifted and fell regularly. Then I saw his lower body. I tore off the cover. The wound wasn't there anymore. He didn't have a knee anymore. They had cut at mid-thigh. I calmed my pounding heart. Of course, what was I thinking? That a young nurse was going to reconstruct his knee? He was alive and that was what was important. I held his hand. It was soft to the touch, and warm. The skin was supple. The nails were clean.

I wondered what they had done with the leg.

While we were unconscious, we had been transported to an isolated house on the shores of the lake that could only be accessed by eight hundred metres of private road that was easy to watch. A docked boat provided us with a means of retreat by the lake in the event of an unexpected visit. In our entire existence, we had never lived in such comfort. Even though the electricity was off, huge reserves of dry wood and a real stove ensured both comfort and food. We lacked nothing. Mistral had emptied the clinic of its medications. Our friends had joined us and Mistral, in an effort to combat idleness, sent them out to pillage the other houses in search of supplies.

Manu began to regain consciousness after three days. But his gaze, foggy with morphine, kept resting on me. Theo explained that he was suffering a lot.

"It will take time for him to recover."

But we didn't have time. Any day now, an army detachment could unload here. And Mistral was anxious to take up the battle again. Manu was no longer of any use to him. He would forget him. He would leave him behind without a second thought. The only ones who counted for him were those who could still fight. In two or three days, the men would have finished regaining their strength.

I spent all my time at Manu's bedside, searching for a bit of colour in his cheeks. I tried to think about what would happen next. One night, I heard a ruckus coming from the living room, then Rossi's voice calling to me.

"Chef! There's a surprise for you."

I came out of the room. In his right hand, Rossi held Pustule by the collar. And in his left . . .

I was . . . I opened and closed my mouth several times over. Finally, when I managed to say something it was . . .

THE LOVE OF WAR

"Hello Maria," I began.

"Hello," she answered, not at all flustered. As though the situation was normal, and simple, and sane – as though she was not the manager's mistress, hiding in the offices for months. As though she had never been, even for a moment, the Monster's mistress.

Rossi and the others were right. From what I had seen through the open door, the manager of the sawmill had, adjacent to his office, a lovely and very large functional apartment that also served as a dungeon for his mistress.

The night before at the hotel, once our discussion was over, Rossi and his companions had returned to their libations without bothering with us again. But word had spread, and without having in any way solicited opinions, other drinkers sat down at our table to blacken Maria's portrait. The women in particular forgave her nothing, mostly for being desirable in a country lacking in men. Traitor, bitch, whore, parasite, despicable, slut: none of these epithets was said out loud, but they underlay the conversation like lines pulling on sails to catch the wind.

"They don't really like her," I said to Josef between two summary executions.

"There are many things and people that they don't like," replied Josef. "But she's easy to name."

Obviously, I had to meet her. But because of the way our meeting ended, I doubted that the manager of the sawmill would cooperate. However, I had a few legal means at my disposal. For example, I could serve him with an appearance notice, and Maria as well.

"Don't do that," Josef said to me.

"And why not?"

"As soon as the process server rounds the corner, Maria will have disappeared, even never existed. In a case like this, it's best not to act, but threaten to act . . . A short letter, for example. Do you have some paper?"

I took out some paper from my briefcase and uncapped my pen, then we set out to write a letter to the manager of the sawmill.

Mr. Gerhart Bolchick, Manager
M.'s Sawmill

Dear Mr. Bolchick,

It is my duty to solicit a private meeting with you, as well as with your wife, regarding Ms. Maria V., a young person that you have welcomed into your family as your protégée, and who is also employed by the sawmill as your personal secretary. We have reason to believe that this person has information on our client that could help with his defence. However, up to now we have not been able to meet Ms. Maria V. For this reason, we are calling on your help, as well as that of your wife, before taking recourse to legal means that would risk rendering certain details public that belong to the private lives of those concerned.

Regards to you and your wife,
François Chevalier
Attorney

"We used 'wife' three times. Is that enough?"

"I think he'll understand," said Josef.

"I'm afraid that his wife will never read this letter . . ."

Josef smiled, then had the letter delivered to the sawmill. The answer came back within the hour. The manager, in the absence of his wife, will make arrangements for us to meet with his employee, Maria V., and would be infinitely grateful if we could keep private whatever possible.

The next day, My Jules was waiting for us at the sawmill entrance. We walked past him as though he didn't exist and quickly made our way to the manager's office where he waited for us, this time, without his buff twins. The manager welcomed us coldly, without making a move to shake our hands. He rearranged the chairs here and there and then moved towards the door to his apartment and opened it. Maria came out, freshly made-up, hair done, well dressed and exhibiting a perfectly engineered timid smile. She introduced herself by holding out a pretty hand with impeccable nails. The manager looked as though he was going to sit down.

"No. This is a private conversation," I said.

He opened his mouth and then closed it. His eyes flashed restrained fury. He withdrew and headed towards the waiting room.

"You too," I said to Josef.

He shrugged his shoulders, took the time to walk around the office, dragging his hand across the wood surface, like a boy who was in no hurry to head to the detention room. He finally left the office, closed the door behind him and left Maria and I alone at last.

We sat across from each other in the manager's office and she waited patiently for me to speak, curled up like a cat in her master's leather chair. She had removed her shoes to tuck her feet under her, and I could easily make out the shape of her thighs that were stretching the fabric of her skirt.

She was a pretty girl, you couldn't deny it. But not a knock-out. To me, a knockout should maintain a slight indifference regarding her own beauty, and not hide behind it or wear it up front.

Maria, I had been told, had long ago decided that life was a permanent battle and the only way to play a good game was to use, at all times, the best weapon she had: seduction.

It showed in the way she twirled a lock of hair around her index finger while looking at me at an angle – a gesture that wasn't intended to chase away her nervousness, but to pro-voke mine. From the outset of our conversation, I knew what I was dealing with: She was gauging me. She was comparing my merits as a foreign lawyer to those of Gerhart Bolchick. She was weighing the pros and cons, calculating, but it had nothing to do with scientific thought. It was purely instinc-tive. She probably had no idea that she functioned this way. And she would adamantly deny that this was the case if it was accidentally brought to her attention.

But it was the case. Like a flea, she asked herself if it was worth jumping from the neck of a furry beast to the neck of another furry beast.

"Are you married?" she had asked me, which was not a way to inquire about my marital status, but rather to lead the conversation towards topics of love and sexuality.

"Yes," I had answered, and the way Maria had nodded her head, I felt as though I had been unfaithful to Florence.

Was it possible that this woman has only one register, flirting? Fifty years of feminism had not only made converts. Some had continued to prepare for battle, and it was sometimes men who had forgotten how to protect themselves.

I knew the type. I had already succumbed to the venomous charms of a courtesan, the difference being that mine had been dyed red rather than blond and she lived as a parasite off the movie trade (I had a crooked producer as a client) instead of corporate officers. I had merely been a passing dog, a human catwalk. But she had done a good job sucking my blood. It was before Florence. Before I understood the meaning of the word "love." Florence taught it to me through patience, by asking nothing more of me than being capable of receiving it – and even then I had disappointed her.

"I don't mean you any harm," I said.

"But you can harm me," she answered, raising an eyebrow and not letting go of her calm smile.

She wasn't in the least bit afraid of anyone. She was only lending me a power that I was supposed to boast about, because men respond to flattery like genitals to a caress.

"Tell me," I said.

"What?"

"What you're doing here. How you got here."

Her father was a judge, she told me, but he died when she was still a child. Lacking resources, her mother tried to work but didn't manage well and ended up remarrying when Maria was fourteen years old. The stepfather was wealthy, the only representative in the country for a German company that manufactured conveyor belts. One day, he took her with him to visit clients. The sawmill was one of the stops. The manager noticed her and offered her a job. And there you have it.

"That's the official story," I said. "What about the other one?"

"What makes you think there's another one?"

"You live in an office."

She sighed.

"I am sensitive and men take advantage of me," she said. "I wanted to get away from my stepfather who had wandering hands, especially when he drank. Gerhart offered to protect me but he couldn't leave his wife who is wealthier than he is. And if I live here, it's because the situation is . . . how can I put it . . . delicate, for the time being. Have you come to save me, Mr. Chevalier?"

"Do you want to be saved?"

"I want to be happy. That's all."

I want to be happy too, I told myself. I thought about Florence, I thought about my children, I thought about the years of my escapes. Despite her anger and pain, never, not even for a moment had I doubted Florence's love for me. If I managed to break her heart, it was because she had one and it beat in sync with mine. Whatever Viktor had done to her, whatever Gerhart had promised her, Maria would never be truly unhappy because in order to be unhappy, you have to first believe in happiness.

Was she magically following my train of thought? In any event, she sensed that the fish spurned the lure. She suddenly became hard, more cutting. The timid smile disappeared from her mouth and her lips formed a bitter crease. She stopped playing with her hair, her body, until then imperceptibly stretched towards me, and retracted. Now she resembled a businesswoman at the negotiating table during a hostile takeover. The change in attitude was incredible. Suddenly, she was ugly.

"And Viktor Rosh?" I asked.

"What, Viktor Rosh?"

"Was he there to save you?"

She waved her hand in the air.

"He wasn't a bad man. What did you expect me to do? When the sawmill closed, the managers left. Gerhart couldn't take me with him so he left me behind, promising to come back to get me. In the meantime, I had to survive."

"And be well fed."

"What's wrong with that?"

"I don't know. What do you think?"

She looked slightly exasperated.

"What should I have done? Let me remind you that there was nothing left here. Nothing. Should I have let myself starve to death in order to look good? Or that I choose a man for his poverty and lack of resources, is that it? Would that have looked better? And tell me, how many extra points if he had been ugly? And if he had been bald? And how many points can be earned in your big book of indulgences if the gentleman had a tiny little penis, eh? How many for a teeny dick?"

"I'm not here to accuse you, but to defend Viktor Rosh."

"So defend him and leave me alone."

"I can't and you know it."

She sunk into her seat and put on a stubborn look that made her appear younger.

"I know what you think of me."

"What do I think of you?'

"You don't like me."

"Why would I like you?"

"Because I'm a human being! You take the Monster's defence, why not mine?"

"Why not?" I answered her.

"Do you know what it's like to be a woman in a country at war? No. You have no idea. You're a man. You are educated. You have a profession. I grew up here. In misery. My father was not a judge. I don't know who my father was. My mother wasn't a judge's woman, although it must have happened at one time or another. I was the daughter of nothing. I can read and count, and not much more because it's wartime. It's always wartime. You have to survive, Mr. Chevalier, and I survive the only way I know how. If I really had a choice, do you think I would be here, enduring the awkward assaults of that pretentious idiot? If I had a choice, there wouldn't be men in my life, not one, and I would be fine alone. But I don't have a choice. In this country too preoccupied with waging war, women don't have many other roles to play than those of mother or whore. And I refuse to bear children that will serve as cannon fodder, and to dedicate myself to a man who will come back to me mutilated, if he ever comes back at all. I refuse to choose the road to pain. Fate made me pretty, that's all I have going for myself. If I had been born ugly, I would have been a mother. And I would spend my days and nights crying over my fate."

At least there, she was perfectly sincere. What a mess, I thought. But what could I really reproach her for?

"Listen," I said to her, "tell me the whole story, and I promise to keep you out of this as much as possible, okay? But I want the real story, not the fiction from before."

She scowled, but perhaps she was suddenly feeling a little respect for me, which required her to be neither mother nor whore, because she began to speak, simply, without embellishment, as if she were outside of herself. She wasn't telling her own story, after all, but the one belonging to the creature she had invented to live in her place.

Since puberty, she had known that she was attractive to men. When her mother remarried, she tested her charms on her stepfather, learning ranges of lascivious looks and evasion, testing behaviours and attitudes, ascertaining through omissions and little white lies the resilient nature of her own honesty. In response, the stepfather showered her with gifts while the mother sought comfort from pharmacists who weren't too concerned with the origin of tranquilizer prescriptions. In short, after two years, the stepfather dumped the mother and set up the girl in a furnished apartment. For a few months, Maria had a dream life, especially when the stepfather went out of town on one of his business trips. But the problem with a man being crazy about you is just that, craziness. And the stepfather's craziness consisted of unbridled jealousy, excessive and not exactly unjustified. So much so that after a while, he decided to take Maria on the road with him in order to keep a hand and an eye on her at the same time.

"It was on one of these trips that I met Gerhart. He was rich and educated. It was a step in the right direction. I did a whole number on him, subtly. After an hour, he was frothing at the mouth. My stepfather looked at us, frowning, but he couldn't say anything. When it came time to shake his hand, I slipped Gerhart a small piece of paper on which I had written: Help me. We finished our trip. But, the next night, I left the hotel while my stepfather was sleeping, and I hitchhiked to get back to the sawmill. I told Gerhart that my stepfather beat me. Since the note, he was ready to pluck me like a flower."

He offered her a job as a secretary on the spot, she who didn't know how to type or write a sentence without making a mistake. But he wasn't paying her to work. For a few years, she didn't want for anything. The Wife was underfoot, but Maria managed to weasel paid trips to the city more and more frequently, sometimes all the way to the Capital, where she planned on widening her hunting grounds. She would have succeeded if there hadn't been war on the horizon and the economic panic that had preceded it.

"The sawmill closed and I was left high and dry. I knew that the Chef had coveted me since our first meeting. He was the most educated of those who remained, the least crude. So, I took up with him."

"To spy on him?"

"Not even. I knew that the war was coming; Gerhart had talked enough about it. But Viktor was gentle, not the least bit aggressive, and he seemed to float kilometres above all of this. He was somewhat reassuring. And I didn't think I could count on Gerhart any longer. Viktor was truly very kind to me. Very attentive, very tender."

"He loved you."

"Yes. That one loved me. Despite the situation and my previous experiences, he loved me regardless. I didn't always understand why."

"Did there have to be a reason?"

She shrugged her shoulders without answering.

"One day, Gerhart telephoned me. He said: I'll be sending for you soon. Be ready."

"Did you want to leave?"

"I can't imagine a whole life in the boondocks, out in the country, raising kids and eating rabbit and cabbage."

"Even with someone who loves you?"

"Especially with someone who loves me," she answered.

"So you told Gerhart that the men wanted to take over the sawmill."

"No. I'm in the manager's pants; I don't share the secrets of the powers that be. The troops arrived in the middle of the night. A car was sent for me. I packed my things and left."

"Gerhart didn't ask you anything?"

"He has other spies. And he wouldn't have dared. He knew that I would have said no."

"Why?"

"It's not what I do."

After several hours on the road, the car drove her to a huge country house on the edge of a lake. It was the Wife's home, but because of the troubles, she didn't dare step foot outside of the Capital. Gerhart was waiting for her, accompanied by Puritz, Pustule, who would take care of her until things settled down.

"At first, Gerhart came to see me regularly, and then all the roads became dangerous. But we had everything we needed and I was in the company of a man who was more interested in my dresses than he was in me, which turned out to be particularly refreshing . . . Then came the war, the attack on M. and the militiamen breaking down the door."

"Tell me about that."

"We hadn't had a telephone or electricity in days. There had been no noise either. I thought we were alone on the lake. But one night, some militiamen broke down the door. I was reading a magazine in the living room. Pustule was taking a bath. I was surprised to recognize people from the sawmill. They seemed delighted to see me. They dragged me by the arm, pulled Puritz from the tub and brought him along, completely naked. They made us walk to another house, and Viktor was there."

"What did he say to you?"

"Nothing. He ordered that we be locked in the boathouse. The guys were laughing at Pustule because he was wearing nail polish on his toes – and that was all he was wearing."

"Were you scared?"

"Yes."

"Did they rape you?"

"No. They wanted to, I could tell. But they left me alone. Then, I was afraid of Viktor's reaction. I had abandoned him without saying a thing – and now he seemed harder, more dangerous, more . . . He found what he was always missing, I think."

"The taste for blood?"

"A certain kind of grandeur. He was very handsome. But he didn't rape me. After several hours, he had Pustule removed from the boathouse and he came in. I thought it was the signal to go to him. I was terrified; I pleaded with him, cajoled him, and even caressed him. He looked at me, listened, let me go on. But nothing happened. His body wasn't reacting and he looked . . . tragic. Since then, I often thought he was saying goodbye to me, or that he was saying goodbye to himself, to a version of himself that no longer existed. Then he left and I stayed alone a few hours. They came to get me in the middle of the night. They put me in a boat with Pustule whose fingers and toes were bleeding. We crossed the lake with the militia men. Once there, they let us go. They disappeared into the forest. I never saw Viktor again, except for in that picture where he looks like a monster."

"Do you believe it? In the Monster, I mean?"

"I don't know. He wasn't a monster to me. But I can tell you what he did to Pustule. Viktor took his chef's knife, he put Pustule's hands and then his feet on a cutting board, and he sliced off the end of every finger and every toe. Not much. Just a little. Just enough to feel the bone in the middle of the cut. He could have killed him. But that's what he did to him. What's worse? I can't answer that."

"Can I talk to this Pustule?"

"His name was Leo Puritz, and no, you can't talk to him. He's dead."

"From his injuries?"

"Pneumonia. Naked, outside, in April. I helped him as best I could but he could barely walk. It took us over ten hours to get back to the inhabited shore of the lake. I got to know him. He was very kind. He dreamed of grand balls, beautiful clothes, of princes and princesses . . . He said that he was a woman trapped in a man's body; a monster in his own way. It's funny, now that I think of it . . . Leo and Viktor are the only two men who loved me for who I am."

"What happened next?"

"I took care of Leo. He died. I waited for Gerhart who finally found me and had me safely driven to the neighbouring province where I waited for the end of the war, listening to records and drinking wine."

"If you told Gerhart everything, I understand why he hates Viktor so much."

"I didn't tell him anything!"

"Why?"

"I can't risk damaging my reputation. If I tell people that I was captured by a band of militiamen, everyone will think I'm lying when I say that I wasn't raped."

"You're worried about your reputation?"

"The problem with rape is that it gives men ideas. They suddenly realize that with a bit of force, all girls are easy. As for me, if I'm easy, I'm finished. Believe me, what I have, Gerhart has to fight to get it every time. I'm the victor as long as that lasts."

I had taken notes. I closed my notebook.

"So I guess you won't be coming to the trial to say that Viktor saved you from rape?"

"I won't go because that incident never happened."

"Well, there's not much left for us to talk about."

"Unless of course you offer me your heart and your fortune," she answered, smiling.

I was moving towards the door, but just before opening it I turned to Maria.

"Listen, I don't have any advice to offer you. I destroyed everything that was important to me. But here's what I think: Even if happiness landed in your lap, you wouldn't know what to do with it. You can't be in a permanent state of war and let happiness in at the same time. Happiness doesn't know how to breach those defences. It's too fragile. As far as I know, anyway. Good luck," I said.

"Good luck," answered Maria.

In the waiting room, Josef and Gerhart jumped up at once when they saw me come out.

"Let's go," I said to Josef.

I didn't even glance at the manager.

Josef was driving. He scrutinized me but my mouth was clamped shut.

"That was very nice," he said after a while.

"What? What was very nice?"

"The frailty of happiness and all that."

I looked at him. He was smiling, more elflike than ever. "Josef?"

"Gerhart is a crafty fellow," he said. "Before he left the office, he pushed the intercom button that communicates with his secretary's office."

"You heard everything?"

"Everything. Gerhart was furious. 'The awkward assaults of that pretentious idiot!' You should have seen his face!"

"Maria's going to have a tough time."

"It won't take her long to talk her way out of it. She's a pro. She'll flip him like a pancake."

"I hope it doesn't take her too long. Time is money for a girl like her. She's banking on her youth and youth doesn't last. She's already lost several years. Regardless of what she says, the war wasn't part of her plan."

"She'll end up marrying a dirty old middle-class man that she'll scorn divinely. And despite herself, she'll turn into a sour old biddy who will try to fill the void of her existence with jewels."

"No doubt, it's her most precious hope," I sighed.

We remained silent for a while. I went over the moment in the manager's office, right before Maria and I were left alone. Something wasn't right.

"Josef?"

"Yes?"

"Are you positive that Gerhart pressed the intercom button, and not you?"

"Yes, at least I think so. I seem to remember that it was him, but I could be wrong."

Looking away from the road for a second, he turned to me:

"My memory is as fragile as happiness," he said.

MARIA

What could I say? Everything or nothing at all. Everything wasn't an option, so I said nothing.

I ordered Rossi to lock them in the boathouse. He looked disappointed; he was counting on getting his fill. Maria also seemed disappointed. Did she think that I was going to welcome her with open arms?

It had crossed my mind. So had killing her on the spot. All that in the matter of a second. I couldn't see clearly within myself. I needed time. This intrusion of my previous life into my new one gave the impression that I was more fragile than I would have liked. The past had to die so that the present could reign supreme. There had to be a clean cut, as though pruning a tree to rid it of dead branches or of those that, being too heavy, compromise its balance. A few sick branches subsisted in my mental structure, prolonging my suffering. Pustule was a small branch that I could snap between my fingers. Maria was another, a framework branch, barely distinguishing itself from the trunk, so much so that I didn't know where my pain from her ended and the simple pain of being me began.

I returned to Manu's side. He had regained consciousness. He also had the time to notice the absence of his leg under the covers. He was pale. He stared at the ceiling without saying a word. Theo changed his bandage. The flesh was swollen; the stub was deformed, red and covered in stitches. But there was no trace of infection and that was a miracle.

"Are you in pain?"

He nodded his head without looking at me. I consulted Theo with a look.

"I can give him another injection but . . ."

"I don't want him to be in pain."

While Theo prepared the injection, I gently told Manu the lies that you tell under such circumstances, the kind lies, visions of happiness that are within reach. I spoke of Jana who was waiting for him somewhere safe. I spoke of the cheese we would make after the war. I spoke of future children, numerous and boisterous, and I spoke of a house full of noise and action that would be his home. But he continued to stare at the ceiling and closed his eyes only when the needle broke the flesh of his arm in search of an artery. While Theo depressed the plunger, his entire body quivered. Manu kept his eyes closed. His breath slowed until it was imperceptible. My voice broke in a whisper. He slept. I leaned over to kiss his clammy forehead, and then left the room.

I called Rossi.

"Show me where you found them."

Maria lived in a house similar to the one we were occupying. A luxurious residence that was merely secondary for the wealthy ones of this world. Too many bedrooms, too many bathrooms, too many richly embroidered pillows on cushy sofas. Summer houses that were warmer and more comfortable than all of those, sole and principal, that my friends inhabited. I asked Rossi to stay outside and I went in alone.

It was dark. My flashlight captured pieces of reality in its cone of light. There were pictures in pretty frames. You could see the manager with his wife, with the governor, with the president. Frozen images of a privileged life that were trying to immortalize the most powerful moments. But all of that was of no interest to me. I lingered on the imprint of Maria's body left in the down of the pillows. She had flipped through this magazine. She drank from this glass that preserved traces of her lipstick. I crossed the living room seeking, with my nose, the smell of her perfume, her hair, her flesh. Three rooms opened onto a wide corridor. On the left was a huge overly decorated, opulent room. Heavy tapestries cascaded down to the carpet in a wave of velvet. The enormous bed didn't have a wrinkle. No one had slept here in a long time.

To the left was a guest room, smaller, almost austere, and reeking of the lemony perfume in which Pustule doused himself. His garb for the evening was laid out professionally on the bed. At the back was a door through which I could see the bathtub that was still full. On the water's surface, the last bubbles were bursting.

Maria's room was the last one on the right. It was untidy, clothes lay on the floor. The chest drawers were open and from them escaped pieces of lingerie. I sat on the bed. Everything she took with her when she left me was here. I recognized the shoes, the dresses, the undergarments. I recognized the beauty products that covered the entire surface of a small rococo vanity. A silk scarf in violet hues was thrown over the lampshade of a bedside lamp. She had thrown this same scarf over the lamp in my room before we would make love, how long ago? This gesture that I thought was for me, she had repeated with Bolchick the manager while welcoming him in this bed of wrinkled sheets. I took a pillow, exploding with whiteness, in my filthy hands with black nails. Maria's head had rested in it, hair spread and vibrant with life after its daily ration of one hundred brush strokes.

Holding the flashlight in my teeth, I opened the drawers one by one, my big paws digging a path down to the wood without finding anything but stockings, garters, slips, thongs, tights and bustiers. I emptied the closets by throwing on the bed the dresses and skirts, suits, sweaters, coats and pants draped on hangers. At the very back of the closet, the luggage she had brought here was empty. No secret pocket held messages, letters or diaries.

I had put everything upside down. There was no trace of me in this room. No note, object or souvenir. She hadn't taken anything from our months together. It was as though they had never happened.

The garters with which we had played had been worn for another, before me and after me. What I believed to be mine had never been: neither pleasure nor intimacy. I inserted myself in the place of the man in a routine that was hers and that she had perfected long before we had met. I felt no anger. Not even sadness. I stood in the debris of my sentimental life, my boots muddied by the dresses whose frills had excited me. I felt nothing but a void left by the flat-out lie.

I left that room. I left that house. I had Pustule brought from the boathouse and I stood before Maria, standing straight, and I didn't even grant her the favour of hurting her. Since I was nothing, I did nothing. However much she spoke, and pleaded, however much she hung from my legs and climbed my body with her mouth and her hands, nothing filled the void. It was there to stay, and once I was convinced, I could leave, turn my back on Maria and close the door on that part of my life.

In the living room, Mistral appeared agitated. The lookouts claimed they saw an army patrol, which appeared to have been sent on reconnaissance. We had to hit the road. There was still the problem of Manu. I knew that taking him into the forest was out of the question.

I also knew that I couldn't abandon him.

"There's not only Manu," said Mistral. "The girl, Pustule, the nurse."

In the darkest of night, twenty of us boarded the boat docked on the lake. Towing a rowboat, it took us a little under twenty minutes to make it to the northeast end of the lake, giving us a good hour lead over the government troops because no road reached there. After reaching the shore, Mistral sank the boat with an axe. Pustule was naked. I didn't show him the kindness of giving him a blanket. Maria helped him stand.

"You're free," I told them.

They looked at me without understanding.

"Go home."

I indicated the forest. They moved forward in the dark and the woods, and for several minutes, I could hear the cracking branches. Then they disappeared from my sight.

Manu and I were dressed as civilians. Expensive clothing found in the closets of the secondary residence and which were a pretty good fit. I had a revolver and my knife in its sheath, both slipped in my pant belt, under the flap of my jacket. Manu was unarmed. I carried a travel bag as a bandolier. It was filled with medications, bandages and the entire morphine supply from the clinic. Theo the nurse supported Manu who was leaning awkwardly on crutches that were also taken from the clinic.

I had long questioned myself. Where to go? I had decided to cross the length of the lake, this time in the rowboat, and disembark behind the government troops. Then, on foot if necessary, to make it to the city of M. that we had fled a week earlier after almost conquering it. The wolf doesn't hunt its prey in its own jaws, behind its teeth. It shouldn't be too difficult, in a city half deserted by its frantic population, to find somewhere to stay until Manu could get back on his feet.

We said our goodbyes. Mistral said:

"Are you deserting, Chef?"

"What? Are we in the army?"

Manu's head was nodding and we lay him down on the bottom of the rowboat, well protected by many blankets. His moans were becoming more intense and rebounded like stones off the surface of the lake. I gave him another dose of morphine. Mistral, Rossi and the others waved goodbye one last time and then disappeared into the woods. I pushed out the rowboat and settled myself on the seat.

"Take care of him, and don't make a sound," I said to Theo while showing him my weapon.

I took both oars and we slid into the night, on the black waters that reflected the pale starlight, making it dance.

DO YOU SEE THEM?

I couldn't take it anymore. I left Josef having a heart-to-heart with his litre of red wine and went out to get some fresh air in the poorly lit village square. Nothing lived outside at that time of night. I begrudged their laughter, over there in the jam-packed bar buzzing like a hive. I begrudged their clinking, holding their glasses between their stubs, the day to work and the evening to drink, foraging from bottle to bottle, as though tomorrow didn't exist. In fact, perhaps it didn't.

No tomorrow. No hope. No dreams. Bees didn't dream; they made honey, and too bad if the beekeeper vandalized their honeycombs. They can be rebuilt. That's their life. And if they feel like fighting, they are smoked and that's that. The desire passes, just like everything else.

I begrudged myself as well. Where was my compassion, my empathy? But even compassion and empathy sometimes need to recharge and fall back from the frontline, leaving behind only slight ignorance and a touch of morbid humour. Everything is despicable in war, even the resulting peace.

What had I learned? What had I understood? What was I searching?

I was annoyed. In moments like this, the recourse to general anaesthesia usually applied, but the taste for alcohol seemed to have left me for the time being. In its place, I swallowed gulps of air scented with resin and dead leaves, hoping that this would clear my brain.

I couldn't shake the idea that I was being taken on a wild goose chase from the beginning. I strayed from the square to stroll across the village. Tonight, the sky was partially stopped up with clouds through whose tears trembled the starlight. Everything was tranquil; there was no wind, but an oppressive feeling seemed to rise from the Great Forest, as though closing in on us.

I reflected. It didn't make sense that a defendant who refuses to utter a word would call on an organization such as Lawyers Without Borders. Since he didn't want to defend himself, who did? And most of all, why?

Who had an interest in defending the Monster? Those who had, up until now, mostly contributed to his defence were lawyers from the civil party! By withdrawing Rosalind's story from the charge sheet, they had swept under the rug the most cruel episode from my client's life, the only one that a jury, anywhere in the world, would condemn without appeal as being the product of a sick, rotting mind. They had done more for Viktor Rosh's defence than the defence itself since the beginning of the affair.

And what had Cevitjc accomplished? To my knowledge, nothing. He had handed me the matter like a basket of dirty laundry. At the very least, he introduced me to Josef, without whom I would have been as helpless as a newborn. But Josef knew more than he was letting on. I remembered his guardedness the night before, and most of all his silence that followed.

Perhaps it was logical that an old fraud artist play on several canvases! In any event, he seemed to have a certain affection for me, and the state of his country and its citizens seemed to break his heart at times.

What had I learned from Maria other than the fact that games of love are sometimes cruel and that even a monster can reveal himself as tender and gentle? To me, it seemed more important to know that the manager of the sawmill, a powerful man in the region, may have personal reasons to have it out for Viktor Rosh, and that behind the stories of war and power, two men's jealousy over the same woman could explain many things. Was Gerhart Bolchick assuaging his revenge by singling out my client and unleashing on him the thunderbolts of exemplary justice?

But it wasn't exemplary because it averted its eyes from the worst!

And what about me in all of this? I drew a certain strength from the source of my frailty. As though, by letting the masks fall away, I discovered on my face some kinder traits than I would have expected. Once again, Florence had set everything off. I was spiralling down into the dimension of my ruin whereas I was estranged from her and from my habits, and there was nowhere to take refuge. It was hard to believe that I hadn't had a drink in three days. After we left M., I had behaved like a man, meaning I had done my best – and that hadn't happened in how long? Years probably. My best. No illusions of grandeur, no lies, not neglecting the possibility of failure. Yes, there was a certain grandeur in the simple fact of accomplishing what needed to be accomplished.

The hotel bar was far behind me now; even the ones who annoyed me earlier by denying the tragic dimension of their existence – now they could just as easily pass for heroes in my eyes. Heroes of their own stories. They fed their families. They got back into harness. Wounded, broken, grieving, their dreams of emancipation trampled underfoot; they were rebuilding their lives. What more could they do other than take their own lives? Is suicide a more courageous gesture than rebuilding? Or they could bestow death on others as Mistral continued to do because he refused to wake to another reality other than his dream of war.

At the exit of the village, the road followed a sharp hill that I had started to climb unaware. The village lights shone at my feet, like a solitary, miniscule constellation in infinite blackness. It was nothing on Earth, even less on a universal scale. It was not even a big war on the scale of the century. The city of M. was not big. The dead were counted in tens of thousands, not in millions. But what gave us the right to say that? What was the yardstick? Who could properly establish a scale of the horror? Where does civilization end and barbarity begin when the latter draws inspiration from the first? The laws of the vanquisher always apply retroactively. Cevitjc was right: if my client's party had won the war, a school would have been named after him and his accusers would be the ones in a cell waiting for judgment. The Nobel Peace Prize was given to terrorists because after all their killing, they finally convinced the rest of the world of the legitimacy of their initial cause. But must the dead be forgotten?

Certainly the living couldn't be forgotten. I had mine: Florence, the children. My living. The only ones who could benefit from my love. The only ones that I could help directly, and hold in my arms. The only ones for whom I could slightly ease the burden of living. And by helping them, I was helping myself. The power of love as opposed to the power of death. The simplicity of love as opposed to the complexity of war. The truth of love as opposed to the lies of interest. What use was it to march in the streets waving signs for peace if I was unable to kiss my children's boo-boos – and to believe in the absolute power of kisses to heal boo-boos? It's not enough to be against war; you have to be for something. But peace is nothing. Peace is the absence of war. With what will we fill the absence of war?

I was now at the very top of the hill, slightly winded from the climb. I was a little light-headed. The sky had clouded over. I could barely see my feet and the half-erased white line that separated the road in two. I was far away, at the other end of the world, at the other end of something anyway. If those men, down there, mutilated, injured, grief-stricken, could start their lives over, rebuild their homes and make children to replace the dead, why wouldn't I make it?

"I know who you are," said a voice in the dark.

I felt as though someone had whispered in my ear, but there was no one there. Where did that voice come from? It was a woman's voice, otherwise I would have been afraid. Josef had warned me that the region wasn't safe.

"Here," said the voice.

It was coming from the right. I left the middle of the road to get closer to it. I could vaguely distinguish a light spot that seemed to be suspended in the air. I inched closer to it with small careful steps, feeling for obstacles with my feet.

"Watch the ditch," said the voice.

I heard a scratching noise. A match was struck. A woman was lighting an oil lamp. She was sitting in a rocking chair, on the dilapidated balcony of a lopsided house covered in a tar paper as black as night, rendering it invisible. The woman wore a dress just as black. Only her face, pale as the moon, floated as though it wasn't attached to anything.

"Over there," said the woman.

She indicated a board placed across the ditch which I used to cross to then join her on the balcony. The woman was slight, and under her wrinkles, behind the sadness in her eyes, remained the memory of her beauty. However, she seemed younger than me. Perhaps she was sick.

"You're the lawyer," she said after I approached.

"Yes," I answered. "And who are you?"

Instead of answering, she blew out the lamp. The obscurity blinded me for a few moments. The blackness was so intense that I thought I would fall. I sat on the worn balcony boards, my back resting against the railing of the stairs.

"I like the night," she said. "You can resuscitate the dead. Look, they're all there, in the field, across there. Do you see them?"

I studied the obscurity, squinting, but I saw nothing.

"My children. There are three of them. Two girls and a boy. They are the best of friends. They only have each other. Look – they're chasing each other. They play tag but they change the rules as they go along. Do you hear them laughing? I can hear them. I see them. I can smell them."

She breathed in deeply. She stretched out her neck, as if to see them better, and she rocked at the edge of her seat. In the white spot of her face, I could see the black line of a smile forming. I didn't dare question her.

"Soon my husband will come to sit next to me," she began again, "and when he leans over to kiss me, I'll put my hand on his bottom. A nice tight bottom with just a thin layer of skin covering the muscle. Only I am allowed to touch him there. He is the only one I can touch in that way. He's going to sit there, exactly where you are. And together we'll watch the children play in the field. My eldest never stops running. He spins in circles to get dizzy. Do you see him?"

"No," I said.

"That's because you don't love him. You have to love him to see him. But it's easier in the dark. NOT ON THE FENCE!" she yelled suddenly into the night, half standing from her chair. "There's barbed wire over there," she added to me. "I wouldn't want them to get hurt. Children are crazy. They're attracted to what can hurt them."

Despite myself, I looked out into the kilometres of blackness in front of me.

"The little one has shoulders like round loaves of bread," said the woman. "He's always outside from morning to night. Look how he's having fun! Look how happy he is with grass in his hair! Do you see him?"

"No," I said. "No, I don't see him."

"You know how children run . . . They run for the fun of running even if they have nowhere to go. They run because they're made for running, and jumping, and playing. Now they're throwing pebbles in the pond. Do you see them?"

"No," I said. "I don't see them."

"They're made for that too: for throwing pebbles in the water. And pebbles are made to be thrown, and water to receive them. There, I bet they've found a frog. They're going to scare their little sister . . . What did I tell you! Do you see them?"

"No," I said. "I don't see them."

"But look," she yelled suddenly, "they're there! Look! Open your eyes! Don't let them leave! Look! The two older ones are comforting the youngest who is crying a little. Look – they're taking her by the hand. Do you see them?"

"No," I said. "I don't see them."

But I could see. I could see something. In the darkest dark, I could see my own son crossing the prairie at a run, tanned, naked, his little round bottom covered in mosquito bites. Behind him trotted Margot, still hesitant on her plump little legs, like little pillars of flesh. They both ran towards Florence and the long grass whipped their reddened thighs. They ran and laughed, they ran screaming in happiness, towards Florence.

Florence, lying on her stomach in the green and gold hay, feet in the air and a blade of grass between her teeth. She rolls over, straw stuck to her clothes, she sits up and the children throw themselves into her arms that she closes around them, laughing, then together they roll and roll and tickle each other and hug and I can hear the trio of crystal laughter.

"Do you see them?" asks the woman.

"Yes," I say. "I see them."

"That's good," she says.

I was crying in the dark.

We stayed in silence, each plunged in our own visions.

After a long while, the woman rose and moved toward the rickety door of her house. The door was already half open when she said to me, without turning around:

"Tell Viktor that I want my letters."

She disappeared into the house. For several minutes, I heard her stirring in the dark, moving a chair, placing a cup on the table. I heard a mattress squeak.

I stayed outside, waiting. But it was over. I rose heavily. I crossed the ditch, on all fours, and I found the pale white line on the road. Slowly, I made my way down to the village.

The bar was closed. I went up to bed. The next day, I asked the owner the name of the woman who lived at the top of the hill. It was Jana, Manu's wife. She had lost two children and a husband to the war. After the war, she had lost custody of the third child.

"She's not all there," said the owner, pointing with her index finger to her temple.

She was right, of course, she wasn't all there. But, I asked myself, is anyone all there?

MY SON BY BLOOD

Oh! I would have done anything for him. I could feel his shivers in my flesh. His needling pain pricked my nerves. I would have given my leg to replace his. I would have taken anything so that his forehead could regain the smoothness of serenity. I would have drunk his cold sweat. I would have licked the pus from his wounds. I would have broken my bones to fasten them to his.

Once again, I discovered the powerlessness of my body, limited in space and time, to restrained action and pathetic strength.

For almost six weeks, we lived in the city of M., in a fifth-floor apartment of a building that had been bombed. There was neither water nor electricity but several supplies in the event of trouble: several staircases and an exterior metal ladder. But most of all, the apartment had a gas stove hooked up to a practically full tank, enabling me to make hot soup to build Manu's strength.

At first I thought that his lack of appetite was due to the pain in his leg. But as time went on, the wound covered itself in new pink skin that was a strong contrast to Manu's pale face. If the leg was healing, Manu continued to be sick. Was there a mysterious underlying infection? At times I regretted that Theo wasn't there. His advice had been welcome but I had no choice but to kill him even though I would have preferred to let him live. I couldn't trust him.

The night of our escape, I had rowed for an hour when we ran ashore on the southwest side of the lake. From there, it was easy to reach the outskirts of the town by stealing a vehicle.

But first of all, we had to reach the road across a steep, dense thicket. Theo had helped me to support Manu on the way up, then, still under the cover of the brush, we rested for a minute, watching for possible movement. There were still two hours of night remaining and everything was quiet on the road. Through a folded blanket, I put a bullet in the back of Theo's head. The muffled sound of the discharge made Manu jump.

"Everything's fine," I said to him.

I dragged Theo's body a little further and then came back to Manu. He was propped up on an elbow, looking at me. He seemed terribly young and distressed. He was suffering. I would have liked to take charge of his suffering but I didn't know how. I gave him another injection so that he could sleep, then I left in search of a car to steal, which took me mere minutes.

I was most afraid of all the road blocks. People were leery of two men without papers, of fighting age, especially if one of them was wounded. I could always lie, but lies wouldn't prevent our internment. In the regions under government control, as in the ones in the hands of the militia, the prisoners' camps were death camps without water or food, and their sanitary conditions were unworthy of a pig farm. In his current state, Manu wouldn't survive.

That's why I abandoned the car long before the city's first faubourgs, continuing on foot through a maze of vacant lots, railroad yards and small deserted streets. I had to carry Manu, the medication bag and the crutches. But like a father carrying his child to save him from danger, I wasn't fatigued. However, at daybreak, we had to hide from the patrols that became increasingly numerous as we neared a working-class neighbourhood close to the centre of town. I found the bombed building just before the city awoke and out into the streets would pour the besieged inhabitants, in search of news, food and water. An entire side of the building had crumbled, vomiting a mountain of gravel, and revealing entrails chequered with concrete, sinks suspended from pipes and gutted couches. The rest of the structure, weakened by the impact, was cracked like an old person's face. But a few apartments had more or less survived, well hidden under the ruins, and I made one of them our home.

In the first few days, Manu's condition improved slowly. I hesitated to leave him alone, but we needed water and supplies. I gave him a shot before I slid through the loose rubble of the building's front to blend in with the uprooted citizens queuing up with their plastic water bottles in front of the tank trucks requisitioned by the army, or in front of the tents erected in the middle of the street that distributed rice and milk. But all that took time, hours and hours among the screaming shrews and the offended model citizens who began the day by claiming their due and finished it by begging for handouts. It took me very little time to understand that everything could be found faster on the black market, as long as you had the money, lots of money, cash, because the banks had frozen the accounts and were closed until the new order. However, I had no money.

But I had a weapon.

In the town square was an outdoor black market where buyers and sellers gathered. That's where the goods and the money were. I organized my days so that I bought the meat, vegetables and bread that we needed. But in the evening, before curfew, as the market was closing, wearing a mask, I discreetly followed one of those who had fleeced me that morning, to recover my due and then some, at gunpoint. I was careful never to attack the bigger traffickers who had their own men, seeing as they could afford to buy them. I concentrated on the small-time, solitary negotiators without resources, the old toothless granny who disposed of the six eggs from her chicken coop on a daily basis, or the little public servant who sought to liquidate his bribes, paid in kind since the beginning of the war. I was gone for two hours at the start of the day and two more in the evening. I spent the rest of the time taking care of Manu, changing his bandages, massaging his muscles to maintain their tone, feeding him and keeping him hydrated.

But he wasn't recovering. He didn't get up from the mattress thrown on the floor below a glassless window whose gaping opening was concealed by a blanket full of holes. He spent hours with his eyes lost in the emptiness. When I returned in the evening, most of the time there was no light, or just the quivering halo of a candle's flame whose glow I didn't notice until the last minute. I asked him:

"Are you in pain?"

He didn't answer or made some meaningless gesture. The nights were long. Dozing here and there throughout the day, he slept very little at night and became restless and moaned. I listened to him, searching for some key in his indistinguishable murmurs.

His stump was now perfectly healed. I had long since progressively decreased the morphine injections, and then stopped them all together. I forced him to do some exercises. Some days he was cooperative, others not. I scolded him like a child and he went along with it.

Sometimes, most often in the morning, he would talk to me as though everything was normal.

"I would really like some orange juice," he would say, for example.

I was so happy to see him want something that I ran to the city to fill his request. But when I returned, I would find him down, distant, in a cold desperation that managed to scare me. As for the orange juice, he wouldn't touch it, and I had to drink it before it spoiled.

Manu never looked at his leg. It was as if it had never existed – as if his entire body had never existed. I tried to talk to him, to carry on a normal conversation. I told him about my outings, the news of the war that I picked up in the streets. I would tell him:

"You have to get better. There is fear of a new offensive here. We don't want to be on the wrong side when that happens!"

He had lost a lot of weight and continued to get thinner, which worried me because thanks to my outings, we lacked nothing. Every morning before I went out, I left Manu a full plate. When I returned, it was empty.

But Manu was still wasting away.

One morning, as I left the building, skirting its side, out of the corner of my eye I saw something fall not far off, followed by a sort of plunk! Intrigued, I went to investigate. It was two eggs and a small piece of ham that had cost me a lot. Leftover meat, bits of bread, dried-out pasta were all over the ground. Crows and seagulls, whose presence I had already noticed without questioning it, waited for me to leave before feasting. I looked up. Right above was our window.

I ran upstairs. Manu hadn't heard me coming. He held the end of the tourniquet between his teeth and was searching for a vein by tapping his forearm. The syringe and vial of morphine were set out beside him like jewels on a velvet pillow.

"Manu?"

He lifted his head slowly and saw me. His face was expressionless. Then he went back to what he was doing and I watched without interrupting as he pumped out a powerful dose from the vial, and then injected it in his arm, clenching his teeth. At last, he released the tourniquet and it was as if his entire body relaxed at the same time. He dropped back on the mattress, eyes half shut, appeased – and at that exact moment, despite the bones protruding from his face, despite his luminous pallor, he appeared to be twelve years old, twelve years old always, twelve years old forever. A child who for now, after a last flutter of eyelids, fell asleep.

I went right up to him and pulled the blanket over his skinny chest that rose peacefully. From the floor, I picked up the bag of medications that I had put away in a closet weeks ago. I opened it. There was only one vial of morphine left out of the dozens that it had held. The bottles of codeine and sedatives were empty. Manu was but days away from a violent withdrawal that would have blown the whistle on him anyway.

I tossed the vial and the rest of the medication out the window, and then I stretched out on the bed next to Manu. I listened to his breathing. Tiny beads of sweat shone along his hairline and on his forehead. I lifted his head and slid my arm under his neck while I wrapped the other around his waist. I glued myself to him. Then I waited. A long time. Hours. I waited for the withdrawal. Manu wouldn't be alone.

At first, it was but a quivering of his limbs, like a long shiver that started from the heart and spread through the blood to the extremities. Then came the tremors, and at that moment, I saw that he opened his eyes trying to figure out where he was. On either side of his body, my hands were joined and clasped firmly. I tightened my grip. Manu could see the empty gaping bag on the floor. He remembered me watching him injecting the drug. He started to understand. The truth was coming to light, the cruel knowledge, while each cell in his body begged to be appeased with a fresh dose. He was moaning now, rolling from one side to the other inside the steel hoop of my arms. His good leg started to kick. He spoke.

"Let me go."

He ordered.

"Let me go!"

He begged.

"Let me go!"

"There's no more, Manu. I threw everything away. It's finished."

He sobbed. With his thin fingers, he attempted to pick the lock of my fists. With his nails, he scratched my arms. But I didn't let go while the storm raged inside his body. It was growing, I could almost feel its undulations under Manu's skin, like snakes moving up the current of his veins looking for a way out. The jerking movements were more frequent, Manu moaned louder and louder until he was howling, so skinny, so weak, but the snakes under his skin were driven by such force that I had to use all my strength to not let them escape through all of Manu's pores. How long? There was morning, and then afternoon and finally the evening. At nightfall, each passing second was like a razor blade slicing the skin, the soles of the feet, the cornea of Manu's eyes. His nerve endings threw wild sparks. Every joint in his body felt like it was made of brick sliding against brick, and the bone marrow was changing into glass dust. He was suffering. A skin pouch filled with suffering. A bag of suffering filled with suffering. He was fighting and screaming to escape that suffering. His intestines emptied into the bed, underneath him, underneath me, but I didn't loosen my grip, I didn't let go until the end of the next morning when at last, the exhausted snakes slowly ceased their wild race. The storm moved away. Manu's body was no longer a giant puppet whose strings were being controlled by withdrawal. Exhaustion was justified by the suffering; the tremors diminished in intensity. Manu finally slept.

I disengaged myself with difficulty. My muscles that had been immobile for so long, my fingers that had been knotted for so long, untied themselves little by little. I was covered in shit, exhausted. Manu slept. What kind of victory was this, at the end of a war that could have been avoided?

I drank a glass of water without wasting a drop. I washed standing up and changed my clothes. Then, I gathered the sheets under Manu's body, undressed him and washed him with a cloth without him waking. I moistened his lips and saw a tip of pink tongue move around.

He suffered attacks for another two days. But they were less violent and the lulls in between were longer. We were finally able to talk, and I asked for his forgiveness.

"For what?"

For everything.

He looked at me without understanding, ashamed of himself and what the drugs had done to him. I wanted to chase away that shame, it had no place here. I told him so. He smiled.

We had no more food or water. I had to go out. When I returned, Manu was waiting for me, his gaze clear, standing, leaning on his crutches. He had tidied up a bit. He was hungry. He ate as though he hadn't eaten in weeks, months, avidly, with gluttony. Meat juices ran down his chin and he wiped them away with a piece of bread. I had tears in my eyes. Manu noticed. He was about to speak when in the distance we heard the echoes of the first bombings. I went to the window to see.

"So?" asked Manu.

"It's the second offensive," I said.

"We have to leave."

"Not now. You aren't in any shape."

"When then?"

"Tomorrow maybe. You have to sleep and eat again."

He smiled bravely, but his spent body wouldn't have carried him very far. He crumbled on the bed and fell asleep immediately.

I stayed at the window for a long time, watching the combat progress.

This time, our forces had given it everything they had. But I learned that later. The smoke columns drew closer. The detonations became louder. It was going fast; too fast. Our forces were advancing too quickly and too far without waiting for reinforcements. They were risking being surrounded. And then it would be chaos.

At dawn, I woke Manu.

"Get dressed. We're leaving."

We gathered our measly belongings. As we were leaving the apartment, Manu touched my shoulder.

"Thank you."

We went down the emergency stairwell, fairly slowly, although Manu was managing pretty well with his crutches. We came out onto the deserted street. Everything was hiding. As I determined from my window above, the battle had reached an even point. Our forces were no longer advancing, and the government army hadn't unleashed its counterattack thus far. We had the choice of fleeing the fighting, and in doing so throw ourselves into the arms of the army, or attempt to join the Militia's rearguard by going around the frontline.

For the moment, everything was still, silent, except from time to time an isolated detonation, a reminder that men were dying. We hadn't yet left the relative safety of our half-crumbled building. I explained the situation to Manu. Like me, he felt that we should join our people.

"I could still be useful," he said. "I know how to man the radio . . ."

I was looking at the deserted street.

"You run, keep your head down and hug the walls. Follow me, OK?"

"Yes Chef!"

"Come on!"

I sprang from the building. I took three steps. I heard a gunshot. I turned around. Manu was looking at me. He had a hole in his forehead, above his left eyebrow. He looked surprised. He kept his balance on the crutches for a moment, and then went down like a tree. There was another gunshot that kicked up dust at my feet. I dove and regained the shelter of the building.

"Manu!"

I called to him. But I knew he was dead. I could see the blood trickling from the wound.

"Manu."

I wanted him to answer. I longed for a miracle. But there are no miracles, ever. There are never any miracles.

I caught Manu's ankle and dragged him towards me. His face dragged on the ground and the blood running from his wound was already turning brown. When at last he was sheltered, I placed his head in my lap. But it wasn't Manu anymore. I searched his pockets to transfer his few personal possessions to mine. Slowly, I rose. I lifted Manu's body and hoisted him on my back, his arms around my neck, his head resting on my shoulder. I kissed him on the cheek.

I crossed the street like that. The bullets lodged themselves in Manu's flesh without reaching me. The sharpshooter gave up and stopped shooting even though we weren't even halfway across. In the shelter of a doorway, I dropped my load. Then I continued on my way, alone.

RETURN TO M.

I left Josef at the Black Bear Inn bar, his only company a bottle of red wine. I knew that he wasn't upset with me. I wanted to go up to my room and take a shower before sharing a last meal with him, on me of course. I felt I was done with his services. What would I have used him for? A guide? For what? You don't need a guide when you're going in circles.

We had left the village shortly after breakfast. I was thoughtful, not quite depressed. Obviously, the usual methods of investigation resulted in nothing here. In times of war, all circumstances are both attenuating and aggravating, so much that you can't make heads or tails of anything. If a man is to be judged according to the amount of pain he inflicts on others, the defendant benches would be warmed with posteriors much nobler than those they are accustomed to rubbing against. Asses carefully wrapped in silk drawers and designer clothes. But the court could only judge those indicted and it wasn't the fault of justice if the strategists of a derailed world and the profiteers of massacres were hardly ever brought before it.

I told Josef about my encounter with Jana. He just nibbled his moustache, a gesture that I grew to understand signified, in the limited expressions if his sentiments, profound dismay and great sadness. Without feeling the need to discuss it, we packed our bags to head back to M.

Travelling in silence became a habit, but this time, I wasn't going to let myself be seduced by the landscape's promises of adventure: it was nothing more than earth and trees, a slight amount of venality, a few principles of a market economy and lots of broken hope. I had my fill of the Great Forest. I preferred to look at Josef. He drove with a steady hand, wearing his usual sardonic smile. He knew that I was observing him, and he didn't care. He wasn't curious about my curiosity.

I had become attached to this career military man – a cultured and resourceful man, a giant sprite who protected his heart of gold under an armour of skin that was tanned like leather. If he had seen it all, he hadn't become colour-blind because of it. Beneath his humorous jabs, I sensed a more serious note that he had the decency not to abuse.

Who was he? He knew everyone and everyone knew him. He kept secrets that I never imagined could be extorted from him, even with threats or torture. He seemed to be a free man, whatever that meant. A mercenary is also a free man. I tried to imagine him at thirteen, juggling his sticks of dynamite – and I could see it without a problem. What had all of that cost him? The life of a soldier? The smell of gunpowder instead of jam? Women's skirts lifted over their hips to take them standing up against a wall – and never anyone waiting for him with a bouquet of flowers and children's drawings? But perhaps I was mistaken. One didn't necessarily cancel out the other. It simply seemed strange to me that in the same life one could kill people and make children. Was there a woman baking cakes, waiting for him to return from a campaign? Was she the one who washed and ironed his bloodied uniform and mended the bullet holes? In the evening did she prepare sandwiches and a glass of milk? Did she sit on her side of the kitchen table to ask how his day went? What could he answer to that?

"Well, fourteen dead and thirty-two wounded?"

What is a normal life? Shit! Can someone, somewhere, tell me what a normal life is? Because since the dawn of humanity, we've been killing each other, because we've been tearing each other apart, fleecing each other, torturing each other, abusing each other . . . Because our common history was but a long series of bloody battles and rapes just as bloody, how could we affirm that normalcy resides in love, sharing, fairness and respect? The love for gold? The sharing of the booty? Fairness in suffering and respect for the strongest? What is a normal life?

Is it normal to live an entire life in fear of one's boss; to spend evenings in front of a television and Saturday afternoon at the shopping centre? In the fifties, we were in a hurry to get older; at the end of this century we seek to stay young. What is normal?

No doubt, Josef's life was normal for him. Perhaps he never had a wife, sandwiches and a glass of milk, but rather a string of friends with benefits who one day grew tired of his underarm odour and back hairs. And from one to the next, the years went by without too much suffering, never really alone, never really loved.

Life was elsewhere, in the barracks, in the scent of greased leather and lice ointment. It was in the obedience, not blind but partially so, carefully maintained, because the world is decidedly too vast and too complex, so much so that we can only stand to see a little at a time. Life was in the lines of duty done, whatever the duty, decided by another in the name of who knows what. "I'm only doing my duty." "For the greater good of the nation." "God is with us." Those are good sayings that you can get drunk on without getting a headache, but that reflect only a tiny little part of the world's truth.

And yet, Josef seemed to have his own opinions that were founded on a subtle knowledge of things and people. Or was it merely that they went against my own opinions? Go figure.

Maybe his mystery could be summed up in the fact that he had killed. We say "take a life" and that's not for nothing. As if the murderer absorbed the lives of others; took on the weight of their souls. In my country, the law wanted to qualify them as *less than nothing*, but weren't they *more than us*, and wasn't that precisely what scared us, that additional dimension of murderer? We never spoke of this in the moot halls; we wanted to be objective, *letting the facts speak for themselves.* But the facts didn't speak, they stuttered, they bumped against the first word of a story that would never be told. Who do you listen to when the victims would remain silent forever? The facts didn't speak, they've been repeating themselves for thousands of years. Maybe it was time to give the assassins the floor so they can tell us what it's like to kill?

I looked at Josef. He had lived through three wars. How was he different from me? He had killed. No matter how much we say that killers don't make up the majority, that there aren't that many of them who have crossed that line and therefore have an advantage over the rest of us. The killer as a superior race? The assassin as the next evolutionary step? What is the difference between the piece of scum playing with a knife for a few measly dollars and the God-crazy president launching his troops on an unarmed country to steal its oil? A difference in scale? One is thrown in jail and the other climbs in the popularity polls. Our own moral conviction towards killers is tainted by ambiguity. But never has a journalist stood up at the White House to ask the president what it feels like to kill. He kills, therefore it must affect him somehow, right? I was not a journalist and Josef was not president, but I had to start somewhere.

"Josef?"

"Yes?"

"You've killed?"

"Ah! It took you long enough. What do you want to know?"

"What it does to you."

"Why?"

"Because we never speak about it. We search for the reasons, we condemn the action, we punish it, but we never discuss what killing does, to the one who has killed."

"Perhaps there are good reasons not to talk about it."

He was nibbling his moustache again.

"Listen," he said, "I never killed for pleasure, understand?"

"Yes."

"I never killed to gain something, not out of vengeance or anything else. Those I killed were enemies, and I killed them in the line of duty within an established framework, OK?"

"OK."

"Well, it doesn't change anything. I killed anyway. And in the beginning, even if you don't want to, you feel something very powerful. At first, there is nothing more powerful. Nothing. Remove guilt, the fear of punishment and moral condemnation, and killing becomes the act that provides you with the greatest sense of power there is. Better than an orgasm, which relegates us to our mammal state, whereas killing elevates us to the state of God."

"Do you truly believe that?"

"Among other things. But I also believe in guilt, in the fear of punishment and moral condemnation. Killing is exhilarating, sure, but it doesn't lead to happiness."

"Do you believe that some kill in their search for happiness?"

"I don't know. What I do know is that the sensation of power that is felt when you have someone in your aim and that all it takes is a finger's pressure to erase a life forever. I challenge you to try: Take up position on a roof with a rifle with a telescopic lens and aim at the ants that are innocently climbing the sidewalks to get to work. You don't even have to shoot. They don't even have to know that you're there. You feel the exhilaration of power. It's like a drug. At first, it's a drug. Even without shooting. But what happens in those situations happens, and because you can shoot, you end up doing it."

"We kill like we take drugs?"

"I'm talking about the effects, not the causes. We kill for many reasons, but at first, when we kill, we feel a sense of power that deep down is just exhilaration: a sudden acceleration of your heart rate, a tidal wave of hormones that floods your brain and bathes each cell in your body. Yes, it resembles a drug, and like a heroin addict, the killer is changed forever. Even if the heroin addict stops taking drugs, he has tasted the fruit of paradise and he will keep that burning memory forever. As for the killer, for an instant he has felt what it's like to be God . . ."

"And after?"

"We aren't God."

However, we give life, I thought. We create life. We create beings who could either become the killer's prey or the killer himself.

"Do we ever get out of it?" I asked.

Josef shook his head.

"Do you know that saying by Pascal: *All boredom stems from not knowing how to stay still in a room*? Or something like that. Why do we take drugs? Why do we kill? To feel something? There are people who are crazy enough to throw themselves off a bridge with an elastic tied to their ankles . . . Why? For the adrenaline? There is a difference in substance between adrenaline and heroin, but the goal is the same: exhilaration. As if salvation only exists in exhilaration. But how can we condemn the heroin addict while broadcasting television ads acclaiming the exhilaration of speed?"

"You know very well that it's not the same thing."

"No. And yet yes. I imagine that the feeling of exhilaration began long ago, when one of our ape ancestors grabbed a stick to knock a piece of fruit from a tree that was out of the reach of others. But once he had the stick, nothing stopped him from using it to hit his own . . . Exhilaration and death have always gone hand in hand . . ."

"Like love and life."

Josef made a face that could have passed for a smile.

"Maybe. But I don't know those two very well."

A long time goes by.

The city of M. appeared in the distance.

"Does it bother you? That I ask questions?"

"No. What bothers me is that you aren't the first to ask me these questions. What bothers me at times is when people think I had a choice, that I chose this life, consciously, like choosing a melon on a shelf. But that's not the case; it isn't true. That's not the way it happens. I told you: I was eleven years old. I was a child. Just a child. Do you think that if I really had a choice, I would have chosen to fight and kill before being killed? Do you think that at the age of eleven, you don't dream mostly of a nice bike with a bell on the handlebars? Do you think that you wouldn't rather be playing ball with your friends and gorging yourself with junk food? Do you think that you wouldn't prefer a real bed in your own room, decorated with posters and painted in bright colours? Do you think that you wouldn't prefer a mother's cool hand placed on your forehead when you have a bit of a fever? Do you think that, at eleven years old, you wouldn't prefer your parents alive than dead? War was rammed down my throat, and I had no other choice but swallow it. If I had the choice . . . But what power does a child have, eh? None. He has no power. Rather he does. The power to survive. And that's what I did. I survived. I survive . . ."

"Forgive me."

"That's OK."

"I didn't know."

"No. No one ever knows anything. That's the problem."

My hotel came into view. I didn't want to leave Josef on this sad and slightly discordant note. I invited him for a drink. He accepted right away, regaining his wicked smile, as though his little speech was nothing but a rehearsed number that was often repeated. But I didn't believe any of it. His maliciousness was his way of thumbing his nose at the life he hadn't chosen.

I asked him to wait for me. He answered that he was never lonely in the company of a bottle of red. I knew what he meant but it wasn't for me anymore.

Heading up to my room, I felt immense fatigue; that of the accumulation of all these lives that went wrong and were dragged in the mud and blood. Our common burden that nevertheless must be carried. If the world is as terrible a place as it seemed, then what? If only we could change worlds like we change cars. Wanting a new world like we want a new car, but not just any one, a certain model that would seem to be meant just for us. Dreaming about its shape, the iridescent gleam of the paint, and the smell! That new car smell! And a shiny engine that wouldn't yet have, like us, generated its own grime. Yes, the counter at zero. But should the driver be changed every one hundred thousand kilometres? We could change our skin, bones, heart, and organs, but the counter of our humanity would never be at zero. Cosmetic surgery and a new car: Same desire as new-found virginity. Same illusion.

Good God, I thought, I'm going to die. It hit me all of a sudden. I'm going to die. Not today, not tomorrow, not even soon, I hope. But it would always be too soon. I can already see my death facing me; it bares the name of my children who will outlive me to die in turn, years later. By giving them life, we give them the gift of death, and if you really think about it, it was unacceptable, the worst of all scandals.

We had to live with death and tell it stories at night to put it to sleep. We had to stroke its hair. We had to look death in the eyes and say: I love you.

I hurried to take a shower so Josef wouldn't have to wait; Josef, who was thirteen years old and who, in order to survive, had given death. That's how it is perpetuated. The only normalcy that we have the right to aspire to is to die at the hands of fate or from illness rather than by a bullet shot by a lost kid. I hated war. I hated what it had done to Josef, to Viktor and his parents, and to Jana. War in the name of what? In the name of God? It's substituting yourself for him, to exercise in his place the power that was attributed to him. In the name of a culture? It's more like losing that culture only to benefit another, warring one: sharing with the enemy. For money? Power? Sure. Give a weapon to a child and he'll rule his school in no time, at the risk of having fewer and fewer subjects to push around.

Give him a weapon and you make him a monster. Declare war and you'll have hundreds, thousands of monsters. That's how it goes. So? Say no to war? Then you'd have to say no to new cars and cosmetic surgery. You'd have to say no to everything that conceals wear, fatigue, frailty – our simple, *condemned* mortal condition.

I finished dressing and was about to leave when it occurred to me to check my e-mails. I hadn't received anything. However, I had left my sent messages window open and took a few seconds to reread what I had written to Florence less than three days earlier.

I am still, and will always be, the little boy hunting seal
between the two apple trees in the snow-filled backyard. And
I'll never be armed with anything other than a measly
broomstick.

I couldn't believe my eyes. I was furious. Who was this man refusing to age and grasping at images from his childhood as if he was none the wiser? What had he learned from his entire existence? Or had he lived in vain?

I sat down at the keyboard and typed furiously beneath the original text.

Always means nothing. What I was is not what I will be. I
am no longer a little boy and I'm done hunting seals. A broom
handle is one weapon too many. I accept the idea of being
happy.
I love you.
P.S. Don't kiss the children for me. It's up to me to do it. I'll
be home soon.

I sent the whole thing off and proceeded downstairs to join Josef. I had an idea. In this whirlwind of events in which I felt perfectly useless, who could I really help? To whom could I reach out? Who needed it most?

***

"Josef," I said, "I have a favour to ask of you."

"Go ahead."

"I want to meet Rosalind."

He almost choked on his wine. He wiped his moustache and his chin with the back of his hand.

"I don't know . . ."

"You know everything. You must know where she is."

"But since she's no longer . . ."

"It's not a legal step, it's a human one. She's a young woman who suffered immensely, and although I represent the one who killed her child, I'd like to help her. My profession isn't entirely representative of who I am. I think you can identify with that."

Josef looked at me without blinking. He seemed to be thinking, as if a fierce contradictory battle was unfolding within him.

"I beg of you."

He was sighing now. His decision was made and he seemed more sad than relieved.

"OK," he said. "But I'm warning you, you're not going to like it."

"Who likes suffering?" I asked.

"You'd be surprised," answered Josef. And he emptied his glass.

END OF THE GAME

Madness had taken over the world and we were in the world and we were in madness. I had rejoined our forces, leaving Manu's body baking in the summer sun. Along the way, I had armed myself from the cadavers and the bullets that whizzed by my ears didn't have the power to reach me. I was condemned to live to feel pain, loss and regret. I was condemned to live to feel the death of others in my own living flesh, right into the grain of my dreams.

The battle was lost. We had fought in retreat like wild beasts before a fire, in confusion, using claws and teeth to go faster. On the roads riddled with agitated runaways, a rain of metal pounded down, and flashes of fire, a fog of powder, and a thundering of shells.

I had found Mistral by chance. Or rather it was he who had found me. He was shaking me by the arm and yelling in my ears for several seconds before I understood who he was and what he wanted from me. I saw the others, from the sawmill, black with soot, with crazed looks, clasping their weapons as though they were going to kiss them.

Yelling and slapping, Mistral tried to keep us together, in a sort of caricature of a military unit, but bullets were coming from every direction and the dogs were at our heels, biting our calves.

The universe was turned inside out like a glove and showed its seams. The war was lost, we already knew that, we knew it without a doubt, we knew it to the point of fear. Fleeing the city, fleeing the faubourgs, fleeing by the road where, at every turn, heavy fire was directed against us. Along the way, we lost more men, wounded, killed or deserters, but what were they deserting? From the enemy we had stolen a jeep equipped with a machine gun, and we sprayed the thickets, houses, groves; any obstacle behind which danger could lie in wait. We tossed grenades behind us as if out of vengeance and in the hope that the fires would slow our pursuers. We were surfing on a wave of madness, on the crest itself. It lifted us, carried us, and it lasted, it didn't stop, it didn't want to stop. I remember a scream that accompanied our flight, a shrill scream that modulated in sync with the rhythm of the explosions and the staccato of the bursts. My scream.

My scream and the wave finally broke at the foot of the mountains. I looked up at the naked rock and the steep cliffs. The government troops weren't far behind.

"We have to climb," said Mistral.

"On foot?"

"Do you have wings, my angel?"

"Not yet."

In the end there were eight of us climbing, on hand and foot, up the first slopes, while bursts of rock ripped by enemy bullets tore up our faces. Up higher would be no lack of hiding places: holes, basins, caverns, fissures, crevasses and stone cathedrals. For hours on end we climbed, always higher, always farther into the heart of the chain, in air that became scarcer, exhausted, out of breath and out of heart, to end up crawling under piles of rock, waiting for death to come, fists clamped around the grip of our weapons.

But death didn't come. The government army had turned back. Death had lost our trail. We were alone with the sky, and we could finally sleep a dreamless slumber. The slumber of a beaten beast.

⟳⟲⟳⟲

Licking the water sweating from the cliff. Eating bitter marmot flesh. Dressing wounds with lichen. Eight men, still standing but pierced all over, skinned, trembling with fatigue. Most thought of one thing only: getting out, getting home. And if there was no more home, build another one. Pick up the thread of their lives that had been cut. Rossi, Oscar, Vlad and Youri, mostly, but Stitch too, and Karim. Two defeats were enough for them. Suddenly, their previous condition that had so enraged them seemed desirable again. But wounds needed time to heal.

To make fire in a country without wood, we had to gather the dried feces of animals, big and small, even our own, that we lay out in the sun on scalding rocks. Mistral was remarkable. He exerted himself. He seemed to be at the service of those he commanded. Sinewy and rake-thin, he willingly gave up his rations to those who were going mad from hunger. To the others, he spoke softly, with dignified words. He was blowing on the embers of revolt. He would say, "The combat continues. Every day, others are rising to reclaim justice."

He said, "What they took from us, our land, our dignity, our culture, regardless of whether they robbed us one hundred or a thousand years ago. The age of the crime never exonerates the blame. Everything that goes wrong in the world stems from not being master of your own house."

Most listened to him because there was nothing else to do. As for me, I stayed for hours on end, sitting there and looking at the mountains. This lunar landscape crawled with life. The animals seemed happy. However, slightly lower down they would have thrived. Like them, I wanted nothing that wasn't of my lot. I looked at the shadows change, lengthen and then shorten. At night, the sky was extraordinarily pure and I contemplated it, lying on my back while sucking on a pebble to fool my thirst. I was nothing but a tiny insignificant point on the surface of another tiny insignificant point gravitating around a star among billions of stars drowning in an infinity of nothing. My thirty-something years of life weren't even a bat of an eyelash in the universe's existence. And yet, I had put so much energy into living and loving. But everything I had loved had been ripped away from me and I was left with only the painful memory – like the luminous echo remaining of a few dead stars, reaching me here on earth. What I see is already dead. What I love is already dead.

The owl's hooting startled me. I propped myself up on my elbows, searching the night. A field mouse had just met its end in the darkness and in nature's perfect indifference.

I rose and walked towards our camp, our hole. A fire of feces warmed a grass soup. Mistral had finished with his speeches for the evening. Rossi was sharpening his knife on a rock. Stitch seemed hypnotized by the flames. The others were sleeping. The men didn't want to fight anymore. Mistral turned to me.

"Will you come?"

"Yes."

What did it matter?

To describe the weeks that followed, the newspapers spoke of terror campaigns. Why? Reality is much simpler. If every day, in the field, the war was getting its fill of blood, it was because peace was already being negotiated in the headquarters of power. The two camps tried to rival each other in savageness in order to provide their leaders with the power of persuasion that they needed. The massacre of innocents could be worth a minister. The takeover of an oil facility could result in political impunity. At the end of the game, the opposition's true power lay not in the capacity to win the war, but rather in the power to stop the atrocities. That is, if there were still atrocities to stop.

We had followed Mistral down from the mountains to meet up, after nights of walking, with a Militia camp where the dispersed forces from across the region had assembled. There we found Commander Cousteau, as well as other officers whose names and titles I didn't know, no more than I knew their roles in this whole story. In any event, they seemed very busy and professionally unrolled maps on tables that they studied late into the night under the glow of the lamps.

However, the camp revealed a distressing scene. We weren't even a thousand men surrounding a village wedged between three bare hills and a muddy river. Ill-equipped men carrying deficient weapons and low moral. Only beings gifted with a powerful sense of self-suggestion could see in that the flourishing seeds of power rather that the rotting remains of a routed army. We hadn't been there for twenty-four hours when Rossi and the others had taken off without a word. Three days later, of the almost one thousand men at the start, barely half remained.

Those who stayed were the strongest, the most determined, the most idealistic or the sickest. There were certified psychopaths among the lot. Never look a gift horse in the mouth . . . The flag of the rebellion would be waved very high by those men.

I was resting when Mistral entered the tent, followed by Commander Cousteau.

"We have to get out of here," said Mistral.

"They're coming," said Cousteau.

"Where are we going?" I asked, even though I didn't care.

"All over the place," replied the commander.

The idea was to break up our few hundred men into tiny independent guerrilla units. In the absence of an army to direct, the command would dissolve. The only order:

"Keep causing chaos, Chef," Cousteau said to me.

He was solemn, serious, grave. He took me in his arms and gave me a long hug.

"Goodbye, my son."

"Goodbye, Commander."

He had tears in his eyes. He had believed in his war and the possibility of victory. Anyway. He died a month later during a skirmish in the north.

Under Mistral's orders, with three other men I didn't know, we left the camp one October night. The first light snowflakes of the season fluttered in the sky, revolving in slow motion, as if refusing to touch the ground and melt. Snow also wants to live forever, I suppose, just like anything else.

The snow also made me think that the war was merely a year old, even though it had become my whole life.

What else could be said? We hit to the left and to the right, never from the front. It wasn't war anymore, but organized terrorism. We had travelled the province to blow up power plants, grain silos, railroad tracks and food warehouses. We were neither numerous nor powerful enough to attack military targets so we beat up on civilians, and too bad if the victims were precisely those for whom we were supposed to fight.

After each attempt, we returned to the Great Forest, the only place in the world where Mistral felt at home. For years, he had hidden weapons and food supplies there. I understood that what was a nightmare to some was Mistral's dream, and for him, the war was an end in itself.

One night, a patrol interrupted our meal. I jumped on my weapon and rolled far from the fire, among the dancing shadows of the foliage. But someone had targeted me and I had to move deeper into the forest. There was gunfire, footsteps and treading. I heard Mistral barking his orders.

I began to crawl around in a circle in order to take the patrol from behind. But as I crawled, the noises moved away. I moved towards the fire. No one was there.

I went off in their pursuit, but it was as though the patrol had disappeared into thin air. There was no more noise, not a gunshot, not a sign of life. In precaution, I went back to the camp and settled in as best I could, just beyond the circle of light, back against a tree trunk and weapon in my lap.

I waited. If Mistral escaped the government troops, I thought, he would do like me and we would find each other a little later.

The fire went out due to a lack of fuel. Only the embers under the ashes gave off a faint glow. No one came. The forest had reclaimed its serenity, little by little. I could hear it living around me. I fell asleep.

I woke in a jolt just before dawn. The light was grey and the camp was still empty. I yelled:

"Mistral!"

I waited a long time for an answer that didn't come. I was alone.

I stirred the last embers and blew on them to ignite the fire. Flames soon spread, bright and clear, and I sat on the stump to wait a little longer.

I waited for hours. It had been so long since I had been alone. I was hungry. I rummaged through my pockets searching for something to eat. My fingers felt Manu's letters that I had placed in a plastic bag to protect them. I took them out. On the envelopes, I recognized the writing as if it was my own. Letters to Jana. They were sealed. Manu's tongue had moistened these envelopes. All these letters, about fifteen in all, several pages each. I had never opened them. What could he have found to write about with his round, childlike scrawl? A single word, repeated a thousand times over? Love? A single word to say everything? He was so careful to conserve paper. He had so much to say to his Jana.

And as for me, who did I write to?

I stood up. No one else would come here. I was alone and my war was over. I looked around me. To the north, a road, villages, men and women. To the east, mountains. To the west, the city. To the south, nothing but the Great Forest covering thousands of kilometres.

I placed the letters back in my pockets. I spread the fire with my boot. I turned to the south and, without a moment's hesitation, I began to walk.

I went into the forest, never to come out.

ROSALIND

The door opened allowing us to discover a tall, slightly plump woman with dyed blond hair, who wore her fifty-something lustful years well. She moved aside to let us in and then moved out onto the landing.

"Has she eaten?" asked Josef.

"A little. Not much. She's sleeping."

"Thank you."

"It's nothing. You know where to find me."

He had to get up on the tips of his toes to kiss her, and then Josef closed the door. It was a tiny little apartment on the sixth floor of a high-rise apartment building that had seen better days. In the hallway, a rust-coloured carpet showed its filling, and two out of three wall-blocks were missing. The building was old, worn, slightly poor, but it wasn't squalid.

The woman who had greeted us, with her bright red lipstick and large breasts contained in a corset that was too tight, had a nice smile. When he kissed her, she had squeezed Josef's cheeks between her two hands as if they were cream-filled pastries.

"This way," said Josef.

He wasn't himself. Or rather, maybe he was. He had spoken very quietly, and he walked, careful not to make noise.

The vestibule gave onto a room that combined a kitchenette, with a table and two chairs, and farther over, a living room furnished with a couch and television. On the couch, I noticed a pillow and a carefully folded blanket. To the left, the door that must open onto the bedroom was closed. Before opening it, Josef turned to me.

"I . . ."

But he couldn't finish his sentence, as if he had come upon an invisible obstacle.

"Try to understand," he ended up saying, and he opened the door.

Illuminated by the faint blue light of a night light, Rosalind slept, her face turned towards us, an arm hanging over the side of the bed. How old was she already? Eighteen or nineteen? I couldn't remember. But she could have been thirty, because despite the peace of sleep, her face bore the stigmas of misery. She must have been very pretty before. She had black hair, cut very short and messy. Her reddened eyelids bounced as if her eyes were rolling underneath. She breathed while emitting a slight whistling sound. A string of saliva trickled from the corner of her lips.

On the night table beside her, a candle, a spoon, silver paper, a rubber band, new syringes in their packaging, and several small bags filled with white powder. I looked at Josef, alarmed. I approached Rosalind and knelt to look at the inside of her arm. It was covered in needle pricks, some old, others more recent. Those that needed it had been disinfected.

"Why?" I asked Josef. "Why?"

"It's what she is. You know that. A drug addict."

"Not like this."

"Lower. You're going to wake her."

I pointed to the nightstand.

"How can she afford that?"

Josef didn't answer.

"Who pays for it? And why?"

He remained silent.

"Who sees the advantage of keeping a young woman drugged from morning until night? Who?"

But he didn't answer. He chewed his moustache looking me straight in the eyes – an impenetrable look, as if I was very far away and he couldn't hear me, or too close, a pile of colour stains in motion that filled the horizon.

I stood up. At the back of the room, near the window, there was an easel. Leaning against the wall were canvases of all sizes. Brushes in a pot. Tubes of colour on a low table. I looked at Josef.

"You live here!" I said. "It's you! You're the one drugging her! You're paying for her shit every day! You're the one who's killing her!"

"Not so loud!" he roared.

He took me by the arm before I had a chance to react and dragged me from the room, whose door he closed with great care.

"You!" I accused.

"I told you to try and understand."

"I understand everything."

"Nothing at all. You have no idea."

Rage prevented me from thinking, a primal anger, a sense of failure, an atavistic pain.

"All of your speeches!" I threw at him out of spite.

"Which ones? Those for or those against? Unless it was those in between? Listen to me for a minute . . ."

He took a step towards me. I backed away.

"No!" I said. "You are a killer, and that's exactly what you're doing. You're killing. Only this time, you're doing it dose by dose."

"Yes," he said. "You're right. I am a killer. And I was asked to get rid of her."

"Who?"

"You know very well. You've suspected it for quite some time. But tell me, is she dead?"

"It's the same."

"No. I picked her out of a sordid hole, a syringe planted in her arm. You know what was in that syringe? Mouthwash. She was lying in her own shit. I carried her in my arms and brought her back here. I spoon-fed her. I treated her wounds."

"And you supply her poison."

"I make sure that she isn't in too much pain. I spread out the injections, I slowly reduce the doses. When she's strong enough, I'll try to wean her. She is so weak, withdrawal would have killed her. Do you think there's a place for her somewhere? Do you think the hospitals would free up a bed for her? We're more than happy to let her kind die. It's cheaper. So yes, I supply her heroin with the money I was given to make sure she was never heard of again. And that's exactly what's going to happen. She won't be heard of again. I'll make sure of it."

"You're going to keep her locked up here?"

"I'll go away with her if she wants. Elsewhere. Far away. She'll make a new life and I'll help her."

"Love at first sight?"

"Don't be ironic. It doesn't suit you. You know very well what I mean. Build instead of destroy. Help instead of hinder. Heal instead of wound."

I went to the window to look at the city. Everything seemed so peaceful when seen from above! I pressed my forehead against the glass. How many inhabitants were there in this city? One hundred thousand? One hundred thousand births, one hundred thousand deaths, and in between, this. My anger subsided. In its place, I felt an immense weariness.

"But why, Josef?"

"I don't know," he said. "A soldier doesn't question orders. He carries them out."

"And yet Rosalind is alive."

"Yes. I've had enough. I've seen too much. I don't know if it's age or fatigue, or simply if I've reached my limit . . . I'm not eleven years old anymore. And now, I have a choice. It took a long time for me to figure that out. I think I'm ready to give up my career of weapons to begin my life as a man."

I indicated the bedroom door.

"What can I do?"

"Nothing," Josef answered. "I'll take care of it. I promise you that. I'll watch over her. I won't let her down."

"So you don't need this anymore," I said, reaching out my hand to take the automatic pistol that he had slid through his belt.

Josef stiffened but let me complete my gesture.

"No," he said, as though with regret. "I guess I won't need it anymore. But you don't need it either, I can assure you."

"That's what we'll see."

I moved towards the exit. I opened the door.

"Goodbye, Josef."

"Goodbye, Mr. Chevalier."

"François."

Josef smiled.

"Be careful, François."

And I walked out of his life forever. I hope he succeeded. I hope he's living somewhere in a peaceful country and that Rosalind has gone back to school, and that their respective wounds are slowly scarring over. I hope.

As for me, I had made a decision. I was going to give up this whole affair and go home. But before I did that, I had to have a clean conscience and notify Viktor Rosh that I would no longer be representing him, not that this would make a big difference in the current state of things.

First, I made my way to Cevitjc's office. The bouncer who acted as his secretary told me that he couldn't see me at the moment. I couldn't care less. I entered his office without knocking. Cevitjc was reading the newspaper, smoking a cigar. He was the same as the first time I saw him. But not me. I was a different man.

"Mr. Chevalier!" he exclaimed with his customary cheerfulness.

"Mr. Cevitjc!" I exclaimed in return. "A few questions for you."

"Of course."

"Who are you working for? Why do you want to get rid of Rosalind? Why doesn't her child's murder appear on the charge sheet? What's the real reason for this trial? What role was I supposed to play? Who will benefit from Viktor Rosh's conviction?"

The smile disappeared from Cevitjc's face as if it had been wiped with a wet rag. He rose from his chair and leaned his fists on the varnished wood of his huge desk.

"I think," he said, "that we have nothing more to say to one another."

In this way, he confirmed that he was tangled up in all of this.

"Oh yes," I answered. "We have lots of things to talk about, and I suggest you tell me right now."

I pointed Josef's pistol at him. Cevitjc sat back down, looking surprised.

"Are we going to do this the hard way or the easy way?" I asked.

"You're making a mistake, Mr. Chevalier."

"It's about time, Mr. Cevitjc."

He was sweating now. He didn't take his eyes off my weapon. He probably didn't doubt my inexperience when seeing my white, rigid knuckles. And that didn't comfort him, on the contrary.

"You should calm yourself," he said to me.

"The hard way or the easy way?" I repeated, waving the gun around.

"Who cares!" he yelled.

"Let's try the easy way. Who are you working for?"

"I'm paid by the State. I work for the State."

"As a lawyer?"

"Not only."

"Why would you want to get rid of Rosalind?"

"Some people in high places seem to believe that she wouldn't make a good impression at the trial. Her lifestyle, her appearance. They believe that she could hurt the prosecutors instead of helping them. But they were also afraid that she would show up uninvited and turn the trial into a circus show."

"That's a reason to kill a poor girl?"

"Who said anything about killing her?"

"Don't play with me."

"The word 'kill' was never uttered."

"Why does her child's murder no longer appear on the charge sheet?"

Cevitjc sighed. He took the time to relight his cigar before answering me. He was regaining his strength, the little bugger. He probably thought I would never have the courage to pull the trigger. He was wrong there.

"Listen, I'll tell you everything. But don't go making illusions for yourself. It won't change anything. This isn't a trial for war crimes, but rather a political trial. Viktor Rosh was chosen because he is Evil incarnate. The rebels are the forces of Evil. It's not about condemning a man, but about discrediting a party. Rosalind's story didn't fit in perfectly with the sketch of a terrorist who is ready to do anything to take power. My employers didn't want a spectacle spoiled by an alienation defence, however temporary. Rosh's action of killing Rosalind's child created a gap in the appearance of a cold and calculating killer that we wanted to pass off as the truth. So, we had to remove Rosalind from circulation and remove the murder of her child from the charge sheet. It's simple. As for the real reason for this trial, it's just as simple: discredit the opposition and show the international community that the party in power doesn't hesitate to clean house. That's the reason we called on you. Yes, us, not Viktor Rosh. We believed that the presence of a foreign lawyer would draw the media from here and there, which we weren't wrong about. By asking you to defend the Monster, we were targeting two objectives. The first was to reassure foreign observers that we were respecting the rules of our judicial system. The second objective was even more important: by giving a foreigner the task of defending the Monster, we wanted to promote a sense of indignation among the population regarding the way we are treated by wealthy countries. What gives them the right! They defend killers and let us die of hunger! Well, you get the picture. A jingoist population is always easier to manipulate. And the international community, guilty through you of clumsy interference, would perhaps resign itself to open its purse strings. But," he sighed, "now we'll have to do without you. What a pity! Well, you know everything. But it goes without saying that I know nothing and that this conversation never happened."

"You're a bastard."

"I'm a politician, Mr. Chevalier."

"Not me."

I stood up. Cevitjc was smiling again. I pointed the gun at his forehead. His smile froze and, without a single muscle coming into play, changed into a horrible grimace. He was scared now, oh yes, he was scared.

"Between Viktor Rosh and you, who is the most monstrous?" I asked. "No! Don't answer that. It's no longer my jurisdiction. Consider this my letter of resignation."

And I pulled on the trigger.

"Bang! Bang!" I said.

Cevitjc had closed his eyes. The pistol had only produced a metal click. I let it fall on the desk and it scratched the surface. From my pocket, I took out the magazine that I had been careful to remove from the pistol after leaving Josef, and threw it in Cevitjc's lap. He jumped. On the front of his pants, I saw a urine stain that was spreading.

I didn't feel better.

I left Cevitjc's office. I hailed a taxi and was driven to the prison of M. I was escorted to the same small room and I sat in the same small chair right in front of the same white wooden table. While waiting for Viktor Rosh, I took out my pen and a piece of paper. I wanted to put my ideas in order, take a few notes. I wanted to tell the Monster everything. Tell him what I had done, what I had understood. Explain to him the kind of vipers' nest in which he was at the centre, held captive.

He entered and sat in front of me without saying a word. And I told him everything. I told him about his brother over in Africa. I told him about Josef, the observatory and Maria. I told him about the men from the sawmill and the nights at the bistro. I told him about Jana. I told him about Rosalind. I told him about Cevitjc. And when I was finally finished, he still hadn't opened his mouth. I had done everything that I could have done. I readied to leave.

"Oh!" I said suddenly. "I almost forgot. Jana wants her letters."

I stood to move towards the door, and it was at that moment that I heard him. I heard his voice for the first time.

"Wait," he said.

I waited. And in a flat voice, a hoarse and distant voice, a voice come from very far, the Monster began to tell his story.

THE TREE OF POSSIBILITIES

I walked for a long time. I think I remember a night without fire on a bed of moss. Maybe there were others, I don't remember very well anymore. It was at the end of the second or third day that I found my house. It was a small, rocky promontory covered with trees and at the foot of which opened not a grotto, but rather a crevice, as tall and as wide as a man, and as deep as two. It dug like a corner into the heart of a stone. I fashioned a door of supple branches, camouflaged by leaves. Cracks in the ceiling of my den allowed the smoke to escape in thin imperceptible ribbons through the stone's thickness.

I immediately organized my life with a serious lack of passion. I needed a bed to isolate the floor of my shelter, to gather a large quantity of dry wood and to find something to eat. I sometimes stopped my work to watch the squirrels play. With a branch from a walnut tree and a thin band of fabric taken from my coat, I made a small bow. Sharpened sticks served as arrows. With patience, I killed two squirrels that were my first meal and whose skins I kept after scraping off the fat with my knife.

I knew I could survive anything.

With other bands of fabric coated with squirrel fat, I made collars that I laid out in the surrounding area. I didn't want to use my weapon, which wasn't adapted for hunting, but I would be happy to have it in a pinch and I kept it at home on a bed of dry leaves. If it was the season for it, I would have eaten nothing but plants and roots. I had seen enough blood. But those scruples didn't last long. I had to live.

I wasn't any less cautious. I avoided the clearings where, from the air, I could be seen, and even in the middle of the day I never built a fire outdoors.

At the end of twenty days or so, I had enough squirrel and rabbit skins to make myself a sort of cape that I had sewn using a bone needle and fine leather laces that I had cut out. As of then, I was almost never cold and I could enjoy the rediscovered solitude a little more. I had plans. In the spring, I wanted to dig a pit covered with pilings to capture a deer or maybe even a bear. I needed skins to make clothes, and I needed fat to soak a wick to light my needlework at night.

It was February, maybe even the beginning of March. The sun climbed a little higher in the sky every day, and in the air wafted the smells of spring.

From a bark plate I ate a gruel of rabbit, devoid of salt or herbs, that I had cooked in my old dented lunch pail. I took pleasure in this undressed meat, I who, all my life, had sought to perfect my recipes, found the true meaning of food, which is to take the life of another in one's mouth by tearing its flesh with one's teeth. I didn't give a thread of fat the chance to escape. It seemed to me that in this way, I paid homage to the beast that I had sacrificed for my own survival. I felt its strength penetrate me, its warmth spread through my stomach while high in the sky buzzards circled in search of prey.

I didn't think. My brain no longer functioned with words, but with sensations. Thus developed in me a primal vocabulary of scents, colours, textures, heat and cold, of well-being and urgency. I didn't feel the need to speak out loud to convince myself of my own humanity. I existed, that's all.

Then it was spring. In one night, the stream that had been stuck in the ice and in which I rinsed my billy-can, transformed into a torrent. From above poured the meltwater, hauling seeds, mushrooms, fruit pits and fish no bigger than a finger. With violence that belonged only to it, nature shook itself free of the snow that had covered it and extended its twigs to the sun. The earth was splitting with everything that wanted to gain access to light. The buds exploded in the air. I relieved myself of my cape and then my coat. My skin called for sun as well.

Bare-chested, bearded, hairy, I hunted every day because every day you have to survive. During the winter evenings, I had made a bigger, more powerful bow, and about ten fletched arrows equipped with bone tips. It's while hunting partridge that I saw signs of the bear. He had sharpened his claws against the trunk of a tall pine tree three hundred metres from my dwelling. From then on, I monitored his tracks, his droppings, his habits. Had it come down from the mountains to get closer to the trout streams, or rather had it come up to escape the biting insects that came down in a cloud, buzzing around everything with warm blood? Over the following days, it seemed that the bear was marking its territory and that it overlapped mine. I had had enough. Now I could dig my pit.

I made a fairly rudimentary wooden shovel, and then I selected the site: the bear often passed along the border of a clearing in a place where the ground seemed loose. But I wasn't kidding myself. I was going to encounter matting of roots and rock. I would have to dig deep, maybe two metres or a little less. The beast, falling on the tapered pilings, would impale itself using its own weight. At least in theory.

I dug for about two hours a day, every day for long enough that it was summer when I was finished. I had to move the pit three times when faced with the stubborn rocks that met my shovel.

One morning towards the end, while I was clipping a root the size of an arm, I heard the sound of voices. I hoisted myself up to see. In the clearing, two children stumbled towards me. One of them, no more than ten years old, was crying his eyes out. The other, a little older, carried a small calibre rifle. They were both filthy, their clothing torn, and on their faces and arms were scrapes, some of which were infected. Kids who had gone out hunting and had become lost in the forest. For how long?

I could have disappeared into my pit and let them pass without being seen. But they had lost all sense of direction and were plunging deeper into the forest, turning their backs on civilization.

Why did I show myself to them? If I hadn't done anything, would the authorities have organized a search to find them? In so doing, I would have been throwing myself to the lions. The truth is, I emerged from the pit because I had had enough of death and I was thinking of Andreï.

I must not have been very nice to look at, but when they saw me, the children ran over screaming right away. They were both talking at once.

"We're lost, mister."

"We're hungry, mister."

"My little brother is sick, mister."

"We're hungry, mister."

I had a piece of dried meat that I threw to them. They shared it right away.

Then, I held out my canteen. They each took a long drink. They started to speak again. I don't know why exactly, at the time it seemed like a good idea – I hadn't spoken in such a long time! – I pointed to my throat saying no with my head, as though I couldn't utter a sound. That made the children quiet.

Then, I pointed to my chest with my finger, and with my hands and head, I tried to make them understand that I didn't exist, that I wasn't there, that they hadn't seen me. Their eyes opened wide, as if it was a game. They finally understood that I was offering them a deal which they quickly accepted. Then, I pointed to them, and moving my index and middle fingers to mimic walking, I showed them a brook in the forest. They just had to follow it all the way, I motioned to them. They would end up on an old forest road that crossed others. They always had to veer right. I drew a map on the ground. To the north, I insisted with both hands. To the right, and head north!

They would really have liked it if I had gone with them. They were scared. But I had already done too much. Grunting, I signalled for them to leave. They crossed the clearing, turning around often. Just before reaching the brook, the younger one waved his hand to say goodbye to me.

I waved in return.

Of course, I had to move immediately. But I had fled enough. I lived in a hole of rock lost in the forest: from here, where was I to flee?

For a few days, I was on guard. In the morning, I opened the door to my den with circumspection, expecting to see an entire battalion pointing their guns at me. But no. Instead I heard the sound of a stream splashing down over the round, polished rocks. Above, the birds' songs gave way to war games. The wind rustling through the treetops. The peace of the untouched forest.

It was the first days of summer and I was gorging myself with young shoots whose sap seemed to have euphoric virtues. There was no place in nature for worry or anguish. This didn't mean that I didn't have to think about the coming days. I wanted the bear's skin and fat to diffuse the coldness of the imminent winter.

I finished digging the pit. The pilings with fire-hardened tips were planted solidly, and then I covered the hole with a slat-shade. Of course, the bear walked around it several times without ever agreeing to fall in. He knew the area. He had seen me working. He was suspicious. I had to bait him.

As soon as they were ripe enough, I picked a pile of berries that I placed in the centre of the slat-shade. The birds had a feast.

I tried the raw livers of three partridges. In the morning, the livers had disappeared but not the slat-shade, which remained intact. I wasn't any more successful with pieces of meat and the brain of my rabbits. Raw or cooked, meat held no interest for my bear. However, an ant colony and several thousand flies had a fabulous time.

What could I bait him with? What did my bear want to eat? It was a nice challenge for a cook. But aren't bears omnivores like us? How do they differ from the lumberjacks that I fed daily at the sawmill? Between the bear and Rossi, in the end, what was the difference? Which led to the following question: How would I succeed in luring the real Rossi to the centre of a trap that he suspected existed? What could I have used to tempt him enough so that he would take the risk?

It was clear. First I needed a container, as hermetic as possible.

Using embers, I managed to dig out a deep enough hole in a log, which held approximately three litres. With greased skins and leather laces, I fashioned a tight-fitting cover. Then I picked berries. I chose only the ripest, the sweetest. I needed a lot and it took me three days.

I crushed the fruit from my harvest without pity, mixed it, reduced it to a purée, and with this purée I filled the hollowed log. I adjusted the cover and then, at the foot of the cliff beside my dwelling, in a cranny that the sun never lit, I dug another hole in which to bury the hollowed log, which I then covered with earth. There was nothing left for me to do but wait, tending to my other occupations and resisting the temptation to check too soon on the results of my experiment.

At the end of fifteen days, I couldn't wait any longer. I unearthed the thing, removed the cover and dunked my finger. I tasted it. In fermenting, the fruit sugars had produced a sort of alcoholized pulp that must have been three percent. Not bad. But for Rossi, not enough. I had decided to name the bear so, in memory of my old buddy who it resembled.

I buried the hollowed log and waited another week at the end of which I exhumed it once again. It was maybe six or seven percent now. I estimated that it would never go any further because of the low sugar content in wild berries. It would have to do.

I poured a good litre of the alcoholized pulp into my bark plate, which I placed in the centre of the slat-shade, exactly vertical to the middle piling, and then went home. There were two litres left over that I reserved for other attempts. I could have drunk them myself – I was an omnivore as well – but I worried that drunkenness would lead me to the narrow paths skirting the vertiginous chasms at the bottom of which milled about nightmarish beasts. The advantage of life in the great outdoors was a dreamless, refreshing, functional sleep.

In the morning, I was wakened by an almost human scream that stretched all the way to a tearing, mounting into a sharp pitch. I had the time to leave my den and travel three-quarters of the distance that separated me from the pit before the scream changed into a growl so low, so muted that I seemed to sense it through the pores of my skin.

The thin slat-shade was staved in. I unsheathed my chef's knife and cautiously leaned over to look into the pit.

It was almost black. Its pelt glimmered in the shadow like silk. Two hundred kilos of muscle, fat, claws and teeth. The tip of a piling had pierced its chest and came out through its shoulder. Bubbles of blood sweated from the wound, swelled and fell with each breath. The bear couldn't turn its head, but it watched me with a black, tearful eye. It was still growling, although less and less loud, like a storm moving farther away.

I picked up a solid, stick of hard wood and beat it on the head with all my strength, over and over, until its eye became fixed and stopped staring at me. I felt no pleasure from this victory, quite the contrary. Leaning over it, I reached out my hand and stroked its shoulder. My fingers felt its strength, still warm, the suppleness, the intelligence of the body adapted to its surroundings. I stayed like that for a moment to catch my breath.

Now I had to get it out of there.

This proved to be impossible. I hadn't thought of everything. Without rope and a hoist, the beast's weight itself exceeded my physical capacity, especially if you added the resistance of the piling on which it had impaled himself, and along which it continued to sink.

I removed my shirt and descended into the pit. I had no choice but to carve it up on the spot, in this diminutive space that soon filled with the bear's blood when I began to empty it, by incising with my knife what I believed to be its femoral artery. I opened it from belly to throat to remove its entrails which I placed at the edge of the pit on a carpet of leaves. Only then did I attempt to skin it. But you don't skin a bear the same way you skin a rabbit, removing the skin like a tight sweater. It was a thankless, bloody and frustrating task, complicated by the presence of the piling and my own lack of experience. I was obsessed with the idea of preserving the fur close to intact, and the care with which I proceeded no doubt explained why I heard nothing before it was too late. A voice ordered:

"Come out of there. Hands in the air."

Approximately ten submachine guns appeared over the pit. The metallic clicking of the bullets engaging in the barrel confirmed the seriousness of the situation and the urgency of obeying. I extricated myself from the pit and stood up. I heard the click of another order. Someone had taken a photograph. Surely you've seen it. It's famous. Before I was even asked, I gave up my knife.

Later on, I learned that it was July 8th. I had lived for close to seven months all alone in the forest. I would still be there if I hadn't been arrested. But the lost children had spoken of this strange mute living in the woods. The story made the rounds of the schools before reaching the ears of the authorities. They had hoped to capture Mistral. Many were disappointed upon discovering my true identity.

They didn't learn it from me. I was led, covered in the bear's blood, all the way to the prison of M. I was interrogated. I was threatened. I was hit. They finally assigned a lawyer to me but I still said nothing. There was nothing to say, nothing to explain, words couldn't describe reality, only mislead it, reduce it, deface it. I wasn't what those words would say of me. Since then, I have lived in prison as I lived in my den, in silence and in solitude. I am fed and clothed. The pallet that serves as my bed is more comfortable than the layer of leaves in the rock hole over there. I miss the sun. I accept it. And then one day, you arrived, but you were like the others. You had nothing but words and never the reality behind the words. And you came back, and it was still more hot air.

But now it's different. You are here in front of me, and you tell me that you're no longer my lawyer, and you tell me about my loved ones, those I knew and loved, and the others.

You saw Jana. Without Jana, I would never have spoken to you, but you had to understand all of this. You had to understand why I am here and why Manu's letters stayed over there, buried at the foot of the cliff beside my home. I would have had a thousand uses for the plastic bag, but I wanted to keep those letters intact forever, because their love was so strong, despite Andreï and his blood mixed with sugar and despite the hole in Manu's forehead, right above his eyebrow.

You have to tell her, please. Tell Jana. She can't think that I threw them away. Nothing else matters since she is still alive. I didn't know. I didn't know that Jana was still alive because all the others are dead.

I don't know, Mr. Chevalier, how to explain this. Sometimes I feel like I'm the last living being on Earth . . ."

THE INSURMOUNTABLE

We remained quiet for a long time. I contemplated my stiffening hands. The long speech explained nothing. Viktor Rosh could have become someone else one hundred times over in his life. The hot dog king, for example; what was so shameful about that? And what would have happened if his big brother had taken care of him rather than take to heart the abstract peace cause? Where would he be now? At the zoo? On a picnic with his children? In love with a woman that he would never tire of looking at?

What could you add to all that? The world was sick and Viktor Rosh was merely a symptom. How would punishing him change the problem? However, he had to be punished, right?

By pure professional habit, I had taken notes throughout Viktor Rosh's discourse. What purpose did they serve now? I was certainly not going to pass them on to Cevitjc so that he could use them against the one he was supposed to defend. Viktor Rosh was a man very much alone. He was also a horrible murderer, despite the candour of his narrative.

"What are you going to do?" I asked him finally.

He shrugged his shoulders.

"From what you've told me, I've already been condemned."

"Plead insanity."

"I'm not insane."

"But you're not of sound mind."

He looked at me, intrigued.

"Say that the war made you mad," I added.

"I don't think so."

I shook my head. Was I the one who was mad? Oh yes, in my own way, I was. But I wanted to recover my health.

"May I ask you a question? What happened at the observatory, the one from your childhood?"

He looked at me without understanding, and then his mouth stretched into a shy smile.

"Oh that! That's an old story."

"Your mother says that this experience changed you."

"I fell from up high."

"I'm referring to your state of mind."

"So am I. Do you remember being twelve years old?"

"Yes."

"I was a dreamer. Everything seemed possible. I was the centre of the world. I wanted to gaze into the telescope to see the stars up close. But what I saw were even more stars, so far away . . . I was dizzy. It was the sense of my insignificance."

"So you fell?"

"In a way."

"You *let* yourself fall?"

"Things are never as clear as that, don't you think?"

Was he playing with me? Who did he think he was fooling? Was he trying to convert his experience as a militiaman into a challenge to the stars? Was he trying to justify his murders by some sort of personal mysticism in which the sense of his own insignificance was applied to others, no matter who they were?

"So twenty-five years later, you set fire to another observatory filled with wounded and dead, is that right?"

I wasn't sure what I was getting at. But Rosh was looking at me without answering, which was an admission in itself. He closed his eyes. I imagined that he was playing back the scene, that he was hearing the screams, that he was contemplating the shower of sparks swirling around in the air.

"You see, there are things that you admit, and others that you keep quiet. You recognize a hierarchy of your crimes: you explain some and not others . . . And you claim that you aren't mad?"

"Can you stop with that!" he said, and he leaned over the table, grabbed the pen and paper out of my hands (I hadn't stopped taking notes), opened my jacket and stuffed it all into the inside pocket. "Stop behaving like a lawyer if you're no longer mine!"

The violence of his gesture startled me. I had had enough.

"OK," I said. "Plead insanity; it's your only chance before the court. But I know that you are no more insane than the next person. And you know it too. Only, you have made the choice. You have chosen to surmount the insurmountable. You have chosen to believe that a human life is nothing, unless it is close to you. Your love for Manu, for Jana, it's all very good, it's very touching. But it's always about *your* feelings, *your* agony. Because that's all that matters to you, right? The others are of no value unless you grant them one. That's the reason you were such a fearsome war machine. No feelings. You didn't love Maria. You loved the effect love had on you. You didn't love Manu. You loved loving him . . ."

"That's not fair!"

"I don't care. Why should I be fair? Are you? You described the bear's death in such luxurious detail! But the humans you've killed, you don't give them a second thought. What gives you the right? What gives you the right to decide who deserves to live and who dies?"

"The war . . ." he began.

"Thousands took part with a bit more restraint. You had the choice."

"That's not true – I didn't have the choice! You said it yourself. Power manipulates, kills and lies! I'm being given a trial that is lost before it's begun. You find that fair?"

"It's true, you can't repair one injustice with another. I am sorry that you are at the centre of a . . . conspiracy. But don't ask me to sympathize with you. It's not the government in power, nor the manager of the sawmill any more than Cevitjc who burned the injured alive at the observatory. You did. You, out of vengeance, sliced Leo Puritz's fingers. You assassinated Rosalind's child."

"No."

"You slit its throat with a knife to shut it up."

"No!"

"Not an enemy. A hungry baby! Rosalind's baby!"

"Stop talking about her!"

"Why? Because you're ashamed? That's new."

"Because I don't remember it."

He was shaking his head, leaning over the table, his eyes filled with tears.

"I don't remember it . . . I've searched, tried to remember, but I don't remember it . . ."

He lifted his eyes towards me.

"There were so many . . ."

"You're lying," I said. "How can anyone forget something like that? You're lying because you remember those moments very well when you stopped belonging to the human race. Only, you don't want to feel shame and regret. It's too painful, isn't it? It's too normal? This is where your humanity catches up with you. Oh no, you can't escape it. And I hope that this pain grows in you until you want to scream. But I doubt that will happen, and that's too bad. Regret would be the only way for you to recover a fragment of your lost humanity."

I was disgusted. I wanted to get out of there. I wanted to go home. But Viktor Rosh straightened up and his eyes shone with rage and indignation.

"You know nothing," he spat. "But perhaps one day you will, when the squadrons holding foreign power disembark in your homeland, assassinating all those you love, one by one. You will see hatred flourish. They'll take everything from you. They'll burn your home. They'll rape your wife while your children watch. Then they'll rape your children, and then they'll smash their heads against the wall and their brains will splatter all over you. Then, perhaps, only then will you be able to tell me: I understand. You will understand the desire to kill and the absence on Earth of any power that would be able to stop you. Then you'll be on the other side of the border, in a dimension exempt from the justice of men."

I stood. I had heard enough.

"The justice of men," I said, "is all that we have."

Rosh smiled as I moved towards the door. I knocked to call the guard.

"If ever that happens," I turned and said, "if ever war explodes in my homeland and my entire family is massacred,

I think I would take up arms. Yes. I would surely take up arms. But I would keep one name in mind, a name which I would repeat like a warning, and that I hope would prevent me from crossing that line."

"My name?" asked Rosh with an intolerable smile.

The door opened. I was already out.

"Rosalind."

ROSALIND

At nine years old, she is adorable with her red and white checked apron. At parties thrown by her parents, she serves, always smiling, content, and bubbly. No one sees her taking a sip here and there, and sucking on half-melted ice cubes rather than emptying the glasses in the kitchen sink.

At nine years old, she has a way of being drunk that passes for irresistible drollness.

At ten years old, her parents are slightly worried about her mood changes. Not much. The father drowns his worries in alcohol. The mother calms hers with pills.

At twelve years old, Rosalind spends more time out of the house than inside. When it is commented upon, she says, "Let me live."

For her, living meant drinking, smoking hash and sampling all sorts of pills that have all sorts of effects on her.

At thirteen years old, her mother dies in a car accident, her reflexes slowed by the sedatives. From then on, her father never sobers up, which suits Rosalind fine.

At fourteen years old, after a huge screaming match with her father, who discovers scruples a little too late, Rosalind leaves the house for good. She is happy because she is finally free.

She hangs out with seedy people who she calls her *friends*. They give her drugs in exchange for services she provides because she likes *it*.

She lives with girls and boys in a succession of tiny and filthy apartments, with lots of music and no heat. It's a perpetual party, a life of just getting by, filled with bursts of laughter, of get-togethers and incredible stories. One night, someone introduced her to the White Lady. It's love at first sight. It's as if giant hands were shaking the planet until everything was reinstated to the place that was initially intended for it. What a smile on Rosalind's face! She feels like an angel that has just understood what those things are on her back. Wings!

The next day, she is troubled. She's cold. She only sees ugliness, the humidity stains on the walls, the ring of dirt around the sink, the rips in the carpet covered in cigarette burns.

At fifteen years old, Rosalind loses twenty kilos. She floats in her boy's clothes. She uses a hand to lean against an alley wall and vomits on a pile of garbage. She wipes her mouth with her sleeve and goes back to selling her body for little money.

The White Lady is a harpy.

Rosalind would so much like to rest. If only she could. One morning when she has nothing left, a horrendous morning, she goes to her father's house to beg him for help. She tries to stand up straight. She runs a dirty hand through her lifeless hair and then rings the doorbell.

A pretty woman in her twenties opens the door. Rosalind asks for her father. But he's not there. He sold the house over a year ago.

The door closes.

Rosalind doesn't know where to go. But she needs money, otherwise the giant hands will grind her bones and ring her entrails and squeeze her skull until her brain comes out her eyes and ears. Her father abandoned her. She wants her daddy. She is all alone. She's in pain. She wants to die.

At sixteen years old, she hides from the soldiers on patrol. She doesn't have her papers. She only has a bottle of solvent and a plastic bag. She sleeps with other kids on the concrete floor of an abandoned warehouse, not far from the train station. For some time now, life has become harder. Soldiers are everywhere, demonstrations, fights in the streets. It hinders the business of selling her body. There are no more White Ladies in the street.

One night, soldiers chase her, corner her behind a building, and take turns raping her, except for one who is happily smoking a cigarette and looks at her with disdain while the others work her, their machine guns strapped across their chests.

At sixteen years old, Rosalind is pregnant. She didn't think it was possible. She hasn't had her period in a very long time. But she has to go with the evidence: something is happening inside of her, her stomach is already rounding, under the overhang of her rib cage through whose skin each one of her ribs can be seen. For an entire day, Rosalind cries, sitting on the ground, chin on her knees.

Yes, something is happening inside her. A child. She cries over this child to be born. But over the days, she surprises herself by crying less and talking to it more and more. She starts getting hungry, a hunger that seems to come from very far away and from long ago. An ancient hunger. Now, she can't inhale the solvent fumes. It makes her nauseous and gives her a headache. So she stops. The thing growing in her stomach helps her to stop. She doesn't feel the need to fill the void anymore as she is fulfilled by the child in her belly.

She leaves the abandoned warehouse. She has to find a home, a nest somewhere to welcome the child, with blankets and hot water. She only has a vague idea of what to do, but that's already a lot.

She asks for help from the people who run the soup kitchens, the same people she was suspicious of not so long ago. Now she accepts their bowl of soup, their piece of bread, but no one knows what to tell her about the child. They explain the situation to her: there's a war going on. She had no idea.

She walks around the city keeping a hand on her belly, asking if someone can help her. She would never have done this for herself. She's doing it for the child.

One day, someone takes her by the hand and leads her to an old house where there are three other girls like her, at various stages of pregnancy. She has to share a room with one of them. It's wonderful! A small bed with blankets and a pillow with a bright white pillow case.

Before sleeping, she is forced to take a bath. A fat woman in her fifties washes her hair, scrubbing very hard with her nails. After, when her hair dries, Rosalind feels as though there are ants marching across her head.

In the small oval mirror hanging on her bedroom wall, she looks at herself. The bones in her face stretch her yellowed skin. Her eyes seem faded. She smiles. She's hungry. She's very hungry.

At seventeen years old, Rosalind gives birth to a little girl who has Chinese eyes and an impressive tuft of hair that forms a kind of parasol on the top of her head. Rosalind was scared, because of the solvents and the White Lady, but when she sees her daughter's small eyes seemingly searching for her mother, when she feels the strength of her child's tiny hand gripping her mother's index finger, she feels a sense of happiness she didn't think was possible. Who needs wings on your back when you can have this?

Her body is thin, she doesn't have much milk. That's a problem in wartime, the fat lady tells her. Anyway, we'll manage.

At seventeen years old, Rosalind is sleeping when some ten soldiers barge into the house and chase out its occupants. They take up position in front of the windows while Rosalind wraps her baby in a shawl and goes out into the street with the others. Shells start to fall, they have to get away. Other soldiers, with other uniforms, are coming around the corner. The shooting begins and Rosalind weaves between the houses and starts running to escape the bullets.

She runs for a long time. There are people everywhere, running like she is. No one worries about her fate, with her bag lady clothes. Finally, exhausted, she slows. She walks out of the city among this whole crowd in which she feels somewhat safe.

Her baby is crying. She has to stop often to give her a breast, but she wants more right away and Rosalind has no more to give her. After a while, there are only old people and mothers dragging their children by the hand around her.

Her baby is crying. Her baby is howling. Her baby is all red with frustration, pain, the desire to live. She is hungry.

Rosalind can't take it anymore. She sits on an overturned road marker. She extends each of her nipples to her hungry child's mouth. But three mouthfuls empty them and the crying starts again. All at once, from every direction, she hears the shots and explosions that don't succeed in covering the child's screams.

She sees soldiers crossing the road, hunched over, weapon in hand. Only one of them walks straight, as if on a healthy stroll. He approaches Rosalind. His face is blackened from smoke and, at his belt, the handle of a kitchen knife is sticking out of a leather sheath.

"Why is it crying?" asks the militiaman.

"She's hungry."

The militiaman looks at Rosalind, but his eyes don't see her. He looks past her. Suddenly he leans over, takes the baby from Rosalind's hands and removes the shawl wrapped around it. The child's screams go up a tone.

The militiaman moves his hand to his belt. He unsheathes his knife. Then he passes the blade over the baby's throat, under the chin, slowly, like a caress.

The screams cease immediately. In their place, an awful gurgling is heard. There isn't much blood. Then even the gurgling stops. The militiaman returns the baby to Rosalind. The small head hangs backward.

"There you go. It's not hungry anymore," says the militiaman.

He leaves, walking at first, and then moving faster and faster. He disappears, running.

Rosalind holds her baby's body to her. Her mouth is open, but she can't scream. She can't cry. She's beyond screams and tears. Her baby.

The militiaman's name was Viktor Rosh.

Her baby hadn't been named yet.

THE PEACEFUL COUNTRY

The day after our meeting, Viktor Rosh was found dead in his cell. During the night, sheltered from the guards under his blanket, he opened his carotid with the help of the pen he had stolen from me while pretending to put it back in my pocket. When they discovered him at morning roll call, his mattress was completely soaked with blood.

Naturally, there are many other ways of dying, even in prison. It was his way of answering my accusations, I suppose. I want to believe that remorse played a role in his suicide, and that way, while the blood ran out of him, he reintegrated the human community.

Stealing my pen to commit suicide was, for Viktor Rosh, the equivalent of a good joke. I learned of his death when the police knocked at my hotel-room door to question me. They suspected me of having knowingly slipped him the weapon used in the crime!

The inspector's manner was brutal, and I don't dare imagine the awful time I would have spent in his company if I hadn't been but a foreign national, moreover a lawyer.

Viktor Rosh didn't believe in the justice of men. But it's in the hands of a man that, in the end, he placed his destiny.

His hands. Even though he was a monster, he was nonetheless a man, and his monstrosity was that of men.

For over an hour, I went up against the inspector's arrogant stupidity. Finally, I had to resign myself to call on Cevitjc, who appeared delighted.

"Tell the commissioner to call off his pit bull," I said to him.

Cevitjc made jokes, affable, as though nothing had happened between us. It's true that Viktor Rosh's death made the whole matter fall apart and I couldn't hurt him in any way. Like Rosh, I had done my time. I imagine that Cevitjc had other pokers in the fire, other political schemes. I wasn't worried for him. I was worried for the others.

After an hour or two, the telephone rang and the inspector left, boiling with rage after he was ordered to let go of his bone.

I was alone. I felt strangely guilty. After all, it was my pen. What did another death solve? Who knows if in a few years, Viktor Rosh would have become another man, able to feel the pain of others?

There was nothing left for me to do here. I reserved a plane ticket over the telephone for the next flight and then I packed my suitcases. I sent Florence an e-mail to tell her I was coming home. Then I wrote a note to Josef. I told him what Viktor Rosh had told me about Jana's letters and gave him the location where they were buried as best I could. If anyone could find them, it was Josef. I had my letter delivered to his apartment. On the envelope I had written: *For Josef and Rosalind*.

I didn't doubt for a second the great efforts that Josef would make to get Manu's letters to Jana. It's the paradox of this man, back from the land of the dead.

I imagined Jana reading the letters, crying over the love that should have prospered instead of being ruined in vengeance and being lost without any hope of returning. Was it a good idea to give them back to her? Perhaps the letters would do her more harm than good? But who was I to judge what was good or bad for others? The letters belonged to her. The memory of love is still better than no love at all. She could recite passages to her children, at night, under the sympathetic blackness of her madness.

I was going home. I was going to see Florence and the children. I would beg for clemency from the jury. And whatever the verdict, I would have to learn to live with its consequences.

I boarded a bus that would take me to the Capital. I slept in spurts, having nightmares. I woke when we arrived, sweating and trembling.

I had a little over two hours ahead of me. I headed towards a telephone booth and looked in the phone book. The Art Café still existed.

I hailed a taxi. It dropped me off in front of a pretty little restaurant in front of which a jam-packed terrace echoed with bursts of laughter, buzzing conversation and the clinking of the spoons against the porcelain cups.

I sat down and ordered a coffee which turned out to be delicious.

Viktor Rosh's dream had outlived him; another struggled to keep it going, demonstrating more courage and determination.

I stayed there. The sun lit the terrace and I turned my face towards it. War? Where was the war? All around, life went on, like grass springs back after it's been trampled. Life would be

unbearable if we didn't have the ability to forget. And life is unbearable because we do forget.

Hurried people crossed the street, avoiding the cars with
matador-like contortions. They had appointments, money
worries, vacation plans. I sipped my coffee. I wanted another,
which I drank just as slowly, closing my eyes and absorbing
each burst of laughter that shot out from the surrounding
tables.

Another taxi dropped me at the airport. I checked my bags.
I crossed the security cordon.

I was looking at perfumes in the window of the duty-free
shop when the bomb exploded. A huge noise, then a violent
rush that threw me in the air. The blown-out windows stabbed
me with shards of glass. When I came to, I was lying on my
back, unable to move, and a whitish halo seemed to emanate
from everything.

I couldn't hear a thing. Then, my hearing returned gradually, screams, crying, howling. I tried to stand up but my body
refused to obey me. I turned my head. A confused heap of
bodies and blood. The beginnings of a fire.

I saw things in slow motion. A woman entered my field of
vision, hands extended in front of her, as though she was begging for forgiveness. She didn't have a face. Her sockets were
empty and, through the gaping wound, I could see her tongue
thrusting around in search of a palate. She came closer letting
out a muted plea. She bumped into my hip and fell onto me.
I still couldn't move. With a massive effort, I managed to lift my
hand to rest it on the nape of the woman's neck. Moaning, I
stroked her hair. I don't remember anything after that.

I woke up on a stretcher. A paramedic examined me. He
asked me to wiggle my toes and they moved way down there.

I wasn't a critical case. A concussion, shock, multiple lesions and cuts, but for the most part they were superficial.

Seventeen had died and forty-six were wounded. The investigation revealed that the bomb had been brought in in separate pieces in several carry-on bags and then assembled in the men's bathroom. It had exploded inside the duty-free shop, symbol of capitalism at its best. In his own way, Mistral wanted to mark my departure.

Mine or someone else's, what difference did it make? For people like him, it's not important who dies, as long as there are lots of deaths and that the idea of death brands the spirit of the living.

I was driven to the hospital where I was sewn up. I was given pills that I swallowed without question. I was worried about Florence who was perhaps waiting for me and who had no doubt heard the news.

As soon as the doctor gave his authorization, I called home. There was no one there. I left a message saying that I was alive and that I would be on a flight tomorrow.

I left the hospital late the following morning. My luggage had left without me the day before. I bought new clothes and tossed the old bloodstained ones in the garbage. I returned to the airport where, already, the duty-free shop was back in business in a neighbouring location.

I wanted to leave as soon as possible. I wanted to go home, to my peaceful country that had seemed so dreary.

I was awake for the entire trip, haunted by the woman without a face whose gaping wound was a silent cry. I was shivering. A flight attendant held out a blanket. I saw a blood-soaked mattress. Finally, the plane landed. I had nothing to declare at customs.